ASTRALIS
CORE

SEAN L. HOLMES

FORWARD

Honestly, this project started as a personal challenge—just to see if I could bring a story to life in book form. I mean, how hard could it be, right? I'd love to say I poured over classic literature, channeling the works of literary greats to create something profound. But let's be real—I'm not that guy. The truth is, books have always been a bit of a struggle for me. Most of what I "read" is through audiobooks, often while doing other things. Like that one time I was doing the dishes, half-listening to Mr. Serkis narrating Tolkien, and—boom—an idea hit me. Suddenly, there I was, scrubbing away at pots and pans, thinking, "What if I could make this epic world-building stuff happen for my own story?" And, just like that, the seed for this book was planted.

But, if we're talking about inspiration, I'd be remiss not to mention my 7th-grade days. I was the kid who wrote a short story called *StarCon*, about an ultra-powerful artifact that could destroy the world, because apparently, that's what you do when you're a 12-year-old with a lot of time and imagination. This kid's imagination was packed to the brim with aliens, space exploration, and zappy guns. I thought I was onto something big.

Fast-forward to college, and I try to turn it into a script, and my professor, with his most sarcastic tone, tells me, "Sounds like a real cheap movie." (Yeah, it stung a little, but hey, I'm over it now.)

I could've left *StarCon* in the past, relegated to my adolescent ambitions, but when that dishwashing moment happened with Tolkien, I thought, "You know what? Maybe it's time to try again." So here I am, finally turning that long-lost story into something that, hopefully, is more than just a "cheap movie" waiting to happen.

If you are reading this, you may be thinking of your own project or idea that you want implement with the very overused and vague, *Someday*. Let this book be a reminder that it can be done with a tired but direct, axiomatic saying. If this thirty-something, cheeto-dusted, expanded-universe-loving nerd can write a book, then I should be able to as well. To which I unequivocally and enthusiastically say, yes with a small request. After you read, share, and review my book, go for it.

Now that you are here, I would like to explain that you do have options on the method of reading other than the cover-to-cover method. If you are stickler for the details, lore-before-story kind of reader, I would suggest you read the Appendices first and then the main story. If your traditional, read Prologue to Epilogue and then read on if you're still interested. If you don't read past the Epilogue, its fine with me, I'm just glad you picked this up.

Whether you're holding this book in your hands or reading it on your device, the fact that you've chosen to spend time with this creation of mine means the world. Seriously. Whether it's collecting dust on your book shelf, in your earbuds, or wherever you like to read, I'm beyond grateful that this story has a place in your life. Thank you. You are part of this journey now, and I can't wait for you to dive in.

TABLE OF CONTENTS

APPENDICES

NAVIGATION SYSTEM MAPS

PROLOGUE:

BENEATH THE CRIMSON SKY

Under the fiery red-orange glow of a Néalian sunset, young Elara Nova, barely ten years old, darted along the quiet stream at the edge of Astralith. Laughter filled the air as she and Oriana chased after each other, their feet kicking up soft sprays of water while the sky above blazed in hues of orange and gold, painting a magical evening spell around them.

Elara's father had just shown her how to channel energy through her palms, a secret lesson they shared whenever they had a spare moment. He always reminded her, 'This power is our legacy. Use it wisely, Elara.' The words echoed in her mind as the ground quaked beneath her.

Without warning, the sky seemed to tear apart as a dark, angular ship burst from the warp and descended rapidly toward the horizon. One moment, it wasn't there, and the next, its shadow stretched across the ground like a stormfront. The air filled with a metallic tang, thick and harsh as the ship's thrusters scorched the ground. Elara choked on the fumes, tasting ash on her tongue as the vessel loomed over them, blocking the last light of the crimson sun.

Elara's breath caught. "What is that?"

"I don't know," Oriana replied, her voice tinged with excitement. "Let's go!" She ran, her feet kicking up fine Neálian dust.

"Oriana!" Elara strained her voice, her heart pounding as she raced after her friend. Oriana had always been the daring one, but Elara couldn't shake the need to shield her, as if protecting her friend could somehow protect her own heart.

The ship's descent was alarmingly fast. Its massive form plummeted from the sky, blocking the sun as it lowered itself with a thunderous roar. The air vibrated as the ground quaked beneath them, loose rocks shaking underfoot. It wasn't landing—it was claiming the ground as its own.

As they reached the outskirts of the village, the ship touched down in a clearing with a bone-rattling thud. Its sheer size made Elara feel small and insignificant as it towered over the village's stone huts. Its black hull gleamed like onyx, easily dwarfing the entire settlement.

Elara's stomach tightened as she and Oriana slowed their pace, moving carefully now. From the other side of the ship came distant sounds—shouting, screaming, the clamor of chaos. She'd heard whispers of the Obsidian Order, dark figures who left entire planets in ruin. Some said they were more monster than man, their hearts as black as their armor.

"What's happening" Elara whispered, her voice swallowed by the ship's eerie hum.

"I don't know…" Oriana stood up, her curiosity too firm. She stepped out from the cover of the looming kalivaki bush, her eyes fixed on the ship.

Elara reacted instantly, grabbing her wrist. "Oriana! Get down!" she hissed, the urgency in her voice unmistakable.

But Oriana yanked her hand away, her eyes burning with reckless determination. "We can't just hide!" she snapped before sprinting toward the source of the commotion.

Elara's heart pounded as she watched Oriana dash ahead, the ship's shadow stretching long across the village like a harbinger of what was to come.

Oriana sprinted ahead, her figure barely a blur as she darted between the stone huts, closing in on the chaos. Elara's breath came in shallow gasps as she pressed herself flat against the wall, feeling the cold stone scrape against her skin. The cries of her neighbors echoed through the village, each one a knife twisting in her gut. She squeezed her eyes shut, willing herself to stay hidden, even as every fiber of her being screamed to run to her parents.

Elara's pulse thundered in her ears; she needed to run faster. But before she could catch up, a dark figure emerged from the shadows—a soldier cloaked in the obsidian armor of the Order.

"Oriana, stop!" Elara shouted, but it was too late.

The Obsidian Order agent moved with terrifying speed, grabbing Oriana by the arm and lifting her off the ground as if she weighed nothing. Her scream was cut short as they pressed something—a device—against her neck, rendering her limp in their grip.

Elara gasped, her heart seizing with panic as she rushed forward, but she halted abruptly when more soldiers appeared, rounding up the terrified villagers. Shouts and cries filled the air as the Obsidian Order forced the villagers into tight, terrified clusters.

Elara swallowed hard, her eyes darting around for any sign of hope. She couldn't save Oriana—not yet. Her legs shook with fear, but she knew what to do. She couldn't risk getting caught.

Moving quickly, Elara ducked behind the nearest stone hut, slipping through the narrow back alleys where no one was watching. The screams were louder now, agonizing, but she pressed on, sticking to the shadows as she crept around the village, heart in her throat. Every breath felt heavy in her chest.

Peering from behind a crumbling wall, she witnessed more villagers being forced to their knees, her heart twisting in dread. She needed to locate her parents and warn them, but her blood ran cold when she finally spotted them.

There they were, just beyond the chaos, their faces etched with fear as the Obsidian Order surrounded them. Her father stood protectively before her mother, but there was no escape. There were too many soldiers, and their weapons were raised and ready.

Elara's breath caught in her throat as she crouched lower, her mind screaming to act—but she couldn't move.

They took them. Without mercy, the soldiers seized her parents, pulling them roughly into the crowd of prisoners. Elara bit back a sob, every muscle in her body tensing as she watched, helpless. Tears burned in her eyes, but she forced herself to remain quiet. They'd find her if she made even the slightest sound.

The sight of her parents being dragged away was too much to bear. Something inside Elara snapped. Without thinking, she bolted from her hiding place, the fear in her chest replaced by pure desperation.

"Mom! Dad!" she screamed, her voice cracking as she ran toward them, her legs moving faster than they ever had. Tears blurred her vision, but she didn't care. She had to reach them.

Her father, hearing her cry, turned sharply. His eyes widened, and in an instant, he broke away from the crowd, shoving through the soldiers as they tried to push him back.

"Elara, no!" he shouted, but she couldn't stop. She was so close now, just a few steps away.

One of the Obsidian Order guards whirled around, his eyes locking on Elara. The air shimmered as the guard raised his hand, a crackling surge of red energy forming in his palm, aimed directly at her.

Elara froze in terror, her feet glued to the ground. The glowing energy swirled, ready to strike, and in that split second, she knew she wouldn't make it.

But her father sprang into action before the guard could release his blast. His hands glowed with bright white energy, and he unleashed it toward the guard with a sharp, fluid motion. The force of it collided with the guard's red energy, neutralizing it in an explosive flash of light.

Elara stumbled back, stunned by the sudden burst of power. The guard was thrown off balance and staggered backward. Her father stood tall, eyes blazing with determination.

"Elara, come on!" he called, his voice steady now, no longer filled with panic. He reached out for her, and she ran to him without hesitation.

They met in a fierce embrace, her father pulling her close as her mother rushed over. Elara's breath came in ragged gasps, tears spilling as she clung to them. Her mother's arms wrapped around them, holding them tightly together, the three of them lost in the safety of each other's presence for a fleeting moment.

Their moment of reunion was abruptly shattered by a voice that cut through the chaos like a blade, "Bring them to me."

Elara's heart dropped as she turned to see Veyra, the leader of the Obsidian Order, stepping forward with an unsettling calmness. Her black skin crackled with red energy, contrasting her unnerving, cold gaze. The guards obeyed immediately, dragging Elara's parents away from her and forcing them to their knees in front of Veyra.

"Back off!" Elara's father growled, struggling against the guards' grip. His hands sparked with the white energy he had just used moments ago.

Veyra smirked, her lips curling into a wicked smile. "So, this is where the insurgence is hiding. How quaint." She tilted her head, her eyes gleaming with sadistic amusement. "Go ahead. Both of you. Fight me."

Veyra smirked, watching their futile attempts with a look of cold amusement. "Do you really think your little rebellion matters? You're just dust beneath our feet." Her eyes flickered with an unsettling hunger. "The Order has plans for your kind," she sneered, as if she could see through them to a destiny that they couldn't even fathom.

Elara's parents exchanged a glance before springing into action. Their hands ignited with fierce energy, and without hesitation, they hurled blasts of light at Veyra, desperate to protect their daughter.

But Veyra didn't flinch.

She dodged effortlessly, her movements fluid and graceful. Each energy blast sailed past her as if in slow motion while she darted and weaved through them with the ease of someone toying with her prey. Elara could barely process what was happening—her parents were moving as fast as they could, yet Veyra seemed impossibly quicker.

They lunged, their hands blazing with energy, but Veyra was already moving, her figure a blur as she sidestepped their attacks. Every blast of light seemed to slow in the air, suspended just long enough for her to dance around it. Elara's heart hammered as she realized—her parents were giving it everything they had, and it still wasn't enough. They continued to press forward, blasting attack after attack, but it was as though time slowed for Veyra. She danced around their strikes with a cruel smile, her eyes locked on them the entire time.

As they closed the gap, mere feet from her, she made her move. With a single swift motion, Veyra extended both arms—dark crackling energy shot from her palms. The beam struck Elara's father and mother before they could react.

They didn't even have a chance to scream.

Their bodies flew back, collapsing to the ground, the force of the blast knocking the breath from their lungs. The clearing fell into a deafening silence.

Elara stood frozen, her mind reeling, her heart pounding in her chest as she watched her parents lying motionless, their energy drained, their fight over in an instant.

The village lay in ruins, its once lively streets now transformed into a haunting panorama of debris and desolation. Shadows stretched long and eerie as the sun slipped beyond the horizon, ushering in a night thick with despair. Hours had crept by since the massive, intimidating ships of the Obsidian Order disappeared into the distance, leaving behind only devastation and a heavy silence that hung in the air like a shroud.

As hours passed, Elara knelt on the cold ground, her body heavy with exhaustion and deep grief. She clutched her father's pendant, its silver surface cold against her skin. Adorned with complex Sidereal symbols now dulled by soot, the pendant's glowing blue jewel in the center flickered in the moonlight, as if whispering the stories of the lost.

The oppressive stillness of the night contrasted sharply with the earlier chaos. Faint crackles from smoldering embers and the mournful howl of the wind echoed through the village, as if it were grieving the lives and laughter lost.

Tears that had streamed down her face were now dry, leaving tracks on her cheeks, but the emotional ache within her remained deep and unrelenting. The pendant felt heavier with each passing moment, burdening her not just with its metallic weight but also with the profound love she had for her father, the immense loss of his presence, and the crushing finality of events she could never hope to change. With trembling fingers, she pressed it to her chest, the action merging into a silent plea for strength and a desperate need for comfort amidst the chaos.

Above her, the stars emerged against the night sky, casting a cold glow on the surrounding wreckage. Time lost meaning, marked only by the chilling earth beneath her knees. The stillness enveloped her like a shroud, isolating her in her mourning amidst the ruins.

Though her body screamed for rest, her spirit clung fiercely to the pendant, unwilling to let go of the memories it embodied. As the hours dragged on and the night deepened, Elara found herself tethered to this moment, drowning in the overwhelming tide of her sorrow and the bittersweet remembrance of all she had lost. The world around her faded into the background, but the weight of her grief held her firmly in place, a testament to her love and enduring connection to her loss.

CHAPTER 1:

THE HISTORIAN'S INVITATION

THIRTY YEARS LATER...

The grand hall of the Néalian Symposium buzzed with anticipation. Scholars and engineers filled the space, their murmurs weaving through the charged air. At the edge of her seat, Elara Nova leaned forward, her sharp gaze fixed on the stage. Despite decades of experience, her Sidereal heritage kept her youthful, a contrast to the wisdom gleaming in her eyes.

Dr. Elara Nova's turquoise skin shimmered faintly under the symposium's lights—a hallmark of her Sidereal lineage. She was barely aware of the hum of conversations around her as Verus Clemens, the enigmatic historian, stepped onto the stage.

Elara fiddled with the pendant, her fingers tracing its contours with a mix of restlessness and reverence. It was more than an ornament; it was a tangible connection to her past, a fragment of solace she carried everywhere. The pendant, once belonging to her father, held mysteries she could not unravel, its origins veiled in obscurity. Yet, its presence anchored her, providing a quiet assurance amid the chaos of her life.

Scholars and engineers from across the galaxy filled the hall, their whispers in a dozen languages weaving through the charged air. As the lights dimmed, all eyes turned to Verus Clemens. The renowned historian stepped into the spotlight, his presence silencing the crowd.

The air seemed to grow heavier as Verus Clemens took the stage, his silver eyes sweeping the audience. Even among the diverse crowd, the Tetrealin historian stood apart, his melancholic aura a lingering echo of his people's tragic past. At 300 years old, his kind's slow aging imbued him with a timeless authority.

Verus Clemens exuded precision, from the sharp cut of his dark robes to the deliberate grace of his movements. His piercing silver eyes seemed to see through the crowd, each gaze a calculated study. The streaks of gray in his jet-black hair added to his timeless presence, a reminder of centuries of knowledge and experience.

Despite his composed exterior, there's an intensity beneath the surface. His mind is constantly at work, processing every detail around him. His movements are deliberate, and his gaze sharp, making him both an enigmatic and intimidating figure.

Verus paused at the podium, his gaze sweeping across the hushed crowd. The silence was palpable, vibrating with anticipation as he drew a slow, deliberate breath, savoring the moment before speaking.

"The Terranovians." he began, his voice steady and measured, "were a civilization unlike any other. They were master engineers, architects of both matter and mind. Their understanding of the universe extended far beyond the physical; they sought to grasp the essence of existence, the threads that wove together time, space, and consciousness. This pursuit led them to their greatest achievements— and, ultimately, their greatest downfall."

Elara was captivated as Verus began weaving tales of ancient Terranovian technologies and their lost secrets. He spoke of energy matrices and cosmic alignments with a passion that resonated deeply with her research interests.

He moved to the side of the podium, gesturing to a holographic display that flickered to life. It showed a series of complex structures, ancient and alien, that once dotted the surface of Zynthar.

"These structures," he said, pointing, "are remnants of Terranovian society. Their cities were marvels of design, built to harmonize with the natural energy flows of their planet. They believed every action and creation had to be in sync with the universe's natural order."

The holograph shifted, showing detailed images of symbols and carvings on the walls of the ruins. Verus continued, "They were also philosophers and mathematicians, embedding their knowledge into every facet of their world. These carvings," he gestured again, "are not just art. They are complex equations of their understanding of cosmic forces. They saw life as a vast, interconnected web where each entity and particle had a role. To them, the universe was a living organism, and they were but a part of its grand design."

The holograph changed again to show an image of a lush, green terrain teeming with exotic flora and fauna. "This is how Zynthar once looked," Verus said, a hint of sadness in his voice. "A paradise. A testament to Terranovian mastery. They cultivated life with an almost divine touch, nurturing ecosystems that thrived in harmony. Their wisdom in these matters was revered by all who knew of them."

He paused, allowing the beauty of the image to sink in. "But for all their wisdom, the Terranovians were not without flaws. Their quest for knowledge led them down paths that were perhaps best left unexplored. They researched into manipulating reality, attempting to bend the very fabric of the universe to their will. Their undoing was their arrogance and belief that they could control the uncontrollable, tampering with forces beyond their comprehension, leading to cataclysms that shattered their society."

As Verus spoke of the Terranovians' cataclysm, his fingers tightened around the podium, a flash of something dark and unreadable crossing his face. Verus's tone became somber. "They thought of themselves as gods, but they were still mortal. They could not foresee the consequences of their actions. The energies they sought to harness turned against them. What was once a world of beauty and enlightenment, became a desert of despair, a silent graveyard of a once-great civilization."

Elara leaned forward, hanging on every word, especially when Verus hinted at artifacts linked to cosmic phenomena.

Verus paused, letting his words echo through the hall before concluding, "For in the ruins of Zynthar lies not only the story of the Terranovians but the story of what we might become. History has a way of repeating itself, especially when we refuse to heed its warnings. I've seen empires fall."

He stepped back from the podium, the room in contemplative silence. The echoes of his words lingered as each listener grappled with the weight of Terranovian history and its implications for the present. Elara felt a sense of awe mixed with urgency, her mind racing with the possibilities and hidden truths buried beneath the sands of Zynthar.

His speech concluded with thunderous applause, and Elara sprang to her feet, eager to approach him with questions burning her mind. However, as she approached the stage, a tide of attendees surged forward, blocking her path. Despite her best efforts, she couldn't get through the crowd surrounding Verus, clamoring for his attention.

A dark figure stood in the vast auditorium, packed with Verus's assorted groveling admirers. Hooded and cloaked in black, with obsidian skin—scarred red—mostly covered except for vacant expression from nostril slits amid a maw of disdain. He was not simply watching Verus like many in this place but focused on Elara in her futile attempts to reach her academic idol.

Cold. There was a sudden withdrawal of heat; Elara felt this from where the cloaked man stood amid the crowd. The chill in the air felt like a ghost's touch, bringing with it flashes of a time she'd buried deep—blood-red skies, screams, and the burning wreckage of her childhood home.

This sudden temperature drop was not unfamiliar to her, as if the chill and air of despair were distant memories from years past when she lost her township, family, and community.

Elara turned her gaze to locate the source. Behind her, nothing but the impatient crowd of Néalians, Sidereals, and academics were still in the queue. The sensation vanished as swiftly as it returned. Frustrated, confused, and weary, Elara fled the symposium.

Boarding the Néalian tram station, she needed to unload her mental cargo as much as a waylaid and compressed freight ship. Her friend would understand in a truthful and unbiased manner. Elara pressed her palm to the port panel as she stepped aboard, which was lit with a green hue and a happy tone. She spoke aloud, "Codex Cantina." A confirm chime sounded. The whirring sounds of the Néalian Fusion engines came to life with a dull but still present roar.

As its name suggests, Codex Cantina is a local establishment frequented by academics. Once, this place had been a beacon for intellectuals, a place where the air smelled of fresh ink and old books.

Now, the low-hanging smoke and dim lights gave it the air of a hideout for secrets and deals struck in whispers. Currently, the pristine shelves of Codex Cantina are now somewhat neglected, with several books missing, others disheveled or dust covered. The wooden tables and chairs showed more wear and tear, bearing the marks and scratches from less careful patrons. Once adorned with treasured manuscripts and maps, the walls featured darker, more enigmatic art pieces, hinting at the bar's shift to a more clandestine atmosphere. The lighting in Codex Cantina had grown dimmer, the bulbs less frequently replaced, casting deeper shadows into the room's corners. The air was thick now, tinged with the smell of stale smoke and more potent liquors.

Elara slumped into the chair beside Mira halfway through her third drink. Mira's metallic-blue skin shimmered under the lounge's ambient lighting, making her look almost ethereal. Her sharp wit and sarcasm were a familiar comfort to Elara, a stark contrast to the frustration she was feeling.

"Rough day?" Mira asked, her smirk betraying a hint of knowing amusement.

Elara sighed heavily, rubbing her temples. "You could say that. I missed my chance to talk to Verus. And now, the academy's blocking my access to key texts on the Terranovian energy conduits. It's like they don't want me to get to the bottom of this."

Mira took a thoughtful sip from her glass. "They might just start hiding the important stuff behind a labyrinth guarded by ancient riddles next time."

The touch of cold silver of the pendant under Elara's fingers evoked a sense of calm. This contrasted with the warm and loud bar as her thoughts always wondered during conversation in crowds. The remnants of Terranovian history seemed to hold within them a crucial part of the intricate symbols Elara's father had endeavored to impart to her. She wasn't simply seeking information; she was endeavoring to revive a heritage.

Elara managed a weak smile. "I wouldn't put it past them. It's just so frustrating. Another barrier pops up whenever I think I'm getting close to something significant."

Mira paused after she took another swig of her drink, "You know, sometimes I wonder if these 'academic protocols' are just a front. The things they hide—maybe some of them are better left untouched. Or so they'd like us to think."

Mira's grin widened; her tone laced with sarcasm. "Sounds like they're keeping something juicy under wraps. Or maybe they just enjoy making you jump through hoops. But hey, if you're determined, you might find a way around their little roadblocks."

Elara's expression grew more serious. "I've thought about it, but I'm wary of crossing any lines. I don't want to resort to anything that could compromise my integrity or get me in trouble. I'd prefer to find a legitimate way to access the information."

Mira raised her eyebrow, her sarcastic edge softening. "Fair enough. But if you ever need a nudge in the right direction, I've got a few contacts who might offer some insights—legally, of course. We don't need you getting into hot water over this."

Elara looked relieved. "I appreciate that. I'm just trying to tread carefully. I don't want to jeopardize my reputation or the credibility of my research."

"Understood," Mira replied, her tone turning more earnest. "I'll see what I can dig up through the usual channels. And if you end up chasing Verus, ensure you get something out of it. He's notorious for disappearing before people can dig into his secrets."

"I can't believe I missed my chance to talk to him," Elara sighed and went on, venting more of her frustration. "I had so many questions for Verus! He mentioned the Terranovian energy conduits. It's exactly what my latest research touches on!"

Mira sipped her drink thoughtfully. "You know he's heading to Calix City next, right? Maybe you'll have better luck catching him there."

Fueled by determination, Elara traveled to Calix City to wait patiently at Verus's following lecture. This time, she planned to approach him directly as he exited the stage.

Calix City is a bustling metropolis on Elara Nova's home planet, Néalian. Known for its advanced technology and shimmering architecture, it is a crucial hub of trade and politics. Its energetic glowing skyline reflects the energy-manipulating abilities of the Sidereals who inhabit it. However, beneath the city's surface, power struggles and hidden agendas simmer, with various factions attempting to control the future of Néalian.

Elara arrives at the symposium and sits through the same lecture. This time, she takes a seat where she will time her approach. After the lecture concludes, Elara confronts Verus.

"Dr. Clemens," Elara began, catching his attention amidst the thinning crowd, "I'm Dr. Elara Nova. I attended your Néalian lecture. Your discussion on Terranovian energy matrices—how they might align with quantum field theories—was particularly intriguing."

Verus paused, clearly interested. "Ah, Dr. Nova, yes, I recall your enthusiasm. Quantum field theories, you say? That's quite a specialized area. Tell me more about your work."

Elara explained her hypothesis, detailing the technical aspects of her research that suggested a possible reinterpretation of Terranovian technologies. "But I keep hitting walls. The more I seek out sources, the more the academy restricts access, citing preservation concerns or academic protocols."

Verus nodded, understanding the situation all too well. "It's a common plight among us who chase the shadows of ancient knowledge. Dr. Nova, how would you like to see some of these sources? I have access to the Exclusive Library of Ancient Scrolls here in Calix City. It's not open to the public, and we must keep this invitation." Verus looked from side to side while casually waving to his fans, turned back to Elara, and whispered, "Discreet."

Elara's eyes lit up with a mix of surprise and excitement. Catching herself, she nods in solidarity with Verus. "Thank you, Mr. Clemens. There's so much I believe we can learn from direct sources."

"Indeed," Verus agreed, a hint of a smile playing at his lips. "Meet me tomorrow at the library entrance. We'll explore knowledge together, away from the prying eyes of the overprotective academy."

As Elara left the venue, her mind buzzed with the possibilities ahead. Verus's invitation wasn't just a chance to access rare texts but an opportunity to break through the barriers that had long hindered her quest for knowledge.

Elara felt it was a great opportunity but also a sliver of unsteadiness. She knew how Néalian Academics protected their secret knowledge of Zynthar and what wrath they perpetrated to protect it.

CHAPTER 2:

THE WILL OF THE KEEPERS

The Arcanius Academy Library is a colossal stone structure in an otherwise brilliant steel city. It stands out as an ancient, spire dome. Armed guards, plasma fields, and drone surveillance guard the surrounding campus.

Inside, the atmosphere contrasts sharply with the modern, sleek exterior of the city. The library's towering shelves, carved from dark wood, stretched into infinity, filled with ancient tomes and holographic data scrolls. Dim, orange fusion lights hover above, casting a warm glow that creates a sense of timelessness. The air hums like the knowledge stored within the walls hums with life. In the center of the grand hall stands a statue of a robed figure, the legendary founder of the Arcanius Academy, holding a crystalline orb symbolizing enlightenment.

Verus is waiting in the restricted archives section, a secluded area accessible only by the highest-ranking members or those granted special permission. Powerful energy barriers and biometric scanners protect the room. When Elara enters, the tension between the ancient knowledge and the high-tech security resonates.

As Elara approached the guarded entrance to the restricted archives, one of the guards stepped forward, blocking her path. He was a tall, imposing figure, his armor reflecting the faint glow of the plasma field behind him. His eyes narrowed as he looked her up and down, as if assessing her worth—or perhaps her intentions.

"Dr. Elara Nova," he said, voice flat but laced with suspicion. He didn't step aside immediately, instead letting his gaze linger, his face hardening. Elara could almost feel him weighing her every move, trying to gauge what a Sidereal like her could want with the ancient knowledge hidden behind these walls.

For a tense moment, he simply stood there, his hand resting on the sleek weapon at his side. Elara felt her pulse quicken, a flicker of unease worming its way into her chest.

The guard turns his head with his two fingers to his ear. He seems to be getting new information. Finally, after what felt like an eternity, the guard stepped aside, his gaze never leaving her. He presses a white crystal embedded on his wrist and says, "Please continue through the main gate."

Elara is startled by the sudden threat. Attempting to subside her adrenaline sense, she continues her path to the gate, wondering what in the universe would have a fortitude for academia and the pursuit of knowledge and bring so much security. Whatever is in this section is worth guarding. This thought only strengthens Elara's resolve to pursue ancient knowledge and technology.

"Dr. Nova!" Verus exclaims, wearing a content grin when he sees a familiar face. Elara smiles and goes to shake his outstretched hand.

"Dr. Clemens! I would love to extend my gratitude and thanks for the invitation." Elara said.

"Oh, you are pretty welcome in the company of true academia. However, Let us not waste time on further pleasantries. Please follow me."

She moved through the space, her eyes tracing the line between some ordinary cases and the newer Academy-approved books, all meticulously organized along cold, steel shelves. A band of inventory sensors lit up, casting a soft glimmer over the rows of literature. Verus approached the wall and opened a hidden passage embedded within it. Elara was intrigued; an ordinary wall concealing a passageway seemed odd, especially in a place where building codes were so strictly followed.

At the Academy where she had studied, all construction was done in-house, relying on trusted interior labor.

In her Academy years, she had spent thousands of hours in her local library back home, but this place felt unique. The moment Verus pressed his hand forward, and she heard the grinding of stone, she knew something important lay ahead.

Elara followed Verus down a series of stone corridors lit by torchlight; it felt out of place, like stepping back into a history her father once shared in bedtime tales. It was both unsettling and oddly comforting. It was a curious blend of the familiar and the ancient. On Néalian, fusion lights had always been her constant companions, their soft, energy-efficient glow defining her environment since childhood. Torches, however, were relics of a time before the expansion of technology, from thousands upon thousands of years ago.

"We're here," Verus announced, breaking the silence. A small wooden door with a rusted keyhole stood at the dead-end of the corridor. Verus reached into his robes and produced a minor, faded gold key. He inserted it into the lock and turned the knob, dust stirring from the aged blackened surface. The lock clicked, and the door swung open with a creaky, rattling squeak.

The room beyond was pitch-black, save for the flickering torch nearest the entrance. Verus took the torch and reached up, the flame licking the stone bowl mounted on the wall. Fire danced through the room, igniting a line along the upper curve of the wall before sweeping around to the other side, illuminating the vast space with a soft, warm glow. Rows upon rows of books sat on ancient wooden shelves, bathed in the gentle light.

The atmosphere felt alive, as if the weight of history and knowledge permeated the air. The smell of old paper and bindings enveloped Elara's senses.

"Welcome to the sacred library of Arcania! Forgive the torchlight. The Academy puts surveillance on most fusion fixtures throughout Calix City. Can't be too careful with non-digital information." Verus chuckled.

Elara's heart quickened the moment the room came to life with the warm, golden glow of the torches. Her eyes widened as they swept across the rows of ancient wooden shelves filled with countless volumes, each a promise of untold knowledge. She felt like a child stepping into a forgotten treasure trove, her mind racing with curiosity and excitement.

Her gaze immediately fell upon a section marked with the distinct glyphs of Terranovian technology. Without hesitation, she rushed forward, her fingers lightly brushing the spines of the books as if they were fragile artifacts. She pulled out one, its cover worn but the title clear: The Mechanics of Elemental Fusion. The weight of it in her hands sent a thrill down her spine.

Elara quickly flipped through the pages, her eyes scanning diagrams of ancient machines, serpentine energy conduits, and forgotten blueprints. She had read about Terranovian technology back at the Academy, but here it was, right in front of her—original works, not just copied data streams. Each book pulsed with the history and brilliance of an era long gone, and she could hardly contain her eagerness.

She moved from one book to the next, marveling at the vast array of knowledge. Titles like Quantum Refracture Engines and Terraforming Techniques of Old Zynthar leaped at her. Her hands worked almost independently as she pulled them from the shelves, creating a small pile of precious volumes at her feet. Every discovery felt like uncovering a piece of the lost puzzle she had been trying to solve since her youth.

"This… this is incredible," she whispered to herself, barely able to tear her gaze away from the notes and detailed illustrations. The more she read, the more she felt the pulse of Terranovian ingenuity coursing through her veins, connecting her to a deeper understanding of the technology that had once shaped entire worlds.

Verus hesitated as he picked up an old book, his eyes shifting as he pondered, "What should I reveal to her?"

He then cleared his throat, accepting his decision, "If you think highly of that old thing, this might interest you." Verus showed her a sizable black tome with ornate and detailed gold symbols. "This is one of the original editions of the 'Will of the Keeper.' They say if the light shines from these symbols, the long-lost location of the Core will be revealed. Of course, it's been just a plain book for me," Verus said with a shrug.

Elara's eyes widened. She had never heard of any tome of the Keepers existing at all, let alone in Calix City. Concern laced her voice as she asked, "The Keepers are a secretive organization. They protect knowledge with their lives. How did you come by this?"

Verus shrugged again. "I honestly cannot recall. I've had it for so long. A hundred years ago, I was organizing this library when it was entrusted to me. It's been here ever since."

He smirked. "Interesting reading for those who find cults like that fascinating." He handed Elara the black tome. As soon as both of her hands touched the surface, the symbols radiated with a bright white light.

Verus, usually composed and unshakable, found himself standing in utter disbelief. Throughout his years in Academia, surrounded by countless ancient tomes and artifacts passed down by the Keepers, he had never before witnessed Terranovian technology spring to life. What could have triggered the activation of a technology that had lain dormant for over a millennium? The seemingly ordinary book he once held countless times now emitted an ethereal glow, illuminating the space around him without any discernible power source. The light it emitted was intense and radiant, reminiscent of the brilliance of daylight. Suddenly, a beam of light shot out from the book's spine, culminating in the formation of a holographic, transparent gold globe displaying the ancient city of Zynthar in exquisite detail.

"In all my years, I have never seen this," Verus said, his voice low with astonishment.

"Is that Agri Solitudo?" Elara asked, carefully setting the book on a nearby table to steady the projection.

Verus' voice took on a strained, fearful tone, an emotion he hadn't felt in years. "For your safety and the survival of us both, I must ask you not to speak of this to anyone. Elara, there are those in this universe who would destroy everything—us, this city, and everyone we've ever met—if they discover what we're seeing right now."

Elara felt a chill at his words. Verus was a man of reason, a man who lived by facts. For him to say such a thing meant the danger was real. She whispered, "I understand."

With a cautious hand, Elara moved her fingers across the symbols on the tome. As she did, the map shifted to a light blue outline of Agri Solitudo. One spot on the globe glowed with a red sphere, marking a location.

"At long last," Verus murmured, awe in his voice. "After millennia, it has been revealed."

"What has been revealed?" Elara asked, excitement mixed with confusion.

"The Astralis Core," Verus said solemnly.

Elara's pulse quickened. She stepped closer to the floating globe, her eyes locked on the red sphere pulsing softly on the surface of Agri Solitudo.

"The Core..." she whispered, barely able to contain her astonishment. "It's real?!"

Verus nodded, his usual air of nonchalance replaced with a gravity she hadn't seen before. "Not just real—dangerous. The Core was hidden for a reason, Elara. There are forces that have been seeking it long before either of us existed. If word gets out that we've found its location..."

He trailed off, but Elara knew precisely what he meant. The galaxy would tear itself apart to possess it.

Her mind raced with possibilities. The Core could change everything—space, power, identity. Its existence could alter the balance of the universe. But was she prepared for what that meant?

"Why now?" Elara asked, more to herself than to Verus. "Why would the symbols light up now, after so many years?"

"I'm not sure," Verus admitted. "It may have sensed something, or perhaps it was waiting for someone... like you."

Elara looked at him sharply, "Me? What do you mean?"

Verus ran a hand through his silvered hair, his fingers trembling with nervous anticipation. "The Keepers' legends speak of a time when the Core would need a guide, someone worthy enough to wield its power or protect it. I never believed the stories, but you—there's something about you, Elara. The way the tome responded to your touch…"

Elara felt a chill creep down her spine. "This can't be right. I'm not even sure I believe in all of this. What if it's a mistake?"

Verus shook his head. "The tome chose you, Elara. Whether you like it or not, you're part of this now. But I warn you—if you choose to pursue this, there's no turning back. The Core is not something to be trifled with. It will test you, and there will be those who will stop at nothing to claim it."

Elara's thoughts turned to the Obsidian Order, the dark forces that had long been whispered about in the galaxy. They would come for it if they learned that the Core's location had been revealed. And for her.

"What do I do?" Elara asked, her voice barely above a whisper.

"You make a choice," Verus said, eyes locking onto hers. "Do you seek the Astralis Core and uncover its power, or leave and let the galaxy remain ignorant? Either path is fraught with peril, but only one gives us a chance to prevent it from falling into the wrong hands."

Elara looked down at the glowing tome. She had spent her entire life in pursuit of knowledge, but this time it felt distinct, burdensome, as if it was a fate she had not consciously chosen. Could she truly take on this challenge? Did she even have a say in the matter?

After a long pause, she made her decision.

"I can't walk away from this," Elara glanced back at the library's warm, golden glow, the familiar rows of books and ancient knowledge bathed in torchlight. It had always been a sanctuary, a place where the pursuit of truth was safe, almost sacred. Yet now, standing on the edge of a path she couldn't turn back from, she felt the weight of all she was about to leave behind.

This life—these quiet, studious halls, the certainty of her research—might slip away the moment she stepped forward. She wasn't just risking her life; she was risking everything she'd ever known. With a deep breath, she tore her gaze away from the comforting shadows of the library, facing the darkness of what lay ahead.

Verus sighed, his expression both relieved and burdened. "Then we begin our search. But know this, Elara—enemies are watching. We must tread carefully."

Elara nodded. "I understand."

As they stood together in the dim light of the library, the golden globe hovered between them, casting long shadows on the ancient stone walls. The journey ahead was uncertain, but one thing was clear: the discovery of the Astralis Core had set a course for neither of them to escape.

Elara's resolve was solidifying, but Verus wasn't finished. His expression darkened as the warm light of the holographic globe flickered across his face. He took a deep breath and leaned closer, his voice low and serious.

"Before we go any further, there's something you must understand," he began, his tone sharp and urgent. "The Obsidian Order—the dark forces I mentioned—are not just a threat. They are the root of a war that has spanned generations, and at the center of it all was a man named Perfida."

Elara frowned, the name unfamiliar to her. "Perfida? I've never heard of him."

Verus' gaze hardened. "Few have. The histories have tried to erase him, but his shadow remains. Perfida was once a Keeper, entrusted with safeguarding the knowledge the Keepers held dear—just as I now safeguard this library. But unlike the others, Perfida's ambition consumed him. He wasn't content with guarding the Core. He wanted to control it."

Elara's pulse quickened again as she listened, captivated by the gravity of Verus' words.

"Perfida believed the Astralis Core held more than just power," Verus continued, his voice heavy. "He believed it could reshape the universe itself—bend reality to his will. He envisioned a galaxy where he alone dictated the flow of time, matter, and energy. A galaxy ruled by him. And he was willing to sacrifice anything to achieve it."

Verus paused, his brow furrowed as the weight of the past settled on his shoulders. "It was Perfida who sparked the decline of Agri Solitudo. The planet was once a thriving oasis, rich with life and resources. But Perfida drained the land dry while pursuing the Core's secrets. He manipulated its energy, twisting its natural laws, and in doing so, he turned it into the barren wasteland we now know as Zynthar."

Elara's breath caught. "... it was... because of him?"

Verus nodded grimly. "Perfida sought to channel the Core's power directly through the planet. But it was never meant to be wielded in such a way. The land rejected him, and the core of the planet fractured. Agri Solitudo was left broken, and its people scattered. What's left of it now is a desert—a shadow of its former glory."

Elara felt a chill creeping over her. "And the Obsidian Order? They were his followers?"

"They were more than that," Verus said, his voice growing colder. "Those in the Order were once Keepers, like Perfida. But when he betrayed the order, they followed him. He promised them power beyond their wildest imaginations, and in their greed, they fell into darkness. They became twisted versions of their former selves. They evolved into beings who abandoned the Core's true purpose and sought only lust for domination."

Verus' eyes narrowed as he recalled the old histories. "Perfida's reign of terror didn't end with Agri Solitudo. His actions ignited a war that stretched across countless systems. The Keepers, who remained loyal, fought back, but the damage was already done. Perfida was eventually defeated—or so the records say—but the Obsidian Order never disappeared."

Elara's stomach twisted as she pictured the fate of Agri Solitudo. She could almost feel the desolation Verus described—the life stripped away, the scenery drained and hollowed. The thought of one man wielding that much power, enough to ravage an entire world, sent a shiver down her spine.

For a brief moment, she imagined Néalian in Agri Solitudo's place: her home reduced to dust, her people scattered like leaves on a dead wind. The chill that crept through her veins felt too real, too possible. She forced herself to steady her breathing, but the fear lingered, curling at the edges of her thoughts like smoke.

"What if…" she whispered, barely able to voice the fear. "What if the Order tries to do the same to Néalian?" She clenched her fists, pushing the words out despite the tightening in her chest. "If they get the Core… nothing will be safe."

A heavy silence fell between them as the gravity of Verus' words sank in.

Elara stared at the glowing map of Agri Solitudo—the holographic sphere pulsing ominously—and shivered. "And now they know it's been found," she murmured.

Verus' expression was somber. "If they get word of this, they'll stop at nothing to claim it. Perfida may be long dead, but his influence still lingers. The Obsidian Order believes they're his legacy. If they were to get their hands on the Core…"

He didn't need to finish the sentence. The devastation would be unimaginable.

Elara's fingers brushed over the symbols on the tome, her mind racing with the weight of what she had just learned. "Then we need to get there first," she said, her voice steely with resolve.

Verus nodded, though his eyes were filled with caution. "But you must understand the risk, Elara. The Core's power is unlike anything you've encountered. And the Obsidian Order is relentless. Once we set foot on Agri Solitudo, we will be marked. There will be no going back. It wouldn't surprise me if they were already watching. They have a way of sensing when power is within reach."

Elara spent her life searching for purpose. If stopping the Obsidian Order and keeping the Core out of the Order's hands is that purpose, she had to do it. Everything she was, and now is, had to be committed to this task. Anything less would be an insult to everything her parents died for. Elara straightened, her gaze hardening, "I'm ready. Whatever it takes."

For a moment, Verus studied her, the weight of her words hanging between them. This Sidereal, whom Verus just met in person recently, but had known from Academy Orphan program files since she was eleven years of age. All those tests she aced, top of her class every semester, A name that appeared as the driving force behind Verus financing that program. He looked in her familiar yet determined eyes, reminding him of the spark he once had. He found a glimmer of what he had before he lost everything he loved dearly, before the Eclipsion War, Hope. Finally, he let out a long breath and gave a slow nod. "Then we prepare. Agri Solitudo waits. But be warned, Elara—the shadows of the past have a way of finding their way back into the light. And Perfida's shadow may be closer than we think."

Elara stepped out of the library, the cool night air of Calix City hitting her face as she walked with purpose. Verus's warning lingered in her mind, but she pushed it aside. There were preparations to make, and her mind needed to be precise. As she strode down the familiar streets, bathed in the soft glow of distant fusion lights, her thoughts were already on what lay ahead on Zynthar.

But something felt wrong. A creeping sensation crawled up her spine, like eyes boring into her from the shadows. She glanced around, scanning the quiet streets. The soft hum of the city had taken on an eerie silence. Her pace quickened.

From the corner of her eye, a flicker of movement. As she began to turn, her eyes locked onto the barely perceptible and sharp-edged emblem sewn into his cloak—the twisted geometric design that unmistakably identified him as a member of the feared Obsidian Order. In that moment, her heart raced, and an all-too-familiar sense of unease washed over her. Standing before her was the embodiment of her deepest fears.

CHAPTER 3:

LUMINESCENCE OF THE LOST

The shadowy, hooded figure—lunged at her, his presence suffocating like the cold grasp of a void. She knew that figure; it was like her first encounter with the Obsidian Order. His eyes glowed with a terrifying intensity; his anger palpable.

Before she could react, he attacked with relentless fury. Elara barely had time to block the first strike. Pain shot through her as she was slammed against the wall of a nearby building. The impact stole her breath, pain exploding across her ribs as she crumpled to the ground. She could taste blood, coppery and thick, pooling in her mouth. Every nerve screamed, but she forced herself to stand, the world spinning around her as the shadow closed in.

Her hand instinctively blasted radiant blue energy from her hand, a talent few Sidereals possess, but the creature was faster, easily dodging her counterattacks.

He growled, his voice low and dripping with venom.

Elara's heart raced. She darted away, weaving through the narrow streets of Calix City, her breaths ragged as the chase began. Her boots pounded against the pavement, adrenaline surging through her veins. The creature was relentless, his footsteps echoing close behind. She ducked into a side alley, hoping to lose him in the labyrinth of the city's underbelly.

But it was no use. He was there, blocking her path, a menacing silhouette framed by the dim light of the alley. There was no escape now.

With a swift motion, he struck. Elara fought back, but she was outmatched. Each blow was more brutal than the last, her body battered, her strength waning. He grabbed her by the throat, slamming her against the wall. Her vision blurred, her consciousness slipping away.

Just as her world began to fade, she heard a distant voice, a familiar voice cutting through the haze.

"Get away from her!"

There was a flash of light, and the creature reeled back, forced to retreat under the sudden onslaught. Elara's body slumped, and the last thing she saw was Mira standing over her, weapon raised, fury in her eyes.

Then, darkness.

Elara awoke to the sound of beeping, her body aching and heavy. She blinked, her vision adjusting to the dim light of her apartment. The sterile scent of medical supplies filled the air, and the soft glow of the city's lights filtered through the window.

Mira sat beside her, arms crossed, with a stern look. "About time you woke up," she muttered, though there was a hint of relief in her voice.

Elara tried to sit up, but pain shot through her ribs, and she winced. "What... what happened?"

"You got yourself beat up by one of the Obsidian Order," Mira said flatly. "He would've killed you if I hadn't shown up."

"Great. Just another day in the life, huh?" Elara groaned, forcing a weak smile despite the pain.

Mira narrowed her eyes. "This isn't funny, Elara. You're lucky to be alive."

Mira's gaze softened, a rare flicker of vulnerability in her steely demeanor. "Elara, you've got a knack for getting into trouble. But this…" She hesitated, her voice dropping. "This isn't just another research trip. They're hunting you now, and they won't stop until they get what they want."

Elara leaned back, her thoughts swirling. The Obsidian Order wasn't just a shadow anymore; they were after her and wouldn't stop. She glanced at Mira, grateful for her friend's timely intervention but worried. The stakes had just been raised.

"Thanks, Mira," Elara murmured, her voice softer. "I owe you one."

Elara glanced at her bandaged arm and shrugged. "Still attached, so I'll count it as a win."

Mira set the supplies down on the counter with a clatter. "You're lucky, that's for sure. I saw the footage—they almost took your entire arm off! You should be resting, not jumping into a research trip."

Elara waved her off, wincing, trying to downplay the event. "You know me. I can't sit still for long. Besides, it's just a research trip, not a battlefront."

"Uh-huh, like your 'research' trips, don't end up with explosions or death threats."

Elara rolled her eyes, though the teasing had a tinge of truth. Her research did tend to lead her into dangerous territory. But this time… it felt different. The weight of what she'd uncovered was enough to wake her up in cold sweats, and the Obsidian Order's involvement only complicated things further.

"Don't worry, I'll be fine," Elara said, trying to sound more confident than she felt. "I've got a team watching my back, and I'll be extra careful."

Mira gave her a doubtful look but didn't argue. Instead, she grabbed a container from the supply box and tossed it to Elara. "Re-Gen serum for your arm. You'll need it if you plan on doing anything remotely strenuous."

Elara caught the container mid-air and inspected it. "You always come prepared, don't you?"

Mira smirked. "Someone has to keep you in one piece. The universe isn't going to research itself."

Elara laughed softly and placed the serum on the table beside her. However, the lighthearted moment passed quickly as the weight of what lay ahead pressed down on her.

"Listen," Mira said, her tone softening, "are you sure you want to go through with this? I mean, I know you're not one to back down, but... this feels different."

Elara stared out the window, watching the streaks of sunlight filter through the familiar towering buildings of Astralith. The horizon shimmered, and she could see the distant spires of the Néalian Academy—her former home—the place where she'd spent years training, learning, and discovering. And now, it felt like a distant memory.

"I have to," Elara finally said, her voice low. "If there's even a chance the Astralis Core is involved, I can't just sit back and do nothing."

Miras looked surprised. "The Astralis Core?! Everyone here says it's nothing but a myth. You think it's real?!"

Elara confirms, "It is a resounding possibility."

Mira paused, astonished, and made a low whistle. "Wow!"

Mira sighed, crossing her arms. "I get why you are going, but do you know what you're up against? These things don't just chase people down for fun. They want something big."

"I know," Elara replied; she wondered if The Obsidian Order had sent them, her gaze hardening. "That's why I can't stop. This is bigger than both of us, Mira. It's bigger than the academy, bigger than anything I've studied before. If we don't find out what they're planning, no one is going to stop them."

Mira stared at her for a long moment, her usual sarcasm fading away, replaced by a rare seriousness. "Then you'd better come back in one piece," she said quietly. "Because I don't plan on having to rescue your butt again."

Elara smiled, but her eyes held a glimmer of unease. "Deal."

Mira embraced her in a tight, brief hug before pulling back. "I'll grab some more supplies for your trip. And for the record, you're the worst patient I've ever had."

Elara chuckled. "I'll try to be better."

"Don't try," Mira shot back, already heading for the door. "Just be better." She paused at the threshold, glancing back one last time. "And Elara? Be careful."

With that, Mira disappeared through the door, leaving Elara alone with her thoughts. The silence in the apartment grew heavier. Elara stared at the regen serum on the table, her mind racing through everything that had happened and was about to happen.

As much as she wanted to believe she could handle whatever the Obsidian Order threw at her, there was a gnawing doubt she couldn't shake. She wasn't just dealing with information anymore. She was stepping into something far more dangerous. Something that could change everything.

With a sigh, she leaned back on the bed and closed her eyes, feeling the weight of exhaustion returning. Tomorrow, she will begin the next phase of her journey. And this time, there was no turning back.

The Néalian Starport shimmered against the Astralith skyline, bathed in the fiery hues of the red-orange sunrise. Elara gazed out from the portside window of the AetherLift, her eyes tracing the sleek towers as they caught the early morning light.

The AetherLift is the latest breakthrough in personal transport technology, utilizing an advanced form of anti-graviton propulsion. Capable of achieving near-silent operation, it maneuvers with remarkable precision, thanks to a series of gyroscopic stabilizers and adaptive navigation AI. The vehicle's sleek, low-profile design minimizes air resistance, while its composite carbon nanotube frame ensures both durability and lightness. Equipped with environmental sensors, AetherLifts can automatically adjust their trajectory and altitude, navigating through dense cityscapes or open skies with unparalleled efficiency. Popular in megacities and corporate hubs, they are the preferred transport for those needing swift, reliable, and discreet travel across any terrain.

As the AetherLift silently descended into Docking Bay 7. Dr. Verus Clemens stood waiting at the landing zone alongside a man absorbed in the glowing interface of a digital slate. The man's olive-toned skin and lean, wiry frame marked him as a Terranovian, a product of a life forged in adversity. Nearby, a small detachment of soldiers—representing a mix of species—stood at attention, their eyes fixed on the new arrival.

With a whisper-quiet touchdown, the AetherLift's side hatch unfurled like the petals of a metal flower, revealing a shallow-sloped ramp. As Elara descended, she became keenly aware of the intimidating presence of the security detail, their watchful eyes and rigid posture far more imposing than expected.

As Elara approached, Verus cut through the noise of the bustling port with his usual precision. "Dr. Nova, right on time. Allow me to introduce my research assistant, Claudio Vega."

Claudio, engrossed in his display, barely registered the introduction. It wasn't until Elara extended her hand that he glanced up, his eyes widening in surprise. He nearly fumbled the digital slate he'd been pouring over, catching it just before it hit the ground.

"Uh—Dr. Nova! Wow, it's… it's a real pleasure," he stammered, scrambling to regain his composure. "Dr. Clemens mentioned your thesis on Waveform Harmonization in Plasma-Based Energy Manipulation?"

Claudio mentally kicked himself. Great first impression, Claudio. Real smooth. He forced a smile, trying to bury the heat rising in his cheeks.

Elara gave him a polite smile, her hand still extended. "That's correct. It's a bit of a niche field, so I'm surprised you've heard of it. Nice to meet you, Mr. Vega."

Claudio quickly shook her hand, a bit more enthusiastically than intended. "Please, just call me Claudio," he said with a lopsided grin, still trying to recover from his earlier blunder. "And, well, niche or not, I've always thought waveform fluctuations respond to data transponders through particle accumulation bias… you know, the observer effect and all that."

Elara raised an eyebrow, intrigued by his enthusiasm, though she couldn't help but wonder if he was showing off. "I see you are familiar with the research."

Claudio nodded, clearly a bit too eager. "Absolutely! I mean, I've... skimmed a few things here and there. Not an expert or anything, but..."

Verus, who had been watching the exchange with mild amusement, finally stepped in, raising a hand to cut Claudio off. "Fascinating as this conversation is, we're on a schedule. Dr. Nova, if you follow the security team, we can discuss particle accumulation bias again."

Claudio shot Elara a quick wink as they began to move. "Rain check on that, yeah? I've got a few theories you might find... interesting."

Elara's polite smile didn't waver. "I'll hold you to that, Claudio."

As they followed the team, Verus leaned slightly toward Elara, his tone deadpan. "I hope you're prepared for more of that."

Elara couldn't help but be impressed by Claudio's grasp of waveform manipulation. However, she quickly picked up on the fact that his cautious yet aloof demeanor likely came from spending too much time buried in research rather than engaging with people. He was sharp, but something about him was... unpredictable. He had the markings of a seasoned scholar but a rogue edge that set him apart from the typical academic types she was used to. Without a word, she followed Verus and Claudio, joining the security personnel.

The security team escorted them to a large interstellar ship. Its matte blue panels absorbed the light, giving it a sleek, imposing presence.

The Galathea loomed before them, an impressive vessel with sleek, matte blue panels that gave it a stealthy, almost predatory appearance. Its hull was built from advanced composite alloys designed to absorb energy and radar signals, making it nearly invisible to detection systems. The ship's surface, adorned with subtle geometric patterns, reflected little light, giving it a subdued, low-profile silhouette against the stars.

It was built for both speed and endurance, with a streamlined design that allowed it to cut through space with minimal resistance. Its elongated central body housed the ship's command center, crew quarters, and advanced navigation systems, while two massive, retractable thrusters on either side provided thrust for long-distance travel and precision maneuvering.

The front of the ship was dominated by a reinforced viewport, offering the crew an expansive view of the stars ahead. A series of angular, glowing ridges ran along the sides, marking the location of its energy shields and weapon systems, ready to deploy at a moment's notice.

The landing bay, positioned toward the rear, was large enough to accommodate multiple smaller ships like the AetherLifts. An array of docking ports lined the side, suggesting the ship's capacity for refueling and repairs in deep space.

Despite its utilitarian design, there was an undeniable elegance to The Galathea, a ship built for exploration but prepared for conflict. It felt like both a fortress and a vessel of discovery, ready to navigate the unknown with its crew.

Elara had always been aware of Verus's extensive connections, but she never realized the full extent of his influence until now. The sight of The Galathea left her genuinely impressed. Mira had once mentioned that the ship was the pride of Néalian exploration, a vessel so revered that even the most respected academics rarely had the privilege to see it, let alone board it for an exploratory mission.

Once aboard, the ship smoothly lifted off, piercing through the atmosphere to rendezvous with a privately owned space station orbiting Néalian. There, they would conduct low-gravity hull inspections, run instrumentation checks, and refuel for the upcoming 200-light-year journey

The bridge deck's conference room exuded a quiet elegance. Soft taupe and earthy tones contrasted against the sleek obsidian holo table at the center. Comfortable, ergonomic chairs were arranged around the table, designed to reduce distractions during long meetings. Elara took a seat nearest the door while Verus sat directly across from her. Claudio, buried in ancient books and scattered maps, occupied the seat next to him.

"Zynthar is no stranger to students, researchers, and others in Néalian academia," Verus began. "However," He paused, his expression darkening. "We can't remain naive. Some of the main districts have seen an increase in faction-related crime in recent years."

Concerned, Elara leaned forward. "Are any of those factions tied to the Obsidian Order?"

At the mention of the name, the air in the room grew tense. Claudio and Verus exchanged shocked glances as if Elara had just uttered something unthinkable.

Breaking the awkward silence, Elara continued, "Because I was attacked by one just a couple of nights ago. On my way back from meeting you, Dr. Clemens."

Claudio, with clear disbelief in his voice, responded, "The Obsidian Order hasn't been seen in our galaxy for over thirty years. It's more likely you were attacked by one of the Astralith factions."

Elara shot him a discerning look. "I've lived in Astralith my whole life. I've never seen anything like what attacked me."

Verus, his expression stern, turned toward Claudio. "Claudio, don't cast doubt or make accusations at our guest." Looking at Elara apologetically, he asked, "Dr. Nova, survivors of Obsidian Order attacks—those who've lived to speak of it—often mention a sudden drop in temperature when one is near. Did you experience anything like that?"

"Yes!" Elara replied, startled by his insight. "I felt it recently, shortly after your lecture at the Astralith Academy Symposium. It was odd, but I didn't think much of it at the time." She hesitated for a moment, then continued, "Dr. Clemens, after our meeting, I was attacked by an obsidian-robed figure covered in ornate geometric red scars. The attack was so sudden and vicious. I didn't even have time to react, let alone defend myself. If it weren't for my colleague Mira, I wouldn't be standing here now."

Verus's expression darkened with concern while Claudio sat frozen, still reeling from the mention of the robed figure. His mind raced. If this were a faction-related attack, there would have been more than one assailant. And yet, Elara's description was disturbingly precise—consistent with the very few accounts that exist. The drop in temperature, the black robes... it all matched too well. The Obsidian Order, notorious on Astralith, might be involved, but they never wore robes, much less exhibited such a chilling aura. Claudio's unease deepened. This was no ordinary attack.

The thought that the Obsidian Order might have returned sent a wave of fear through Claudio. It was them, after all, who had murdered his parents. A truth he kept hidden from everyone—except for Dr. Clemens.

"I'm relieved you're still with us, Dr. Nova," Verus said with genuine concern. "Without you, who knows if this expedition would've even moved forward."

"The Order has eyes everywhere, Elara," Verus added, his voice barely above a whisper. "We'll be lucky if we make it out of Zynthar unseen."

He paused briefly before shifting his focus. "Now, we need to map out our route on Zynthar. Claudio, if you would."

Claudio shuffled through the brittle, ancient maps; his brow furrowed in concentration. "The maps of ancient Zynthar—Agri Solitudo as it was once called—are incomplete. Many regions are missing, particularly those outside the main settlements. Whole expanses of the planet remain uncharted, at least by these records."

Verus, unfazed by the gaps in knowledge, leaned forward. "Claudio, hand Dr. Nova the Will of the Keepers tome."

Claudio's eyes flicked toward the heavy, worn tome resting on the edge of the table. He carefully picked it up and handed it to Elara. As soon as her fingers brushed the surface, the tome emitted a faint glow, illuminating the mathematical symbols etched into the cover. Claudio froze, speechless for a moment, as the light pulsed rhythmically as if the book recognized her presence.

Claudio, regaining his composure, shook his head in disbelief. "It's... extraordinary. The tome hasn't responded to anyone in years. I've never seen anything like this."

Verus watched Elara with a knowing look. "The Will of the Keepers holds ancient knowledge, but it only reveals itself to those who are meant to uncover it. You seem to share a deeper connection to the Core than we initially realized."

Claudio, eager to regain focus, returned his attention to the maps. He spread out a more recent star chart beside the ancient one, comparing landmarks. "Here," he said, pointing to a location on both maps. "The nearest city is Kraedin. It still stands today, according to recent records, and if we triangulate between the old ruins and these updated scans, it should be located here."

He tapped a point on the map where the ancient and modern versions aligned. "It's not far from the original settlements, but the terrain has shifted dramatically since the time of Agri Solitudo. We'll need to adjust for that when we land."

Verus leaned over the map, his eyes narrowed. "Zynthar isn't kind to those who underestimate it. Even the land itself can change in a heartbeat. We'll need to tread carefully if we're to avoid any... surprises."

Verus considered the options, then made a decision, glancing at Elara and the glowing tome in her hands. "Then Kraedin it is. Let's make preparations—we have no time to waste."

CHAPTER 4:

THE OBSIDIAN ORDER

The Galathea sailed through the quiet void of space enroute to Zynthar, its powerful engines emitting a low, constant hum reverberating through the ship's corridors. Inside, the atmosphere was tense but calm, an uneasy stillness that permeated every corner. The crew worked quietly, some absorbed in their tasks at their stations, while others took the opportunity to rest, reclining in their quarters. Despite the apparent calm, there was a subtle, unspoken awareness that something was looming on the horizon—an eerie calm before the storm.

The mess hall aboard was a stark contrast to the chaos that often filled the ship's corridors. Dim lighting cast long shadows across the steel-plated walls, and the polished surfaces of the tables reflected the soft glow of the overhead lights. Elara sat alone at one of the back tables, hunched over The Will of the Keepers. The faint sound of the engines reverberated through the floor beneath her feet, a constant reminder that they were far from any planetary ground.

The usual mess hall chatter was absent—most of the crew had turned in for the night or were still on duty. Elara appreciated the solitude; it gave her space to think. In front of her, the ancient text was written in a language that had long been forgotten by most. The script was alive, glowing faintly in response to her touch as if acknowledging her presence. Every time her fingers brushed over the lines, the text would shimmer, flickering between known words and symbols she still couldn't decipher.

The plate of untouched food beside her had long since gone cold. She absentmindedly pushed it aside, too absorbed in her study. Her thoughts circled back to the same question: why did The Will react only to her? The glowing text felt like an answer just out of reach, teasing her with its mystery.

Elara sat in the dimly lit corner of the ship's cabin; the original copy of the Will of the Keepers spread out before her. Its faint glow pulsed rhythmically, casting soft light onto her focused face. Her fingers traced the ancient lines and symbols; her thoughts were lost in deciphering their meaning when the quiet sound of footsteps broke the silence.

"You think it's a gift, don't you?" Claudio's voice was low, but it carried a weight that snapped her out of her concentration.

Elara didn't flinch, though the question caught her off guard. She hadn't noticed him enter. Without looking up, she replied, "What do you mean?"

Claudio moved closer, leaning on the table across from her, his eyes fixed on the glowing Will. His usual guarded expression softened, but tension still lingered behind his gaze. "That thing—" he gestured toward the book, "—it lights up for you. Only you. Don't you think that's a little too convenient? A little too... chosen one?"

Elara swallowed hard, the words "chosen one" settling uneasily in her mind. She didn't want to be chosen—she wanted to understand, to uncover truths, not to wield power. But the glow of the Will said otherwise. Was she different from the Order, or was she just as drawn to its call?

Elara's fingers froze on the parchment. His words hit deeper than she wanted to admit, but she kept her voice even. "What are you getting at?"

He sighed, glancing at the glowing pages before meeting her eyes. "The Obsidian... they have a history of finding people like you."

Elara raised an eyebrow, her curiosity piqued. "People like me?"

Claudio nodded, his expression darkening. "The Obsidian Order isn't just another faction. They were once part of the Sidereals—Elara, they're your people. They split off generations ago, consumed by their obsession with power. They believe the Astralis Core is the key to unlocking something far beyond what any of us understand. They look for individuals with unique connections to the Core—people who can unlock its secrets. People like you."

He paused, and his voice was quieter. "I've seen what happens when they find someone they think is 'chosen.' They manipulate them and use them to further their agenda. And if they don't get what they want... they don't leave survivors."

Elara's fingers tightened on the edge of the tome. She finally looked up, locking eyes with Claudio. "I'm not them," she said, her voice steady but cold. "I'm not looking to be some savior. I'm trying to understand why this—" she motioned to the glowing Will,"—reacts to me at all. If I don't figure it out, we could be walking into a bigger mess than we realize."

Claudio straightened, his expression firm. "Or maybe you're already in too deep. You're so focused on the Will you're not seeing the bigger picture. This isn't just about knowledge, Elara. It's about survival."

Elara's eyes narrowed. "You think I'm the problem?"

Claudio folded his arms. "This glow, this connection, is more dangerous than you think. The Obsidian Order will stop at nothing to get what they want."

Before she could respond, the ship's alarms blared, shaking the cabin. The steady hum of the engines shifted into a frantic whine. Elara instinctively reached for the Will of the Keepers as it flickered, the glow intensifying as if sensing the attack before it came.

Claudio's voice was grim as he muttered, "They're here."

"The Order doesn't stop once they set their sights on something," Claudio muttered, his voice low. "I've seen them tear through ships, leaving nothing behind but debris. They're relentless, Elara. If they're this close, we're already in their crosshairs."

A loud metallic boom echoed as the ship shook, sending Elara off balance. As she stumbled, Claudio's arms shot out, catching her before she hit the ground. Their eyes met, and for a brief moment, the chaos around them faded.

Claudio's breath caught as he stared into her Siderealian eyes, captivated by the specks of green swirling like galaxies, tiny universes unfolding into stars. She was close enough that he could feel the faint warmth of her presence.

Elara's heart raced as she looked into his eyes, noticing the flecks of orange that flickered like embers against the dark intensity of his gaze. He's always so guarded, she realized. But right now, it's like I can see through that. There's something more...

The intercom tone sounded, shattering the moment. "Claudio! Elara! To the bridge, now!" The comms system commanded Verus's voice. They blinked, both startled back to reality, exchanging awkward filler words before Elara swiftly swept her books into a rucksack and marched down the corridor toward the fusion elevators.

As if it were a different ship, All the personnel were rushing to their battle stations. Elara was barreling down the hall at astonishing speed, and Claudio was barely keeping up with her. Before they knew it, they were at the bridge.

The crew scrambled to their stations, the atmosphere tense as if they were aboard an entirely different vessel. Elara darted down the corridor with lightning speed, her focus unshakable. Claudio struggled to keep pace, his breath quickening as they neared their destination.

Before they even realized it, they burst into the bridge.

"The Obsidian Order!" Verus exclaimed, his voice cutting through the commotion. "We're under attack!"

Verus turned to Elara, his gaze sharp. "Were you looking at the Tome?"

Elara hesitated, then nodded. His expression darkened. "That would explain it."

Elara frowned; disbelief etched across her face. "How could they know?"

Verus sighed. "The Obsidian Order are Sidereals. They can sense energy fluctuations. You're Sidereal too—didn't you feel the shift?"

Elara blinked, taken aback. "Well, yeah, but I thought it was just nerves or something. I haven't exactly been getting much sleep."

Before Verus could respond, Claudio stepped in, his tone practical. "Well, they're here now. Elara, how good are you with weapons?"

"Astralith self-defense courses, about a year ago. It was a required class," Elara shot back.

"That'll have to do," Verus replied, his tone curt. "Claudio, get her to the drone operations vault—now!"

Claudio gave her a quick nod. "Let's move!"

The hull of the bridge trembled even more violently as they rushed into action, the situation growing more dire by the second.

Elara sprinted after Claudio as they dashed through the narrow corridors, the ship groaning under the relentless assault. The lights flickered overhead, and the distant hum of the engines felt unstable. Every step was more uncertain as the hull shook violently around them.

"Are you sure I'm ready for this?" Elara shouted over the sound of blaring alarms.

Claudio glanced back, his expression serious but steady. "You don't have much choice! Just focus and remember your training."

They skidded to a halt in front of the vault. Claudio quickly entered the access code, the heavy doors sliding open with a low hiss. Inside, rows of consoles and holo-displays flickered to life. The drone fleet, their best defense now, lay in Elara's hands.

"You need to operate these remotely and keep them off our tail until we can make the jump to Serathion," Claudio instructed. "Can you handle it?"

Elara took a deep breath, her fingers hovering over the controls. "I'll manage."

The ship lurched violently as another explosion rocked the hull. Claudio steadied himself, glancing at the ceiling row control panel.

Elara quickly remembered her training. She took control of a Viper-Class Drone.

The Viper-Class drones, sleek and compact, are designed with the lethal efficiency of their namesake—a coiled serpent ready to strike. Their matte black exteriors blend seamlessly into the darkness of space, while their aerodynamic form allows for rapid deployment from the Galathea's hangar. Built for speed, the Vipers execute sharp evasive maneuvers with uncanny precision, making them elusive targets. Armed with twin laser cannons for quick-strike combat and guided micro-missiles for devastating close-range attacks, they are perfectly suited for fast, tactical engagements. Specializing in hit-and-run missions, these drones excel at harrying larger ships or intercepting enemy fighters. When deployed in swarms, they overwhelm opponents with their agility and concentrated firepower, proving themselves invaluable in space skirmishes where speed and precision are paramount.

Elara's Viper-class drone slipped silently out of the hangar bay, blending into the dark expanse of space. Her view of the surroundings was fully immersive, the light helmet she wore linking her mind directly to the drone's sensors. As she fired the throttle, the sudden burst of speed startled her, far more intense than anything she'd experienced in her academic training pods. The controls were sensitive—almost too sensitive—requiring a steady hand as she adjusted to the drone's responsiveness. Her eyes locked onto the ship trailing behind the Galathea.

Claudio's voice crackled in her comm, calm but with an edge of urgency. "That's a Dreadspire. The Obsidian Order recently commissioned them for scouting and offensive strikes. Their drones may still be prototypes, but don't let that fool you—they're deadly. You'll need to take down as many as you can. I'll clear a path to the Dreadspire's engines."

Elara's pulse quickened as she guided the Viper closer to the Dreadspire, the massive ship looming ahead like a predator in the shadows. Her fingers hovered over the controls, adjusting to the drone's hypersensitivity. She could feel every subtle movement, each adjustment translating seamlessly into the drone's quick, darting maneuvers. The Dreadspire's hull gleamed in the distance, and the faint, ominous glint of its own drones launching into the void sent a shiver down her spine.

"Elara, incoming—five enemy drones," Claudio's voice warned through the comm. "You've got to move."

Without hesitating, she rolled the Viper sharply to the left, dodging the first volley of laser fire. The Obsidian drones, sleek and aggressive, were already closing in on her position, their movements erratic but purposeful.

Her heart hammered as she gripped the controls, every nerve alive with tension. The Viper-class was fast, but her movements had to be faster—one wrong turn and she'd be space dust. She could feel the sweat gathering at her temples, her breath shallow as the enemy drones closed in.

Elara gritted her teeth and targeted the nearest one, her hand steady as she fired the twin laser cannons. A sharp burst of energy erupted from her drone, slicing through the void, catching the enemy drone mid-turn. It exploded in a flash of sparks and debris.

"Got one," she muttered, more to herself than anyone else.

"Don't celebrate yet," Claudio's voice cut in. "More are on their way. Focus on keeping them off our backs while I work on the Dreadspire's engines."

She pivoted, barely dodging another barrage of fire from an incoming drone. The Viper was fast, but the enemies were relentless. As she darted between enemy fire, the sheer number of drones made it clear: this was no simple scouting mission. The Obsidian Order had prepared for a fight.

Her comm crackled again. "Elara, they're pushing hard. We need to clear them before they break through our defenses. Keep moving and stay unpredictable."

She gripped the controls tighter, weaving through the chaos, laser fire lighting up the blackness around her. The Dreadspire loomed larger with each second, and so did the growing swarm of enemy drones.

Elara pushed the Viper to its limits, weaving through the onslaught of enemy drones. Every maneuver was a razor's edge between survival and disaster. Sweat dripped down her temple as she fired another burst of laser fire, taking out two more drones in quick succession. The tension in her chest only grew as the swarm multiplied relentlessly in its pursuit.

"I see subtlety isn't their strong suit," she muttered, her voice strained through the comm.

Claudio's voice came through hearing her sarcasm, "Focus, Elara. You can complain about their lack of subtlety after we're not dead."

The enemy drones darted in every direction, their erratic movements making them difficult to target. Elara narrowly avoided another barrage, but a sudden realization hit her—she had missed several in her desperate attempt to evade.

Her eyes darted to the corner of her display, a cluster of enemy drones closing in on the Galathea's vulnerable underbelly. She fired a volley in their direction, but one drone slipped through her attack, dodging her shots with alarming agility. Time slowed to a crawl as she watched helplessly.

The rogue drone hurtled toward the Galathea and slammed into one of its rear engines. There was a sudden, violent explosion, and the ship shuddered violently as sparks and debris shot into space. The force of the impact threw Elara's Viper off course, her controls shaking uncontrollably for a moment before she regained control.

"No!" Elara shouted, her heart sinking as she watched the damage unfold.

Claudio's voice came through, more urgent now. "We've lost engine three! Elara, we're dead in the water if we lose another one!"

The hum of the Galathea's engines faltered their once-steady pulse now disrupted by the damaged unit. Smoke and sparks billowed from the engine as the ship struggled to maintain speed. Elara's heart dropped as she watched the explosion ripple across the hull. She could barely breathe, her mind flashing with worst-case scenarios. This wasn't just an academic exercise; real lives were on the line. And she'd failed to protect them.

"I—" Elara's mind raced, searching for a solution, but she was already running on adrenaline. More drones were closing in, drawn to the weakness they had just created.

"You need to cover us! Take them out before we lose anything else!" Claudio's voice was sharp, laced with both urgency and fear.

Elara's hands shook as she adjusted her course, her eyes narrowing in on the incoming drones. The stakes had risen to survival—not just for her, but for the entire crew aboard the Galathea. She gripped the controls tighter and pressed the throttle forward.

"I'm on it," she said, determination flooding her voice.

Elara's focus sharpened as her drone weaved through the chaos. Years of competitive drone simulations came rushing back, the muscle memory kicking in as she slipped into the zone. Each flick of her wrist sent the Viper darting through space, dodging enemy fire with precision. She could feel the rush of it now—the speed, the stakes, the split-second decisions. Her fingers danced over the controls, firing the twin lasers in short bursts, watching as enemy drones exploded one by one.

"Elara, we're still not in the clear!" Claudio's voice crackled through the comms. She could hear the strain in his voice as he, too, was locked in a battle with the swarming enemy drones.

Her eyes flicked to the Galathea on her display, its damaged engine still sparking, the ship struggling to hold its course. They were running out of time.

Claudio's plasma bolts lit up the display, taking out several drones with pinpoint accuracy. His voice returned, more urgent now. "Listen, there's too many of them. You need to send your drone straight into the Dreadspire. Put it in self-destruct mode. That's the only way we're getting out of this!"

Elara's fingers paused for a heartbeat, her mind racing. She'd never used a drone to self-destruct before. "Are you sure?" she asked, her voice tight.

"No choice," Claudio replied quickly. "Get your drone to the Dreadspire and blow it. I'll clear a path."

Nodding to herself, Elara adjusted her controls, setting her sights on the Dreadspire ahead. It loomed larger with every passing second. She could feel the countdown to detonation ticking in her mind as her Viper accelerated toward the massive ship. Her fingers moved swiftly, engaging the self-destruct sequence. The display flashed with a warning, the drone's systems preparing for the final strike.

Claudio fired off more plasma bolts, taking out enemy drones as Elara's Viper surged forward. "You're close enough. Send it!" he shouted.

Elara hit the final command. Her drone locked into a collision course with the Dreadspire, its engines burning at full throttle. The distance closed rapidly, the massive enemy vessel filling her display.

A sudden explosion rocked the Dreadspire as Elara's drone detonated on impact, a blinding burst of light engulfing the ship's hull. Claudio's voice broke through the noise, excitement and urgency mixed. "You did it! Hang on, we're making the jump!"

Just as Elara saw the first explosion ripple across the Dreadspire, a second Viper drone she had missed crashed into one of Galathea's damaged engines. The ship lurched violently, alarms blaring, as sparks and debris shot out from the impact. Smoke poured from the crippled engine as systems flickered.

But before panic could set in, Claudio's voice shouted over the comms. "We're still good. Buckle up—we're jumping now!"

With a sudden jolt, the Galathea's engines roared back to life, propelling the ship forward into the void. The stars around them stretched into blurs of light as they jumped into hyperspace, leaving the wreckage of the drones and the Dreadspire behind.

Claudio ripped off his helmet and strode over to Elara's drone station as she removed hers. His eyes held a mix of curiosity and admiration.

"What rank were you in the Astralith Academy Drone Sims?" he asked, one eyebrow raised.

Elara shrugged lightly. "Twenty-fourth. But I had some help from someone ranked a little higher."

Claudio paused, a slight grin forming as he extended a hand to help her up. "Not bad, considering almost all of our engines nearly blew out. We'll probably have to make an emergency landing as soon as we hit Serathion."

Elara's voice wavered with guilt. "There were just too many drones. I'm sorry... I should've done better."

Claudio smirked, shaking his head. "I wouldn't lose sleep over it. Verus probably knows someone on every planet in this sector. I'm sure he's already cutting a deal with whatever sleazy politician he can find to bail us out of this mess."

True to his word, Verus was already deep in conversation as Elara and Claudio entered the room. On the holoscreen stood a green, scaly figure—a lizard-like creature with sharp, blinking eyes.

"And I believe we can come to an arrangement, Chancellor," Verus said smoothly, his tone full of practiced diplomacy. "Your mechanics are truly the finest this galaxy has to offer!"

The creature replied in a low, guttural voice, its language a series of growls and hisses. "Slachtak Unt Perrrr Gllaccken Coo ha tsssss."

Elara studied Verus's expression as he negotiated with Filar. There was something almost too comfortable in the way he spoke to the Chancellor, as if this wasn't the first time he'd bartered with people on the wrong side of things. She made a mental note to keep an eye on him—he seemed to have a few secrets of his own.

Verus nodded respectfully. "And may you remain safe as well. Goodbye, Filar." The holoscreen flickered off, and Verus turned to them with a satisfied smile.

Verus turned to face Elara and Claudio, his expression one of calm confidence. "Well, that should take care of things for now. Chancellor

Filar is sending a team to meet us on Serathion. Their mechanics will handle the engine repairs as soon as we land."

Elara gave him a wary look. "You seemed awfully comfortable negotiating with him. How well do you know this... Chancellor Filar?"

Verus shrugged, the ghost of a smile playing on his lips. "Filar and I have crossed paths a few times. Let's just say he owes me a favor or two."

Claudio crossed his arms, leaning against the doorframe. "And I assume those favors come at a price?"

Verus's smile widened. "Everything does, Claudio. But don't worry—this deal will hold. Besides, Serathion's government is desperate to keep good relations with the Néalians. They'll make sure we're back in the air soon enough."

Elara sighed in relief, but a trace of guilt still lingered in her voice. "I just hope we can fix the damage in time. I shouldn't have missed those drones."

Verus waved her concern away. "Nonsense, Dr. Nova. Given the circumstances, you did more than well. We're still flying, aren't we?"

Claudio chuckled lightly, pushing off the wall. "If Filar's mechanics are as good as you say, we should be fine. Let's just hope his price isn't too steep,"

Verus's eyes twinkled with amusement. "Credits are not the only cost for this mission."

CHAPTER 5:

THE RIFTBORN SYNDICATE

THIRTY YEARS EARLIER...

Driftspire Station is a bustling hub located on the edge of a volatile star system. It serves as an important stop for travelers, traders, and outlaws due to its reputation as an essential refueling and business center. The station is a complex of towering spires and interconnected docking platforms, where legitimate trade and black-market deals coexist.

Driftspire is known for its shady back-alley deals and the presence of unsavory characters from across the galaxy, making it a favorite haunt of smugglers, mercenaries, and bounty hunters. The dimly lit corridors and under-the-table exchanges where fortunes are made or lost in an instant, often accompanied by the clink of credits and the whisper of confidential information.

The air was thick with the smell of used oil and burnt metal, punctuated by the occasional whiff of exotic spices from street vendors. Voices mingled with the hum of engines, creating a constant, dissonant symphony of business and barter.

The station is frequently used by The Obsidian Order for their clandestine operations, as it allows them to blend in with the crowd of opportunists and criminals. Driftspire also houses information brokers who deal in whispers and rumors, offering access to rare and illicit goods and knowledge. For those with the credits to pay, Driftspire Station is more than just a port; it's a gateway to power and influence in the galaxy's darker corners.

The prisoner transport ship of the Obsidian Order ominously looms into view at Driftspire Station. As the vessel docks, heavily armored enforcers escort shackled prisoners off the ship, casting an atmosphere of fear and unwavering control. The arrival of the transport serves as a chilling symbol of authority and terror at the infamous outpost.

Jax Teralis stood in front of a shady dock bar, two or three docks away, his eyes scanning the transport ship. To his left stood a short Terranovian, staring incessantly at a datapad.

Jax is an imposing figure, standing close to seven feet tall with a broad-shouldered build. His skin has a light shade of purple, almost lavender, with a smooth texture that reflects the dim light of space stations. His most striking features are his slit nostrils, giving him an imposing, almost reptilian appearance, and a wide, squared chin that adds to his intimidating look. His eyes are dark and always seem to be scanning his surroundings with a quiet intensity, as if he's sizing up everything and everyone around him.

He is the muscle of his crew in the Riftborn Syndicate, specializing in brute force and physical solutions. When it comes to cracking open safes, breaking down stronghold doors, or smashing through fortress walls, Jax is the go-to guy. His strength is legendary, and his reputation for getting the job done, no matter the obstacles, makes him highly respected in underworld circles.

His species, Brulvian, is known for their physical resilience and their ability to thrive in low-oxygen environments, making him especially suited for high-risk jobs in space. His light purple skin, wide chin, and slit nostrils are key characteristics of his race, which is rarely seen outside of dangerous and hard-to-reach parts of the galaxy.

"Well, Jax," Grevlak said, adjusting his slick hair, "the task at hand demands a more delicate and subtle approach." Grevlak, a middle-aged Terranovian with a Napoleon complex stemming from his short height, emphasized the need for caution in their approach.

"Some of my crew is off doing a different job now, Give me this, Grev. I'll get it done." Jax said, watching the busy dock.

Grevlak looked at him suspiciously, "A solo job? Jax, you haven't boosted alone for the last 50 cycles." He shook his head, "Plus the boss said," Grev putting on an impression of a Thessari., "No Brulviansss! The ultra fusion couplings have to be manually...", He was interrupted by Jax's massive hand on his mouth. "Shut up a sec. I might have an in."

A young Oriana is being escorted off of the Obsidian Order transport. As she is being escorted off the prisoner transport, the two heavily armed guards tower over her. Their confident demeanor suggests that they don't anticipate any trouble from the petite prisoner. For a split second, doubt clawed at her. She was alone, far from home, with no one to turn to. But then, the memory of Astralith, of Elara's face, flashed in her mind. She steeled herself. This was her chance—she couldn't afford to look back. As they make their way through the bustling crowd towards a temporary holding area for prisoners awaiting transfer, Oriana's sharp eyes catch a fleeting opportunity. Drawing upon her Sidereal powers, she deftly manipulates the ambient energy, creating a momentary distortion that causes the guards to stumble, momentarily loosening their grip on her.

In that split second, Oriana seizes the chance and breaks free, swiftly disappearing into the throng of people. The bustling station provides her with cover as she expertly weaves through the crowd, skillfully navigating between vendors and dubious characters to evade capture. For a brief moment, she manages to elude the pursuing guards, but the tranquility is shattered as the Obsidian Order raises the alarm, prompting a frenzied search for the escaped prisoner.

Intrigued by her determination and the fact that she's just a kid, Jak's curiosity was piqued as he watched her skillful escape. Despite her small size, Oriana moved with a sense of purpose, clearly not fitting the mold of an average runaway.

Jax, who had a soft spot for underdogs, made the decision to intervene as he observed the guards pursuing her and moved to intercept.

The way she moved, with small, determined steps, evoked memories of his own past days of fighting to survive on the fringes of society. It wasn't just her youth that caught his attention; it was the resolute look in her eyes, a familiar gaze that spoke volumes about her experiences and resilience.

"Hold that thought, Grev," Jax said as he made his way over to the dock where the prisoner queue was forming. He grabbed a bottle off the ground and approached the guards while they were searching for Oriana, pretending to be drunk. "Hey, you guys can't park here, this is a union spot!" Jax slurred his speech as he shoved one of the guards with his half-filled bottle of green liquid, spilling some of the contents on the guard.

Oriana smirked and took the opportunity to slip away into the nearby crowd and into a small alley.

"Citizen, back up!" the Obsidian Guard pointed his glowing palms at Jax threateningly. "We have safe passage in Driftspire. If you wish to file a formal complaint, do so with the Port Master!"

Jax saw where the girl went out of the corner of his eye. "Alright, alright," he slurred again, "I was just making sure. I'm gonna go now." He faked a stumble toward the alley.

Oriana found herself at a dead end in the alleyway. Two figures emerged from the darkness behind her.

"Where do you think you're going?" a voice grumbled. Her heart was pounding with an electrified force. She was about to engage her powers, her hands started to glow.

"Talos! Ronin! Go back to the other district, you filth." Jak said as he walked into the alley.

"Ja Jax!" Ronin said nervously. "I didn't know you were around the portside."

"Yeah, well I'm not asking again," Jax stepped into one of the streetlights. His towering figure is silhouetted by fusion illumination.

Oriana was shocked and terrified at the size of him, almost comical in comparison to Talos and Ronin.

Talos and Ronin darted away like a swift breeze, running in fear. Jax watched them until it was just him and Oriana. He turned to face her, then crouched down to be at eye level with the child. "What's your name, young Sidereal?"

He was massive, and she was nervous to speak. Summoning her courage, she managed to say, "Um… Oriana." She gulped, "Huh… um… How do you know I'm a Sidereal?"

"Not many of you guys come around here that aren't a part of the Order," Jax said with a smirk as he sat down on the ground to be at eye level. "Let's get you to some place safe."

Jax rose up, back to his towering height, and motioned for her to follow him. Oriana hesitated, unsure if she could trust this towering stranger, but with no other options, she followed his lead.

Jax expertly guided her through the crowd, using his size and presence to shield her from view. They weaved through busy sections of the station, slipping into side corridors and service tunnels that only someone familiar with the underbelly of this place would know. Oriana stayed close, watching how he effortlessly commanded the space around him.

After eluding the guards, Jax takes Oriana to a secluded, dilapidated section of the station—an old warehouse that the Syndicate occasionally uses as a safe house. He closes the door behind them, ensuring they are out of reach of the guards.

Oriana is still tense, but Jax, surprisingly gentle for his size, crouches down to her level. "You did well, kid," he says, his voice gruff but not unkind. "How did you manage that back there?"

Oriana doesn't fully trust him yet, but she's also smart enough to know she needs help. "I had to escape," she says, guarded. "They weren't going to let me go."

Jax chuckles. "Yeah, I know that type. Stick with me, and I'll make sure they don't find you again."

Unbeknownst to her, this marks the beginning of a strong bond. Jax, accustomed to using brute force to crack safes and strongholds, sees something in Oriana—a potential beyond just her Sidereal powers. And for the first time in a long while, he feels like there's someone worth protecting, beyond the jobs and the take.

Fifteen years later, the echoes of that fateful night had faded, but its consequences lingered like a shadow over everything that followed.

The acrid smell of burning oil permeated the air as Jax leaned against a grime-streaked wall in a dimly lit boiler room. The seedy underbelly of the city often hid spaces like this, and Graenik always ensured to have a few scattered throughout the sub-levels. This room was situated beneath the temporary quarters of the Ambassador of Néalian.

Unlike his high-strung colleague, Dax, Jax valued patience. This job, Orianna's first, was not one to be rushed. Everything needed to go flawlessly.

"What's taking Karra so long?" Dax demanded, his pacing growing increasingly erratic. "You know we don't have all night!"

Jax cast him an unimpressed look. "Karra's a pro. She'll keep the Ambassador distracted. Trust the process," he said, placing a reassuringly heavy Brulvian hand on Dax's shoulder. "We rehearsed this a dozen times in the simulator, remember?"

"Simulations don't mean jack when we've got rookies on a million-credit job," Dax muttered, his tone laced with skepticism.

Jax exhaled, tired of the doubt. "Orianna's ready. I trained her myself."

Dax shot back with sharp sarcasm. "Oh, well, that just fills me with confidence."

Ignoring the jab, Jax flipped open his communicator and tapped the side switch. A crisp electronic chirp echoed in the room. "Ori, status?"

Orianna's voice crackled to life through the device. "Descending to sub-level two. ETA, two minutes."

"Copy." Jax turned to Dax with a gesture that said, See? Everything's under control.

"Finally," Dax grumbled, rolling over a rusted metal cart laden with a sleek silver cylinder, its surface gleaming beneath the boiler room's dim lights. A keypad was embedded at its center.

"Just shut up and line up the drill," Jax ordered, steadying the cart as Dax reluctantly keyed in the sequence. The device beeped in response.

"Position three, ready," Dax confirmed.

"Setting the compiler now," Orianna reported through the communicator. Moments later, the faint thud of metal against concrete resonated as she placed a compact, silver disk on the floor above.

Phase-shift Matter Compilers were a rarity, their use restricted to the elite ranks of the United Néalian Fleet. These military-grade devices could rearrange matter at the atomic level, allowing precise manipulation of even the most fortified structures. They were worth fortunes—and worth stealing.

"Set," Orianna's voice came through again.

"Copy. Locking location," Jax responded, nodding at Dax.

Dax pressed the final sequence on the cylinder's keypad. The machine hummed to life, its low rumble resonating through the room. "Locked."

"Confirmed. Activate," Orianna instructed.

Dax flipped the activation toggle, and a bright green light pulsed from the compiler. A loud zap cut through the air, followed by an explosion of steam and smoke that engulfed the room, rendering visibility near zero.

On the level above, hurried footsteps reverberated against the metal grates. The door flew open with a metallic clang.

Karra strode in a gleaming red evening dress, her voice sharp and commanding. "Change of plans. We've got ten minutes—max."

Dax emerged from the freshly cut hole, dusting off his hands and muttering, "I knew something felt off..." He glanced down, extending his arm into the opening. "Jax, get up here."

A powerful Brulvian hand clasped Dax's forearm, and with a heave, Jax pulled himself through the smoky gap.

For a moment, the room was eerily quiet, save for the hiss of steam rising through the floor. Jax's eyes narrowed, confusion etched across his face. "What?"

Dax let out a weary sigh and gestured to Karra. "You tell him."

Karra didn't hesitate. She turned to Jax, her tone grim. "We've got less than ten minutes."

Jax wore an expression of disappointment, "Can you tell us why?"

Karra didn't flinch. "Ran into one of the Crimson Syndicate operatives at the benefit. Rin. Recognized me instantly and sounded the alarm before I could stop him. Security's already mobilizing. Graenik Force response time is usually ten minutes, but we'd be stupid to count on that."

Dax let out a low curse, running a hand through his already-disheveled hair. "Of course. I knew this was too clean. What now?"

"We stick to the plan," Jax said firmly, his calm demeanor cutting through the rising tension. "Orianna, you in position?"

"Affirmative," Orianna's voice crackled through the communicator. "Vault entrance secure. No sign of additional guards yet."

Karra moved swiftly, her heels clicking against the metallic floor as she led the way. "Let's hope it stays that way. This Synthex tech is worth more than all our heads combined."

The group moved with precision, navigating the labyrinthine halls beneath the Ambassador's quarters. They arrived at the vault door, a sleek, ominous barrier humming faintly with energy. Orianna stood guard, her firearm gripped tightly, her young face set with determination.

"Vault's sealed tight," she said as they approached. "Jax, you're up."

Jax crouched beside the door, his broad frame blocking most of the view as he pulled a tool kit from his belt. His fingers worked swiftly, bypassing the first layer of security.

"This isn't your typical safe," Jax muttered. "They've upgraded since the intel we got."

"Can you crack it?" Karra asked, her voice tight.

"Already on it." Jax replied without looking up, his focus unshaken. "Just keep an eye out."

Minutes stretched into seconds as the sound of faint clicking filled the air. Dax and Orianna kept their weapons trained in the hallway. Karra adjusted the strap on the case they'd brought for the tech.

Finally, a low hiss escaped the vault door, and it slid open to reveal the prize: the curved cylindrical piece of Synthex tech, glowing faintly with an unnatural blue light.

Jax stepped back, letting Karra approach. "There it is. Don't touch it without the case."

Karra nodded; her movements careful as she slid the tech into the protective container. The room seemed to dim as the glow was obscured. "Got it. Let's move."

The moment they turned, the sound of boots echoed in the distance. Graenik Security was closer than expected.

"Company," Orianna said, her voice low but steady.

The team broke into a run, Karra leading the way as Orianna covered their rear. Shots rang out, plasma bolts scorching the walls around them. Orianna stopped in her tracks, spinning to return fire, her aim precise.

"Go!" she shouted over the chaos. "I'll hold them off!"

"No!" Jax turned, his expression torn. "We don't leave people behind!"

"You have to," Orianna snapped, her tone brooking no argument. "If they get that tech, this mission is for nothing. I've got this. Just go!"

Karra grabbed Jax's arm, her voice sharp. "She's right. Move!"

Jax hesitated, his heart warring with his instincts. But Orianna's fiery determination left no room for doubt. He nodded reluctantly, following Karra and Dax as they disappeared down the corridor.

The last thing Jax saw before they turned the corner was Orianna, her fiery hair blazing like a banner as she faced the oncoming guards.

An hour later, the hideout was suffocatingly quiet, save for the hum of the stolen Synthex tech sitting on the table. Jax paced the room, his steps heavy with guilt.

"She didn't have to stay," he muttered, his fists clenched. "We should've done something—anything."

"Don't start with that," Karra said, her voice unusually soft. She sat on the couch, her expression unreadable. "She knew the risks."

Jax shook his head, his jaw tight. "Doesn't make it easier."

A sudden knock at the door cut through the silence. The three exchanged wary glances, hands moving instinctively toward their weapons.

Karra approached the door cautiously, her body tense. She cracked it open, her breath hitching as she saw who stood there.

"Orianna."

Orianna leaned heavily against the doorframe, her face streaked with soot and her clothes torn. Her gaze found Jax immediately, a tired smile tugging at her lips. "Miss me?"

Jax surged forward, pulling her into a fierce embrace.

Karra stepped aside, watching as the two clung to each other. For a moment, the weight of their mission faded, replaced by the relief of a victory they hadn't dared to hope for.

Five years had passed, but for Orianna, that night still lingered in her mind like a fresh wound. She often found herself tracing the scars on her palms, reminders of the split-second decisions that had kept her alive. The world had moved on, but the memory of her sacrifice—and the relief in Jax's embrace when she returned—remained vivid, a constant tether to who she had been and what she had fought for.

Oriana leaned against the railing of the dimly lit docking bay. The neon glow from the station's exterior cast long shadows across her face. The station hummed quietly in the background, with the distant clatter of dockworkers loading cargo barely audible over the steady thrum of the ship engines nearby.

She stared out into the void, her thoughts wandering to Astralith—her home, or what once felt like it. So much had changed, and yet, her memories of that place, of Elara, had remained untouched. They lingered like whispers in her mind, calling her back.

Jax's heavy footsteps approached from behind. The familiar sound was like an anchor, grounding her in the present. She knew his stride anywhere—the measured, deliberate pace of someone who had seen too much and still bore the weight of every decision. Oriana didn't turn to face him right away; her fingers tightened around the cold metal railing.

"You've been quiet," Jax's gravelly voice broke through the silence, his tone laced with concern. He stopped beside her, his towering form casting a shadow that stretched over her.

Oriana exhaled, her breath fogging slightly in the cool air. She had been quiet, yes, but her mind had been anything but. For weeks now, the idea of returning to Astralith had gnawed at her. The more jobs they pulled, the more time passed, and the deeper they sank into the Syndicate's world, the stronger the pull became. And with each passing day, the memory of Elara grew sharper, more vivid, until it was no longer something she could ignore.

"I've been thinking," she began softly, her voice almost lost in the low hum of the station.

Jax's eyes narrowed, already sensing where this conversation was headed. "About what?" he asked.

She shifted, finally turning to face him. His broad shoulders seemed to fill the space; his light purple skin gleaming faintly under the neon lights. His expression was guarded, but she could see the worry etched on the lines of his face. Oriana felt a pang of guilt—he had done so much for her over the years. He had been her protector, her mentor, her only real family since the day they met. But this... this was something she had to do, whether he approved or not.

"Astralith," she said, the word hanging between them like a fragile thread. "I need to go back."

They stood in silence, the weight of her words hanging between them. Jax's expression softened, a rare crack in his usually unyielding facade. She knew he was afraid—not for himself, but for her. And that was why she had to go.

Jax's expression hardened almost immediately. He crossed his arms, the scars on his forearms catching the light as he shifted his weight. "We've been over this, Oriana," he said, his voice low and firm. "It's not safe. The Obsidian Order's all over Néalian. You know that."

"I've seen what they do to those who cross them," he muttered, almost to himself. "They don't just capture their enemies—they break them. If they knew you were back on Néalian, they'd come for you, and they wouldn't stop until they had you."

She had known he'd react this way. He always did, ever since she first mentioned the idea of returning. But she couldn't just let it go. Not anymore.

"I know it's dangerous," she replied, stepping closer to him. "But I'm not the same kid who ran off a prisoner transport. I've changed. I'm stronger now, and I must find her. Elara—she's still out there, and she's my only connection to home. You know how much that means to me."

Jax's jaw tightened, and for a moment, she saw a flash of something in his eyes—fear, maybe, or something deeper, something that cut to the core of his protective nature. He turned away, running a hand over his squared chin, the tension in his body unmistakable.

"I know what Elara means to you," he said, his voice rougher now. "But you don't understand what you're asking. The Obsidian Order isn't just dangerous—they're relentless. If they catch a hint that you're back on Néalian, it won't matter how strong you've become. They'll hunt you down, and they won't stop until they have you."

Oriana swallowed, the weight of his words settling over her, but it didn't quell the fire inside. "I can't keep running forever, Jax," she said quietly. "At some point, I have to face them. And if that means risking everything to find Elara, then that's what I'll do."

Jax turned to her then, his dark eyes full of an intensity that made her heart race. "Face them?" he echoed, his voice incredulous. "You don't know what you're talking about, kid. You think you're ready to take on the Obsidian Order? Do you even know what they'll do to you if they catch you? You've barely scratched the surface of your power, Oriana. They've been doing this for centuries."

The words hit hard, but she stood her ground. "You taught me to fight," she said, her voice steady despite the lump forming in her throat. "You taught me to survive, and now I'm ready to fight for something that matters to me. This isn't just another job, Jax. This is my life."

For what felt like a long time, Jax remained silent. He stared at her, his expression unreadable, while the tension between them felt thick and suffocating. Oriana wondered if he could hear her heart pounding in her chest and if he could sense just how much this meant to her. She needed him to understand that this wasn't a whim or a reckless decision.

When he finally spoke, his voice was softer, almost pained. "I don't want to lose you, Oriana."

His words cut through the air like a blade, causing Oriana's resolve to waver for just a moment. She hadn't expected that—the vulnerability in his voice, the way he looked at her as if she were slipping through his fingers.

"You won't," she said, stepping forward, her hand resting lightly on his arm. "But if I don't go, I'll never be whole. I'll always wonder what happened to her, and I can't live like that."

Jax looked down at her, his eyes searching hers, and for a moment, she thought he might relent. But then his gaze hardened again, and he shook his head, stepping back.

"I can't go with you," he said firmly. "Néalian is crawling with the Obsidian Order. They've got eyes everywhere. If I set foot there, it's over."

Oriana's heart sank, but she wasn't surprised. She had known, deep down, that Jax wouldn't agree to this. He had spent years protecting her, keeping her safe from the very thing she was now willingly walking toward. But she had to do this, even if it meant going alone.

"I understand," she said quietly, her voice steady but filled with quiet sadness. "But I'm going."

Jax stared at her, the silence between them stretching out, heavy and unbreakable. And then, with a deep breath, he nodded, though the look in his eyes said more than words ever could.

"I won't stop you," he said, his voice low, almost a whisper. "But don't expect me to pick up the pieces when it all falls apart."

Oriana swallowed hard, her chest tight with a mixture of fear and determination. "I won't ask you to."

CHAPTER 6:

WELCOME TO ABHANNOR

Chancellor Filar's forked tongue flicked across his lips as the holoscreen shifted from Verus's smooth negotiation to a darker, more dangerous figure. His reptilian eyes narrowed as he keyed in a special code, one reserved for this specific connection. The screen flickered, and there she was: Veyra Tenebria, her presence commanding the entire room despite the distance between them.

Veyra Tenebria appeared through the flickering holo window, a towering figure of darkness that distorted the light around her. Her skin, impossibly black, swallowed the dim glow of the hologram's projection, making her look less like a person and more like a shadow given life. Fiery red veins pulsed faintly beneath her surface, rippling with every movement, as though barely containing the immense energy within. Her sharp, angular features were only partially visible through the projection's haze, but her swirling black eyes pierced through with chilling clarity. Even through the holo, her presence was overwhelming—her voice smooth and deliberate, each word delivered with a precise, almost clinical calm that made her menacing. Watching her through the flickering light, it was clear that Veyra Tenebria was a force of nature, one who controlled every conversation and saw the world as a board where she moved pieces long before anyone realized the game had begun.

Filar leaned forward, his long, clawed fingers tapping rhythmically against the armrest. His voice was low and guttural, his native language a harsh collection of hisses and growls. "Slachtak Unt Perrrr Gllaccken Coo ha tsssss." The sound rolled from his throat, betraying his nervousness in front of this Sidereal of immense power.

Veyra's lips curled into a knowing smile as her dark, void-like eyes fixed on him. Though she spoke in the standard tongue, her meaning was clear, and the weight of her authority was undeniable.

"You've done well, Chancellor, ensuring Verus's trust. The Galathea will land on Serathion as planned?"

Filar's tail twitched nervously, his voice trembling as he responded, "Coo channthak, Filar tssssss zha kaftak."

Veyra tilted her head, her smile never faltering. "Yes, Chancellor, you'll be compensated. But remember, failure carries its own price. Ensure the crew is delivered, or Serathion's favor will turn to ashes."

Filar swallowed hard, his tongue flicking nervously. "Perrrr Filar shakta verrrr Galathea."

Veyra's gaze sharpened, her red veins glowing ominously as her final warning echoed through the chamber.

"Then I trust I won't be disappointed. The Obsidian Order is patient, Chancellor—but only to a point."

Filar's sharp, curved claws dug into the plush fabric of the armrest, exerting pressure as the tension in the room mounted. his heart racing despite his best efforts to hide it. In Veyra's presence, his normally unflappable composure seemed as delicate as a fragile piece of glass.

With that, the screen blinks off, plunging Filar back into the darkness. His heart pounded as he sat there, weighing the consequences of his betrayal. He had made his choice, but the looming threat of Veyra Tenebria and the Obsidian Order lingered, pressing on his chest like a vice.

Abhannor, the river city, lay hidden deep within Serathion's jungle, its ancient stone buildings woven with creeping vines and towering roots. The slow-moving river, dark and mysterious, wound through its heart, reflecting the city's forgotten past. Bridges stretched across the water, connecting crumbling structures that were both alive and decayed. Soft bioluminescent lights cast an ethereal glow over the misty streets as if the city itself whispered secrets from beneath the river's depths. In Abhannor, the past never stays buried—and neither do its mysteries.

The Galathea soared over the dense, towering canopy of Serathion's jungle, the green expanse stretching endlessly beneath them. But not without difficulty. One of the engines sputtered, smoke trailing behind the ship, leaving its course uneven. Claudio sat at the helm, his grip tight on the controls, a thin sheen of sweat on his brow as the ship bucked with turbulence.

"We've got to land this thing fast. We're losing altitude," Claudio muttered, frustration clear in his tone as the damaged engine groaned again.

Verus, standing beside him, remained calm despite the tremors rattling through the ship. His gaze was focused, sharp, and unwavering as he watched the jungle below. "Just a bit further."

The mist enveloping the riverbanks appeared to undulate with a sense of determination, transporting faint, nearly imperceptible whispers that caused the hairs on the nape of Elara's neck to prickle with unease.

Claudio shot him a quick glance, his fingers tensing around the controls. "This ship's going to tear apart if we keep pushing it like this."

Verus ignored the comment, his focus entirely on their path. "You see that gap in the trees? Head for it."

Claudio squinted at the dense jungle ahead, seeing no such gap. "You mean the solid wall of trees?"

"No. Just wait," Verus said, his voice level, unbothered by the worsening situation.

Claudio gritted his teeth, pulling hard on the controls to keep the ship steady as it lurched forward. The Galathea shuddered violently, and the damaged engine whined loudly. "We won't make it!" Claudio's voice strained with urgency, the ship's controls fighting against him as he tried to keep it airborne.

The treetops parted as if the canopies were tied to ropes pulled from below, revealing a narrow gap, barely large enough for the Galathea to squeeze through. Claudio's heart raced as he steered the ship down toward the almost invisible opening, the canopy closing in around them. The ship skimmed the treetops, and he held his breath, fearing the Galathea would be ripped apart by the dense branches. A loud scraping sound reverberated through the hull, and the ship jolted violently. Claudio swore under his breath but held firm, wrestling with the controls.

With a final lurch, they broke through into a small, hidden clearing. The Galathea slammed down hard, the landing anything but smooth. The ship shuddered and tilted as it settled, one of its landing struts crumpling from the impact. Smoke hissed from the damaged engine, and the crew was jolted violently in their seats.

"Is this it?" Claudio asked, bewildered, his hands gripping the controls as the tension slowly drained from him.

Verus gave a small, knowing smile, unbothered by the rough landing. "Not quite."

Before Claudio could respond, a section of the ground below shifted. Vines and leaves slid aside, revealing a trap door beneath the forest floor. The door creaked open, and an entrance large enough for the Galathea appeared. Despite the ship's damage, Claudio maneuvered it carefully down into the darkness below, the trap door closing behind them, sealing off the outside world.

As they sank into the hidden depths, the space around them expanded. What had seemed like a small underground passage opened into a vast, cavernous hangar, far larger than expected. The walls and ceiling were covered in thick vines, tangled and stretching down like curtains, while bioluminescent plants dotted the cavern, casting an eerie glow across the space.

Elara blinked; her eyes wide with astonishment. "How is this even down here? I didn't know anything like this existed..."

Claudio couldn't help but smirk as he powered down the ship. "Well, I guess you don't know everything, Dr. Nova," he teased. It looks like Verus keeps some secrets after all.

Verus, still unfazed, glanced over at Elara. "Serathion has many secrets, Dr. Nova. This is just one of them."

Claudio gripped the controls tightly, his knuckles turning white as he struggled to steady his breath. A wave of relief swept over him as the ship made contact with the ground, but his body remained tense, the adrenaline refusing to let go, keeping his muscles taut and his heart racing.

The Galathea settled unevenly onto the landing pad, its engines finally powering down with a sputtering hiss. The vastness of the underground hangar was overwhelming, with ships of various sizes docked in the shadows, almost hidden behind the dense growth of vines that clung to every surface.

"How did you know about this?" Elara asked, her voice hushed with disbelief.

Verus gave her a sideways glance. "I told you—Filar knows people." His eyes scanned the cavern. "And this is one of the safest places in the sector."

Elara nodded slowly, still trying to process the sheer scale of the hidden hangar. The air was thick with humidity, carrying the lingering scent of the forest even underground. As the crew began preparing for disembarkation, Elara couldn't shake the feeling that they had just stepped into a far more ancient and dangerous place than they realized.

Amid the moss-covered stone floor stood several Thessari, their towering forms casting long shadows across the ancient ruins. Each Thessari loomed at nearly eight feet tall, their sinewy frames cloaked in a thick layer of dark green and brown scales that caught the light with a subtle shimmer, a natural camouflage perfected over millennia in Serathion's unforgiving jungles. Broad shoulders and long, muscular limbs rippled with raw power, their movements fluid yet deliberate, combining strength with a predator's grace. Bony crests crowned their heads, extending down their spines in a formation that gave them a draconic, almost regal appearance. Their eyes, glowing like molten amber, burned with fierce intelligence, and it was difficult to discern whether they were evaluating a threat or calculating their next move. Sharp claws and long, whip-like tails added to their already fearsome presence, marking them as apex predators in Serathion's wilds. When they spoke, their words were laced with a low, hissing resonance, an eerie sound that only heightened their aura of danger and authority.

Elara, Claudio, and Verus exited the ship to meet their overwhelmingly intimidating hosts. A Thessari translator stood beside them and appeared ready to assist with communication. With smooth, almost disarming grace, Chancellor Filar stepped forward, his sharp features softened by a smile that, though polite, never quite reached his piercing golden eyes. His dark, slate-gray scales caught the light, giving him an aura of quiet authority. Yet his manner remained welcoming, as though he were hosting honored guests.

"Chuu mussstt mudde sssein nachh deinerrr Reissse," he said, his voice low and soothing, with a faint hiss betraying his reptilian nature.

The translator quickly spoke, "The Chancellor says, 'You must be weary after your journey.'"

Filar's posture was relaxed, his hands spread in a gesture of peace, though Claudio, standing to the side, watched him with silent suspicion. Elara, on the other hand, was intrigued, her gaze lingering on the Chancellor's regal bearing and the quiet charisma in his words.

The Chancellor spoke again, his tone warm and inviting, yet beneath it, an almost imperceptible edge lingered, as if every word was carefully chosen, concealing more than it revealed.

"The Chancellor welcomes you," the translator added, glancing between the visitors and Filar.

Elara cast a quick glance at Claudio, whose eyes revealed a hint of uncertainty as they met hers. The smile on Filar's face seemed unnaturally polished, as if the Chancellor used it to conceal something beneath the surface.

"Thank you for accommodating us on such short notice," Verus said gracefully. "As we discussed, our ship requires repairs."

The translator quickly relayed Verus's words in Thessari. Chancellor Filar smiled, replying in his reptilian dialect.

"The Chancellor says it is no problem," the translator conveyed. "He humbly requests that Dr. Clemens accompany him to the Great Hall while the repairs to your ship are underway. Your assistant is welcome to stay here and oversee the progress, as he is the most knowledgeable. Dr. Elara Nova, our library would be honored to have you examine our artifacts."

Claudio's eyes narrowed with distrust at the translator's words, his arms crossing as he shifted his weight. "Splitting us up seems... unnecessary," he said, his tone casual but laced with a hint of unease. "I think it's best if we all stay together—at least until the ship's fully repaired."

Verus turned to him, his expression calm but firm. "Claudio, it makes sense for you to stay with the ship. You're the one who understands its systems the best, and we need someone we can trust to oversee the repairs." His voice was measured, as always, by the weight of authority behind it. "Besides, I trust you'll keep an eye on things here. It's a precaution we can't afford to overlook."

Claudio met Verus's gaze for a moment and reluctantly nodded. "Fine," he muttered, though the tension in his shoulders didn't ease entirely.

Verus turned to Elara, a faint smile playing at the corner of his lips. "As for you, Elara," he said smoothly, "their library isn't like anything you've encountered before. The Thessari have ancient records, knowledge lost to most civilizations. It would be wise to take this opportunity."

Elara's curiosity was clearly piqued, though she glanced briefly at Claudio, who gave her a reassuring nod despite his misgivings.

Filar, who had been quietly watching the exchange, now spoke again, his tone ever warm but with that same careful edge. The translator conveyed his words: "The Chancellor assures you that your safety is his highest priority. You are among allies."

Later that evening, Elara lingered on the landing pad balcony after the others had dispersed, the quiet murmur of Abhannor's energy fields soothing in the stillness. The warm hues of fusion lights cast long shadows across the walls, the city's elegance a stark contrast to the urgency of their mission. She gazed out at the cityscape, her thoughts a whirlwind of unresolved questions and doubts.

Claudio's voice broke the silence, pulling her from her reverie. "I'll never get used to that musty jungle smell." He handed her a bronze cylinder full of steaming liquid, mirroring the one in his other hand.

Elara smirked faintly as she accepted it. "Their biotech is remarkable. I've never seen technology and nature merge so seamlessly before." She sniffed the liquid cautiously. A faint, earthy aroma wafted up.

Claudio followed her gaze to the glowing skyline of architecture and vines, pulsing with a light turquoise hue. "Verus said this place is ancient. He read about it when he was a kid. Pretty sure he had the same fascination in his eyes as you do now."

She raised an eyebrow, feigning nonchalance. "Oh? And what do you see in my eyes?"

He hesitated, caught off guard. Then he chuckled softly, shifting his grip on the cup. "Questions. A lot of them."

A comfortable silence settled between them for a moment. Claudio fidgeted, his thumb tracing the rim of his cup. Then he turned to her, his expression lighter, but still probing. "So, what's your deal?"

Elara looked at him, puzzled and a little amused. "My deal?"

"Why go after this thing? Wouldn't it be easier to let it stay hidden?" His smirk softened the directness of the question, but his curiosity was genuine.

"Something's pulling me toward it. I can't explain it," she admitted, lifting the cup to her lips. The warmth grounded her, even as her gaze grew distant. "Plus, the Obsidian Order is after it. We can't let them get there first. Who knows what that could mean for... well, everything."

Claudio's expression darkened for a fleeting moment, a shadow crossing his face. "Believe me, I know what their reach entails. I don't think there's anyone aboard the Galathea who hasn't been burned by it."

He fumbled with a small silver ring on his finger, spinning it absently. His voice dropped to something quieter, almost confessional. "I get the fight. I just... wonder why you?"

Elara studied him, her amusement fading into something softer. "I've been asking that question ever since the Will lit up in my hands. It's like it chose me." She sighed, her fingers tightening around the cup.

Claudio nodded slowly, his gaze lingering on her a second longer than necessary before turning back to the skyline. "Well," he said, his voice lighter now, "if the galaxy's decided to put its fate in your hands, let's hope it knows what it's doing."

Elara let out a quiet laugh, the tension easing. "Guess that makes two of us."

The next morning, Elara followed Silva down the long, dimly lit corridors of the Thessari stronghold, her footsteps a soft echo against the polished stone floor. Silva moved with fluid grace, her emerald scales glistening as they caught the faint light, each one reflecting an iridescent sheen that made her seem almost otherworldly. Her tall, slender frame was draped in dark, leather-like armor that hugged her lithe form, designed to blend effortlessly with the jungle surroundings of Serathion. A pair of horn-like ridges curved back from her brow, framing sharp, yellow eyes that flicked from side to side, ever watchful. Silva's elongated, serpentine tail trailed behind her, its tip twitching slightly, hinting at a quiet but lethal strength. There was an air of command in her posture, though her silence felt calculated, almost predatory. Something about the way she moved—too smoothly, too quietly—made Elara feel like every step was being judged, like she was walking deeper into a den where prey seldom escaped.

"Your people have a fascinating culture," Elara began, her voice breaking the silence. "I've read about the Thessari, but being here— it's more layered than I expected."

Silva's lips curled into a slight smile, though her yellow eyes remained sharp, almost calculating. "The Thessari have endured much. Our strength comes from survival, yes, but also from understanding the unknown. Knowledge is power, after all."

Elara glanced at the carvings, noticing strange symbols etched into the stone. "I've heard your people have uncovered artifacts that even you can't fully explain."

Silva's smile tightened, and for a brief moment, her gaze flickered toward Elara. "There are things in this universe that defy explanation. Some of these artifacts were not created by our ancestors—or anyone we know of. They are remnants, left behind by civilizations long gone, possibly from before our recorded history."

Elara's curiosity deepened, but she was careful not to reveal too much. "And do you believe these artifacts hold power?"

Silva's steps slowed as they reached the entrance to the library, massive stone doors towering over them. She turned to Elara, her eyes glinting with something unreadable. "Power is relative, Dr. Nova. Some believe these artifacts hold the key to shaping the future. Others see them as relics of a forgotten past—we Thessari. Observe. We study. We do not rush to conclusions."

There was an unspoken tension in her words, and Elara felt a slight shift in the air as if Silva was testing her, waiting for her to reveal something. Elara kept her expression neutral, not willing to give anything away. She knew better than to speak of the Core with anyone outside her trusted circle.

Inside the library, the air grew thick with the scent of ancient parchment and something else—an undercurrent of energy that Elara could almost feel vibrating in her bones. Massive shelves stretched toward the ceiling, filled with scrolls and books bound in leather. But it wasn't just the knowledge stored here that caught her attention—it was the artifacts. Strange, glowing relics sat on pedestals, their shapes unlike anything Elara had seen. Some hummed softly, while others remained silent as though waiting for someone to unlock their secrets.

Silva gestured toward one particularly ornate piece—a stone tablet etched with symbols that shifted and changed when Elara looked at them. "This is one of the oldest artifacts we've uncovered. No Thessari scholar has been able to decipher its meaning. Some say it's a map. Others... believe it to be a warning."

As Elara neared the tablet, she experienced a peculiar sensation, almost as if it held a magnetic pull on her. When she extended her hand, a faint vibration pulsated beneath her fingertips, causing a shiver to run down her spine.

Elara studied the tablet, feeling an odd pull toward it. "A warning of what?"

Silva's smile returned, but it didn't reach her eyes. "That is the question, isn't it? Some things are best left unanswered... for now."

Elara felt a chill run down her spine. The way Silva spoke—calm, measured, and subtly evasive—left her feeling more wary than curious. There was more to the Thessari's collection than they were letting on.

CHAPTER 7:

SIGNALS UNSEEN

TEN YEARS EARLIER...

The grounds of the Astralith Academy hummed with an unnatural energy. The familiar rhythms of campus life persisted—students shuffling between classes, the faint whir of overhead drones—but something was off. Patrols moved with mechanical precision, boots striking the stone paths in eerie unison. Shadows cast by the faintly whirring drones above seemed longer, darker, as if they were watching.

Inside, the Academy's once-bustling halls were subdued. Conversations were truncated into hurried whispers, and even the bravest students avoided lingering near the wide glass windows, which were now sealed tight. A faint hum resonated through the walls—a vibration too steady to ignore. The environmental shield, rarely activated, pulsed with quiet authority, as if reminding everyone they were being protected—or trapped.

Elara sat in her favorite corner of the library's Terranovian section, bathed in streams of filtered sunlight. The data pad in her hands offered her usual distraction, but her focus wavered as muffled marching reached her ears. The cadence of boots was unmistakable: United Néalian Fleet soldiers. Their presence on campus wasn't new, but their timing was unusual. Midday patrols weren't standard protocol.

She frowned, absently tapping the edge of her datapad. Unpredictable schedules meant to keep everyone guessing… but wasn't that predictable by now? The hum in the walls seemed to grow louder, a vibration that resonated in her chest. Her wrist buzzed, jolting her out of her thoughts—a reminder of her next class. With a sigh, she packed her things and left.

The small, grey auditorium filled quickly, students filing into their seats with unspoken urgency. Elara slipped into a chair beside Mira, who leaned in with a knowing smirk.

"You hear about the patrol earlier?" Mira asked, brushing a strand of dark hair from her face.

"Yeah, probably just the UNF shaking things up again." Elara's tone was dismissive, but she couldn't deny the nagging feeling in the back of her mind.

Mira's smirk widened. "That's not what I heard. Word is, something— or someone—got through the shields. They're scrambling."

Elara's brow furrowed. "That's ridiculous. The Academy is practically a fortress. You'd need—"

"An inside job," Mira finished, lowering her voice. "And guess what? High-value artifacts are missing. Gone."

Before Elara could respond, the professor entered, flanked by UNF soldiers. The air in the room thickened, the tension palpable as an older sidereal man stepped to the podium. General Lysar. His light turquoise skin glimmered under the lights, but it was his eyes—bright yellow, piercing—that silenced the room. Each scar on his face seemed to tell a story no one dared to ask about.

"Students," he began, his deep voice resonating. "We at the UNF are committed to your safety." His gaze swept the room, pausing on Elara for a heartbeat longer than necessary. "You've noticed increased patrols. This is not a coincidence. We face a threat, one who believes themselves untouchable. Rest assured—they are not.

He stepped back without another word, his soldiers falling into perfect formation as they exited. The room exhaled as murmurs erupted in the wake of his ominous message.

Mira shuddered theatrically. "That guy? Creepy as hell. It's the scars."

Elara leaned closer. "Rumor has it he fought a Synthex mech bare-handed. During the Eclipsion War."

Mira snorted. "Rumor has it he eats children for breakfast. Keep up, Valedictorian."

Elara rolled her eyes and turned her attention back to the lecture.

After the lecture, the hallways of the Academy were quieter, the evening lull settling over the campus like a thick blanket. Elara and Mira strolled side by side, their conversation gently weaving between topics as they turned down one of the less-populated corridors near the library.

"So, you're not at least a little curious why patrols have doubled?", Mira pondered aloud, her tone half-serious.

Elara shrugged with indifference, "Protocol's change. Not a conspiracy, Mira."

"Uh-huh. And what about the enviro-shields? Very 'Normal', right?" Mira smirked.

"I'm sure there is a very logical explanation." Elara said with a dismissive tone.

Mira shook her head and didn't press any further, skipping a step ahead as they rounded the corner. The moment they turned, a blur of motion collided with them.

"Whoa-!" Mira stumbled back as a figure nearly barreled her over.

Elara caught her footing just in time to see Kael, a wide-eyed and thin Terranovian, scrambling to collect his data pad that fell on the floor, faintly flickering as he quickly scooped it into his arms. His bloodshot eyes darted between them, his disheveled air and rumpled jacket making him look more deranged than usual.

"Kael?"

He froze, his gaze locking onto hers. For a moment, he said nothing, his chest rising and falling like he'd been running. Then he muttered, almost too low to hear, "They're everywhere. You need to watch yourself! He knows about you. He knows everything."

Before either of them could respond, he bolted down the hallway, disappearing around the next corner with surprising speed.

"What the..." Mira muttered, brushing dust off her jacket.

"I... I don't know," Elara replied, glancing down at her hand where her own data pad had fallen. She scooped it up and slid it into her bag, shaking her head. "He's always been—"

"Paranoid?" Mira interrupted, grinning. "More like completely unhinged. I mean, what was he even—wait, wait, what did he say to you?"

"Something about watching myself," Elara said, frowning. The words gnawed at her as she followed Mira's lead down the hallway, but she shook them off. Just Kael being Kael.

It wasn't until they were back in their usual corner of the library that Elara finally powered on her data pad. Mira had already sprawled across one of the chairs, idly flipping through her notes while humming to herself. Elara leaned back, swiping the screen to unlock her pad.

The familiar start-up logo flickered, followed by something unexpected. Instead of her neatly organized files and coursework, a grid of encrypted files blinked into view. Each file was marked with a red warning label, its titles strange and cryptic: "Operation Eclipse: Field Report," "UNF/Obsidian Order Comms Log 3.87," and "Codex Artifact Inventory – Classified."

Elara froze, her stomach dropping.

"Mira," she said slowly, tilting the pad so her friend could see.

"This... isn't mine."

Mira leaned forward, her brow furrowing as she scanned the screen. "Wait. This... no way." She grinned. "You swapped pads with conspiracy-boy."

Elara didn't respond. Her thumb hovered over one of the files, her breath catching as her curiosity warred with her better judgment.

"Go on," Mira urged. "Open it. What's the worst that could happen?"

Elara hesitated, then tapped the first file.

A security screen cap started to play of the Astralith Acadamy Dean's office from a corner UNF surveillance camera. Lysar glides into the room with an effortless motion. The recorded room audio began to play.

"General Lysar! My schedule didn't say you were coming.", Dean Subdolus stood up at rigid attention. A scrawny Sidereal with a nervous expression.

"At ease, Dean," Lysar gestured for him to sit down as we walked toward the desk.

"I'm of the understanding that your post here was conditional to your occasional cooperation with my employer," Lysar began to pick up random items in the room and glance at them, like he owned them.

"Yes! Um. Uh. Yes sir! Anything you need," Subdolus fidgeted with his hands.

"Then why, I wonder, have you not implemented stricter protocols, using UNF troops. We, Afterall are hot off a break in, a priceless artifact of Brulvian heritage being stolen. Don't you even care about the safety of your students?" Lysar had his back turned, a small globe now in his hands, a mischievous smile creeped onto his face.

Dean Subdolus voice started to crack, "Uh yes! General sir! I have a command protocol right here. One that follows the instructions of Mr. Draven..."

Lysar walked over and interrupted him has he swiped the data pad from Subdolus's hand with a swift brutality, "Do NOT say his name!"

Lysar put his hand around Subdolus's neck, "We don't want a repeat of the last Dean, do we?"

"No," Subdolus strained though a now constricted windpipe, "No, General, Sir," Lysar released his grip as Subdolus rubbed his neck and coughed.

Lysar thumbed through the data, "This." He paused in reading, his bright yellow irises shifting, "Is good. The UNF's Unpredictability Protocol. A perfect ruse."

The surveillance feed abruptly cut out, plunging Elara into an eerie silence, her heart pounding. A name echoed hauntingly in her mind, shrouded in such infamous reverence: *Draven.*

"We have to find that Kael kid," Mira said as Elara quickly locked the screen and stuffed the datapad into her bag.

"At the very least to trade back datapads," Elara wore a nervous expression as she quickly packed the rest of her things.

Mira scratched her head, "Do you know where he even is? The rate he was running, he could be on the other side of campus," She started to pack her own things."

"I know see him pass me most evenings, he usually works in the bio lab" Elara already at the door, "Come on. Let's see if I can catch up with him"

Mira quickly finished packing her belongings. They both ran as fast as they could to the next building—through hallway after hallway. After five minutes of second-guessing and getting lost, they found the bio lab on subfloor 3B.

They arrived at a metal door unlike the auto openers on campus to maintain security and air pressure between rooms. This door actually had a knob. With a hesitant motion, Elara turned the knob.

"Is this it?" Mira broke the silence, Elara put her finger over her lips quickly while still holding the door, "Shhh." Mira mimed zipping her lips and throwing away the key as Elara rolled her eyes.

The room was dark, damp, and filled with plants. It contained a variety of species from across the galaxy, including the carnivorous Vulnerus Mortiai from Serathion and Sediment Pods from Brulvian, along with at least half a dozen plant species that she did not recognize.

"...Elara," a strained voice called from behind a row of dense kalivaki pots.

Elara turned toward the faint voice and followed its origin. "Kael!" she exclaimed. Both rushed over to him as soon as they saw him on the floor, covered in blood and wearing a weary expression.

"What happened?" Elara asked, starting to examine his wounds. "Mira, call Med Bay…"

"No!" Kael interrupted; his voice heavy with burden. "No one can know!" Mira started to put away her comm device but didn't let go of it.

"Kael, if you don't get medical help, you'll die," Elara said solemnly.

"You have to destroy the data pad," Kael coughed, more blood splattering from his mouth. "As long as it's in your possession, your lives are in danger."

Mira began to pace; they both knew how dangerous that data could be.

"Who is Draven?" Elara whispered.

Kael's eyes widened. "Shh! Don't say his name," he coughed again. "He was a general in the Eclipsion War. He is brilliant but ruthless. Almost every board member at the Academy is under his influence."

Elara gestured to Mira to toss her a cloth and began wiping Kael's face. "So, what about those security protocols?"

"All an elaborate ruse," Kael replied, his eyes darting around randomly as they began to close, as if he were exhausted after a long day.

"Kael! Stay with me!" Elara shouted; her voice filled with urgency.

Kael drifted out of consciousness, like someone had deactivated him off with a flick of a light switch.

"We need go. UNF security is mobilizing and I don't feel like being framed right now." Mira quipped as she picked up Elara's data pad from the nearby desk.

Elara started to shake Kael's lifeless body in an unavailing attempt to revive him, "Kael?! Wake up!"

Mira placed a caring hand on Elara's shoulder, "He's gone, Elara," Mira helped Elara up, "Let's go!"

They rushed out of the building, their hearts pounding as they navigated through the narrow hallways. Elara's mind spun like a whirlwind, her thoughts racing in multiple directions. Who exactly was this enigmatic figure known as Draven? The questions weighed heavily on her, each one more pressing than the last. Did he truly understand her past, the secrets she held close? The air around her crackled with tension as she contemplated the extent of his influence; it was as if he wielded power that could shape destinies. Why did he command such authority, effortlessly bending those around him to his will? The mystery wrapped around Draven only deepened her unease, leaving her with a sense of impending ruination.

CHAPTER 8:

THE SERENTHIAN LIBRARY

Thessari mechanics swarmed over the Galathea, their guttural, hissing language grating on Claudio's nerves as they barked orders to each other. Parts clanked, tools scraped, and the sound of machinery being shuffled around filled the air. To an untrained eye, it might seem like progress. To him? Chaos. They were moving too fast, too carelessly with every piece of equipment they touched.

Claudio stood with his arms crossed, watching like a hawk. Every movement made him twitch. He didn't trust them—not with his ship. Not with anything, really. The Thessari were skilled, sure, but they were lizards at heart. Opportunistic. They might fix one thing while breaking another, all in the name of keeping the job longer. Hell, they were probably slipping a few surprises into the system right now. Maybe a tracker or two. Wouldn't put it past them.

One of the mechanics grunted something unintelligible to him before disappearing into the engine bay. Claudio narrowed his eyes. He hated that he didn't fully understand their language. They could be planning anything. Sabotage, theft, who knows? The more he watched them fumble around, the more certain he was they weren't fixing the Galathea's engines. They were buying time. Making him rely on them longer than necessary. And it was working.

He clenched his jaw, feeling the frustration mount with every clang and rattle. If they thought they could outsmart him, they were in for a rude awakening.

"What in the world are you doing with that disodium pressure manifold?" he exclaimed, watching one Thessari yank on the sensitive machinery as if it were a stubborn weed, completely ignoring the complex sensor system the Galathea was known for.

"Give me that! Please!" Claudio shouted, but the Thessari looked at him blankly, clearly not understanding. Groaning, Claudio fumbled through his rusty knowledge of their language. "Chu nussst flackakik! Um… Chu nusst flacktek!" He was essentially trying to say, 'Give me the piece,' but grammar was the least of his concerns at the moment.

The Thessari begrudgingly handed over the manifold, muttering something that sounded suspiciously like a snarky comment before stalking off.

Claudio frowned, watching the mechanic's work with growing suspicion. Why were they pulling out this piece of equipment? The disodium pressure manifold wasn't part of the engine system that actually needed repairs. His gaze dropped to the manifold in his hand—a worn cylinder attached to a rectangular base, wires frayed at the ends. As he turned it over, something caught his eye. There, etched into the metal, was a small scratch—deliberate, likely made by a Thessari's claw.

Claudio's gut tightened. He lifted the manifold closer to the light and spotted something tucked underneath one of the plates—a micro-transponder. His heart skipped a beat. Were they trying to bug the Galathea? He had to inspect the rest of the repairs. If one transponder was hidden, there could be more. He needed answers—and quickly.

The faint, flickering light of ancient lamps illuminated the winding passageways of the Thessari library, casting long shadows that danced along the towering stone shelves. Ancient texts and artifacts lined the walls, and the air felt thick with a weighty silence as Elara followed closely behind Silva.

"How much further?" Elara asked, her voice barely breaking the stillness.

Silva didn't turn this time, her pace quickening as if she had a schedule to keep. "We're nearly there. The archives you seek are deeper within."

Elara's senses tingled with unease. It wasn't the first time she'd felt it since they'd entered this part of the library, but the feeling was growing stronger. Something was wrong. The stillness felt unnatural, and her Sidereal instincts—long dormant in peaceful times—buzzed with an urgency she hadn't experienced in years.

As they moved deeper, the quiet murmur of scholars vanished behind them. The lamps grew dimmer, casting weak, flickering light that barely penetrated the dense darkness. The walls and towering shelves looming like silent sentinels.

"Are we alone?" Elara asked quietly.

There was a beat of hesitation before Silva answered, "Yes... just the archivists further back."

Elara didn't respond, but her suspicion only deepened. She focused on her breathing, trying to steady her mind. Her hand brushed against the surface of the old stone walls as they entered a vast, arched room. The space ahead opened into a massive circular chamber, its ceiling lost in shadow. At its center stood an ancient table surrounded by towering columns of stone.

"The Heart Chamber," Silva said softly, her voice echoing in a flutter off walls of stone. "The knowledge you seek is within."

Elara stepped into the chamber, but the moment she crossed the threshold, the energy in the air shifted. It was subtle at first, a faint ripple in the stillness, but it quickly grew into something darker—more sinister.

Her muscles tensed. She glanced at Silva, but before she could speak, the familiar prickling sensation intensified, and she instinctively spun around, just as a cold, mocking voice echoed through the chamber.

"Going somewhere, Dr. Nova?"

Figures emerged from the shadows like phantoms—cloaked in black, their faces hidden beneath dark hoods. Red energy crackled across their hands, pulsing with a sickening familiarity. The Obsidian Order.

Elara's pulse quickened. "Silva—"

But it was too late. Silva lay motionless on the floor, her body collapsed like a puppet with its strings cut. They'd been waiting, and she'd walked right into it.

"You should have stayed hidden, Doctor," one of the figures sneered, stepping forward with a slow, deliberate menace. "Now, it's too late."

Elara's heart pounded in her chest, but she wasn't going to let herself be taken without a fight. Her eyes narrowed as the figures approached, their hands radiating with crackling energy.

For the first time since her journey began, she let her own power surge. Her skin shifted, shimmering like the night sky as she summoned the energy that lay dormant within her. It surged through her veins, and her hands pulsed with a fierce, bright light—a reflection of the stars she once called home.

Doubt flickered in her mind—could she match their raw power? But as the energy surged through her veins, her confidence solidified. She had to. There was no other choice.

The first cloaked figure lunged, but Elara was ready. She thrust her hands forward, and a wave of radiant energy blasted from her palms, striking the attacker square in the chest. He flew backward, slamming into the stone wall with a sickening crack.

Another one darted toward her, but with a flick of her wrist, she sent a pulse of energy that disarmed him, his weapon clattering to the floor.

Elara spun, her movements fluid and precise, her energy crackling with each strike. For a moment, the chamber was filled with bursts of light and shadow as she held her own against the attackers.

But she was outnumbered.

A third figure leapt forward, and though she tried to block the attack, they were faster. A bolt of crimson light shot from his hand, catching her off-guard. It struck her chest with brutal force, and she gasped as the energy surged through her, her body going rigid. She stumbled, her vision blurring as the paralyzing sensation took hold.

Her knees buckled, and she hit the floor hard. The glow around her skin faded, and darkness crept in at the edges of her vision. She fought to stay conscious, to call her energy back, but it was no use. The Obsidian Order had her.

The last thing she saw before everything went black was the red sigil glowing on their hands, a cruel symbol of the Order's power.

Claudio stood in the dimly lit engine bay of the Galathea, his arms crossed, watching as the Thessari repair team worked around the massive engine core. Sparks flew from their tools, and the sound of welding mixed with the low hum of the ship's systems rebooting. But something wasn't sitting right with him. The Thessari repair crew had been taking far too long, and they'd been moving in and out of areas that didn't need repairs. His instincts, usually covered up with sarcasm, screamed that something was off.

"How much longer?" he asked, his tone sharp.

One of the Thessari workers, a scaly, hunched figure with rust-colored scales, glanced up. "A few more cycles, maybe. The damage is more extensive than we thought."

Claudio narrowed his eyes. "Really?" He stepped closer, his boots thudding on the grated floor. "Because it looked like a basic engine recalibration to me. Shouldn't take this long."

The worker's hands fumbled for a moment before he muttered something in Thessari and turned back to his work.

Claudio's eyes flicked to the exposed wiring near the control panel. His gut told him to take a closer look. As he knelt down beside the engine, his fingers brushed along the various components, checking the connections. That's when he spotted it—a small, inconspicuous device nestled among the wires.

A tracker.

His pulse quickened. He yanked it out and held it in his hand, turning it over to study the craftsmanship. It was sleek and hidden in a way that suggested whoever planted it knew exactly what they were doing. His stomach dropped as he realized it wasn't the only one. He'd seen similar devices earlier, brushed off as just routine maintenance tools.

No longer trusting his "crew," Claudio stood up, voice like iron.

"Everyone out. Now."

The Thessari workers stopped, startled by the sudden command.

"You heard me!" Claudio barked; his patience gone. "Pack up and get off my ship. I'll handle the rest myself."

The lead worker hesitated, clearly not accustomed to being dismissed so abruptly. "But the repairs—"

"—Are simple enough for me to handle," Claudio cut him off. "Out. Now."

The repair crew exchanged nervous glances before hastily gathering their tools and leaving the engine bay, murmuring in their native tongue. As the last one filed out, Claudio slammed the hatch shut behind them and locked it.

He turned back to the engine; jaw clenched and began pulling off panel after panel. Sure enough, more trackers. Some were tiny, others blended with the ship's existing components. How had he missed these before?

"Sabotage," he muttered under his breath, yanking another one free. "Sneaky bastards."

After sweeping the rest of the engine room, his mood soured. The Thessari had clearly been dragging their feet on purpose. What they had made out to be a complex repair was little more than a straightforward alignment of the energy core.

He rolled his eyes. "Figures."

As he began adjusting the alignment, a subtle whine in the distance caught his attention. He paused, hands still on the tools, and turned toward the viewport. There, in the faint light of Serathion's dawn, a sleek, black vessel flew silently past—a ship of the Obsidian Order.

His heart skipped. They were here. They'd found them.

Claudio's mind raced, but he knew what needed to be done. Quickly, he finished aligning the engine and slammed the panel shut.

"Computer," he barked, standing tall again, "engage cloaking device and initiate silent mode."

For a split second, he froze, the weight of the situation pressing down on him. But there was no time for second-guessing. Not now.

The ship hummed to life, its exterior shimmering as the cloaking field activated. The Galathea faded from view, blending seamlessly into the shadows of the hangar.

"Move us to a more... secluded spot. Somewhere out of sight," Claudio ordered, watching through the viewport as the ship gently lifted and floated to a different section of the cavernous hangar. It nestled itself between towering pillars of rock and machinery, hidden from any prying eyes.

Claudio took a steady breath, his mind racing. The presence of the Obsidian Order confirmed his worst fears—they were after Elara. His eyes narrowed as he stared out into the hangar, the cloaked ship now hidden from view. Whatever was happening in the library, Elara had no idea what was coming.

Claudio's jaw tightened as he glanced around the empty bay. They could mess with his ship, but they wouldn't lay a finger on Elara—not while he was around. He needed to warn Verus. They had to act fast.

Without wasting another second, Claudio bolted for the exit, his pulse hammering in his ears. The moment he hit the corridor; he tapped into his comm link. "Verus, we've got a problem. The Order is here. Get ready, and we need to find Elara. Now."

The Great Hall of the Thessari was a testament to their ancient heritage, with every stone column telling the story of a people who had withstood time and adversity. Carved with detailed designs, the hall was as much a symbol of their strength as it was of their history. Long banners adorned the walls, and a soft glow from the torch-lit sconces illuminated the vast space, casting flickering shadows across the polished, dark wood table.

Chancellor Filar sat at the head of the table, his posture regal, but his gaze—cold and calculating—rarely moved from Verus. A Thessari translator stood beside him, dutifully echoing Filar's words in a clipped, precise dialect. Filar, ever the picture of control, only allowed a small smile to play across his lips, though it never quite reached his eyes.

Verus Clemens sat across from him, a sharp contrast to the Chancellor's air of superiority. His silver eyes glinted in the firelight as he regarded Filar with a calm, calculating gaze. The air between them was heavy, the silence stretching uncomfortably long before Filar finally spoke.

Through the translator, Filar's voice sounded distant, almost mechanical. "The Eclipsion War," the Chancellor began, slowly sipping from his goblet before placing it deliberately on the table. "As a Tetralin, that conflict took much from you, did it not?"

A memory of Tetrallis surfaced—its sunlit spires, the laughter of his people. All gone. Filar's words twisted like a knife, but Verus kept his face impassive, refusing to give the Chancellor satisfaction.

Verus's jaw tightened, but his face remained a mask of neutrality. "The war took much from many," he said, his tone measured. "But the past is not why we're here, Chancellor."

The translator relayed the words back to Filar, whose eyes gleamed with quiet amusement. He leaned back triumphantly, his fingers tapping the rim of his goblet as though considering his next words carefully.

"And yet," Filar replied through the translator, "the past is what shapes us, Doctor Clemens. It defines what we lose... and what we gain." The translator's voice paused, giving weight to the words. "For some of us, the war was a time of... opportunity."

Verus's gaze darkened, but he said nothing. His mind flashed to the destruction of Tetrallis, his home, and the countless lives lost. For Verus, the war had been a bitter scar, one that left nothing but emptiness in its wake. But Filar's tone—his casual mention of what had been "gained"—sparked a flicker of anger beneath Verus's usually calm demeanor.

"The Eclipsion War wiped out entire civilizations," Verus replied, his voice growing colder. "Opportunity is not how I would describe it."

The translator quickly repeated Verus's words to Filar, who gave a slow, deliberate nod as though savoring the tension that filled the room. His gaze never left Verus's.

"Ah, but opportunity is often born from destruction, Doctor," Filar continued through the translator. "While you lost much—your home, your people—I gained influence. The Thessari emerged stronger. It's curious how war reshapes the fates of those involved, wouldn't you agree?"

Verus's hands tightened in his lap, though his face betrayed a little. "Curious, yes," he answered, his eyes narrowing in an untrusting gaze. "I suppose the question is, at what cost?"

Filar's thin smile widened, but it didn't reach his eyes. "Cost is always subjective, Doctor. But let us not dwell on the past. The present is far more intriguing, isn't it? Your mission, for example—searching for remnants of ancient powers."

Verus's senses sharpened, and his suspicions began to grow. Filar's knowledge of their mission seemed too specific, too pointed. The mention of the Astralis Core hadn't come up, not directly, but the Chancellor's words danced dangerously close to the truth.

The translator continued as Filar leaned forward with curious interest. "Tell me, Doctor Clemens, what is it that you hope to find? The Core, perhaps? Or is it something else entirely?" His tone shifted in a subtle manner, as if testing Verus's reaction, probing for any sign of weakness.

Verus's eyes flicked to the translator, then back to Filar. The Chancellor was prying, digging into matters he should have no knowledge of. The Obsidian Order's involvement, the Galathea's mission, even the Core—it was all too coincidental.

"I wasn't aware you had such interest in our work, Chancellor," Verus replied, keeping his tone neutral. "Our research is strictly historical. Surely that is of little concern to someone in your position?"

The translator echoed Verus's words, but Filar's smirk deepened. "Historical?" he asked, his voice dripping with amusement. "Is that what you tell yourself? I've learned that history has a way of influencing the future in ways we don't always anticipate. The Astralis Core is more than just history, wouldn't you agree?"

Verus's suspicions flared. Filar knew too much—far too much for this to be mere conversation. "You seem well-versed in our mission," Verus said slowly, watching Filar's reaction carefully. "One might wonder how."

The Chancellor's face remained unreadable as the translator repeated Verus's words, but there was an unmistakable glint in Filar's eyes. "As I said, Doctor," he replied, his tone darkening with malintent, "opportunity is born from information. And I make it my business to know what will shape the future of this galaxy."

The silence that followed felt heavy with unspoken threats.

Before Verus could respond, his comm link buzzed quietly in his ear. He glanced to the side, listening as Claudio's voice came through, urgent and low.

"Verus, we've got a problem. The Order is here. Get ready, and we need to find Elara. Now."

Verus's heart skipped, but his face remained still. He cut the link quickly, forcing himself to stay composed. Filar's gaze was fixed on him, curious and watching for any reaction.

Verus stood smoothly, his movements measured. "My apologies, Chancellor. I'm afraid I must take my leave. Duty calls."

Filar's smile was slow, knowing. "Of course, Doctor Clemens. I suspect we will speak again soon. Perhaps when your search... comes to an end."

Verus gave a slight nod before turning sharply on his heel and exiting the hall, his mind already racing. The Chancellor's smug expression haunted him as he strode through the hall. Filar may have his own agenda, but Verus wasn't about to let his crew become pawns in someone else's game. The Obsidian Order was here, and Filar's cryptic words lingered in his mind, casting a long shadow over what lay ahead. The mission had just become personal.

CHAPTER 9:

ESCAPE FROM SERATHION

Elara's eyes flutter open, her vision adjusting to the dim light. She's sitting on the cold stone floor, her wrists bound tightly in glowing energy restraints. The room is ancient—Thessari architecture, judging by the symbols carved into the towering walls. The air is thick and damp, carrying the weight of centuries, but the scent of something metallic tinges her senses.

The stone chamber is still and heavy with age. Elara sits; her wrists bound by energy restraints that pulse faintly against her skin. The symbols on the walls seem to close in on her as if the ancient Thessari temple is watching. She breathes deeply, trying to steady her racing heart.

The door creaks open. Veyra Tenebria walks in, her black skin illuminated by surges of crimson energy. Her gaze locks onto Elara, cold and predatory. Elara straightens her back, unwilling to let her see any fear.

Veyra approaches slowly, her lips curling into a sly smile. "Still playing the defiant heroine, I see." She moves in closer, her voice dropping to a whisper. "But how long will that last?"

Elara glares at her but remains silent.

Veyra chuckles, dark and sharp. "Oh, I know you well, Nova. You come from Néalian, don't you? A proud world... once." She pauses, eyes flickering with amusement.

A shadow of fear crept in, Veyra's words clawing at old wounds she thought had healed. But Elara swallowed it down, straightening as she met Veyra's gaze. She wasn't that frightened child anymore. Elara's stomach tightens, but she doesn't take the bait.

"Did I ever tell you about my travels to Astralith?" Veyra's voice drips with cruel satisfaction. "There was a village. Small, insignificant. On the outskirts." She steps closer, her eyes gleaming as if savoring the memory. "It wasn't supposed to matter. After all, they were just civilians. Innocent. Helpless. But orders are orders."

Elara's jaw clenches, and her hands twitch within the restraints.

"Oh, the begging," Veyra continued, her voice filled with a sick pleasure. "Families torn apart; homes burned to the ground. I could still hear the screams, even as the fires consumed them."

Elara's heart pounds, her breath catching in her throat. That village. Her village. The distant sound of crackling flames creeps into her ears, unbidden, mingling with faint echoes of laughter—her father's, her own, Oriana's. But the laughter twists, breaks, replaced by shouts, the sharp snap of orders barked in a harsh, unfamiliar tongue.

Her fists clench, her nails digging into her palms. The stench of burning wood stirs in her memory, mingling with the scent of singed hair and ash. The lifeless forms of her parents lying in the clearing were still fresh in her vision. Her gaze falls to her hands, trembling now, as though her body remembers what her mind refuses to revisit fully.

The screams come next—shrill, piercing, her mother's voice rising above the others. Her father's defiant shout cuts through the chaos, a single word: Run. Elara's chest tightens, her throat constricting as though it were her ten-year-old self again, frozen behind the crumbling wall, the stone rough and cold against her skin.

She hears it then. The hum of red energy crackling in the air, the low rumble of Veyra's voice—not the words, just the cadence, calm and unyielding. And then the flash of crimson, searing her vision even now. Her parents' bodies jerk backward, their light extinguished as they hit the ground, lifeless.

Elara blinks, and the present snaps into focus. Her chest heaves, her pulse thundering in her ears. The memory of the flames flickers at the edges of her vision, threatening to consume her entirely. She swallows hard, her mouth dry, and looks up.

Veyra stands there, as unshaken as she had been then, the faint trace of amusement curling at the edge of her lips.

Elara's lips part, but the words won't come. Her fingers twitch at her sides, the phantom sensation of ash and blood still clinging to them. Her breath comes in shallow gasps, but she forces herself to stand straighter, her eyes locking on Veyra. She doesn't speak; she doesn't need to.

The faint tremor in her hands betrays her.

The Sidereal guard steps forward, placing the mind probe on the ground before Elara. This time, it's different—the black orb shifts, with small legs extending from its smooth surface. Like a spider, it skitters across the cold stone floor, clicking as it moves. Elara watches, her breath quickening as the device inches closer. The sight of it crawling sends a cold shiver down her spine, but she steals herself, refusing to give Veyra the satisfaction of seeing her fear.

"You remember that day, don't you, Elara?" Veyra's voice oozes mock sympathy. "I wonder if you were that little girl… watching your entire world burn."

The probe reaches her feet and begins its slow climb up her leg. Elara jerks, trying to move away, but the restraints hold her in place. The probe's legs dig into her skin as it crawls up her body. Her mind races, panic clawing at her as it nears her head.

Veyra watches, a cruel grin spreading across her face. "I wonder what else we'll find in that mind of yours. Secrets. Pain. Maybe even the location of the Astralis Core."

The probe settles at the base of Elara's skull, its tiny legs pricking her skin. A surge of energy pulses from the device. Elara gasps, her vision blurring as it tries to force its way into her thoughts. Memories flood her mind again—Néalian, her crew, the fires, the screams. She fights against it, gritting her teeth, her hands clenched into fists.

An icy jolt shot through her skull, as if her very thoughts were being torn apart. Her vision blurred, and for a moment, she could barely remember her own name.

But then, she feels it again—deep inside, a barrier—the connection to the Astralis Core. The energy from the probe is being repelled, though barely. It's like a shield she didn't know she had. Her body shakes with the effort of resisting, but she won't give in. Not to Veyra. Not to the Order.

Veyra leans in, her voice low and taunting. "You can't hold out forever, Nova. Strength is not your strong suit."

The probe pulses again, harder this time, and Elara lets out a pained breath. But her resolve hardens. She locks eyes with Veyra, fury burning in her gaze.

"You don't know me!" Elara bites out, her voice trembling but defiant.

Veyra's grin fades into a sneer, but she powers down the probe with a flick before responding. The device clicks and skitters back to the guard as if retreating in defeat. Veyra glares at Elara, her red energy flaring angrily.

Her voice dripped with frustration. "I will break you."

With a cold glare, Veyra turns on her heel and storms out of the room, the doors slamming shut behind her.

Elara slumps back, exhausted but not defeated. Her breath comes in ragged gasps, her body trembling from the strain, but her mind is clear. She's still in control. She won't break. Not now. Not ever.

Over at the landing bay, Claudio stared at the tracking device he held in his hand, his eyes narrowing as the puzzle pieces fell into place. A grin tugged at the corner of his mouth as the solution hit him, sharp and clear. Instead of simply disabling the trackers, why not turn them against the Obsidian Order?

Claudio stood still for a moment, his mind racing with uncertainty. "What if I'm mistaken?" he pondered anxiously. The weight of Elara's life hanging in the balance made him clench his jaw, bracing himself for what lay ahead. In that moment, he knew there was no space for hesitation or second-guessing.

He quickly scanned the ship's data systems, tapping away at the interface. The plan formed rapidly in his mind: he could reverse the trackers, manipulating the signals to make it appear as though the Galathea was somewhere deep within Serathion's dense jungle or hidden in a secluded hangar. The Obsidian Order would think they had all the time in the world, chasing false signals while he and Verus executed a daring infiltration.

"Verus," Claudio called out, his voice carrying over the gentle hum of the Galathea's engine bay, "I've got an idea—a good one this time."

Verus Clemens appeared from the corridor, his dark eyes reflecting the dim lighting of the ship. "Let's hear it," he said, his tone measured and cautious, as always.

Claudio tossed the tracker into the air, catching it casually as he explained, "I can reverse these signals. Trick the Obsidian Order into thinking we're somewhere else—maybe miles away in the jungle or locked up in some forgotten hangar. While they're busy running around chasing ghosts, we sneak aboard one of their ships."

Verus raised an eyebrow. "And then what? Walk right in and ask for Elara's location. Or hope we don't get vaporized the second they realize we're not where we're supposed to be?"

Claudio's grin widened. "Not Done. We'll use their resources against them. Hack into their systems, find out where Elara's being held, and slip out before they know what's happening. Maybe even disrupt their comms while we're at it. Quick, clean, and without drawing any attention."

Verus crossed his arms, his expression a mix of skepticism and calculation. "You're assuming a lot. Too much. What if the signal falters? What if the tracking data doesn't hold up? The Obsidian Order is not stupid, Claudio."

"And you're overcomplicating things," Claudio shot back, sarcasm lacing his words. "Verus, relax your forehead ridges, will ya? we improvise. You know me. This will work. Besides, do you have any other bright ideas?"

Verus sighed, his eyes narrowing in thought. The air between them thickened as the moment stretched on. Claudio could sense the battle going on inside Verus—the cautious strategist weighing every variable, every possible outcome. But there was no time for that kind of deliberation, not with Elara out there, captured by the Obsidian Order.

"I know the risks, Verus," Claudio added, his voice lower, more serious now. "Elara needs us. We can do this. We have to."

Verus finally relented, though his eyes still held a hint of doubt. "Fine. But if this goes sideways, we'll all wish we'd stayed hidden."

Claudio's smirk returned. "That's the spirit."

Sneaking aboard the Obsidian Order's ship was no easy feat, but Claudio thrived on danger. He and Verus, along with a small group of trusted crew members, moved swiftly and silently through the underbelly of the Thessari city, their footsteps muffled by the jungle's overgrowth. The night provided cover as they approached the Obsidian ship's landing dock.

Claudio crouched behind a crate, his gaze on the sleek, obsidian vessel looming above them. "We're in," he whispered, tapping into the docking system. Verus's technical expertise had proven invaluable, allowing them to bypass the ship's security with ease.

The docking bay hissed open. Claudio led the way, signaling for silence as they slipped inside, their movements coordinated and precise. The Obsidian Order's patrols moved in predictable patterns; their high-tech surveillance systems sharp but not infallible. Claudio and his team knew when to duck, when to freeze in place, and when to move.

Verus remained at his side, eyes scanning for any signs of trouble. "I've got the ship's mainframe," he whispered, tapping into a handheld device. "Locating Elara's position now… and I'm setting up a minor communications disruption. Should buy us enough time."

"Good," Claudio muttered. "Let's keep this quiet. We get in, we get her location, and we're out."

The tension was palpable as they made their way through the corridors of the Obsidian ship, careful to avoid detection. Every footstep, every breath, felt like a risk, but Claudio's focus remained razor-sharp. His concern for Elara drove him forward, refusing to let doubt or fear slow him down.

Finally, Verus spoke up, his voice barely audible. "I've found her. She's in one of the lower levels of the Thessari Temple"

Claudio nodded, determination hardening his features. "Let's go."

In the dungeon, the room is silent, save for the faint hum of energy restraints still binding Elara's wrists. She is alone, or so she thinks. Her body aches from the strain of resisting the mind-probe in the earlier interrogation, and her head throbs with lingering pain. The walls of the ancient temple seem to pulse with the weight of time, adding to her growing sense of isolation.

The heavy stone door groans open. This time, Veyra Tenebria enters alone. No guards, no mind-probes—just her. The eerie red energy that crackles across her skin is more intense now, an uncontrolled rage boiling beneath her cold exterior. There's a dangerous gleam in her eyes.

Elara tenses, trying to prepare herself for whatever's coming next. But she can feel the tension radiating from Veyra. This isn't like the first interrogation.

Veyra circles her slowly, like a predator stalking prey. "You think you've won, don't you?" she hisses, her voice low and venomous.

"You think resisting makes you special?"

Elara says nothing, though her body is taut with pain and exhaustion. She refuses to give Veyra satisfaction.

Veyra stops in front of her, her crimson eyes boring into Elara's. "You cost me time, Dr. Nova. Precious time. And now…" She steps closer, her voice darkening, "I'm going to make you suffer for it."

Without warning, Veyra's hand lashes out, striking Elara hard across the face. Elara's head snaps to the side, the force of the blow sending pain radiating through her cheek. She grits her teeth, struggling to stay upright.

Veyra doesn't stop. She grabs Elara by the hair, yanking her head back to look her in the eyes. "Do you know what I hate more than anything?" Veyra growls. "Weakness."

With brutal force, Veyra slams her fist into Elara's stomach, knocking the breath from her lungs. Elara gasps, doubling over, but the restraints hold her in place. She can't fight back.

Veyra smiles wickedly, watching her struggle to breathe. "We Sidereals of the Obsidian Order have strength. What about you?"

Elara's mind races, trying to think, to fight through the haze of pain. But Veyra is relentless. She strikes again and again—fists, kicks—her red energy flaring with each blow. Elara's body screams in agony, but she refuses to cry out, refusing to give Veyra the satisfaction of her suffering.

Finally, Veyra pauses, panting with a twisted sense of rage. "I could kill you right now," she whispers, her voice dripping with menace. "No one would care. No one would miss another useless academic."

Elara's vision blurs. She's on the verge of losing consciousness, but through the fog, she forces herself to speak. "You're... wrong," she gasps, her voice barely a whisper.

Veyra's eyes narrow. "What?"

Elara looks up at her, her face bloodied but defiant. "I said... you're wrong."

Veyra snarls, raising her hand, crimson energy swirling violently around her fingers. "Goodbye, Doctor Nova."

Just as Veyra's hand comes down, palm glowing with a bright crimson and ready to strike the killing blow, the sound of a shot rings out.

Silence.

Veyra freezes. Her eyes widen. Slowly, she looks down at her chest. Blood begins to pool, spreading across her dark skin, and she stumbles back, her energy flickering weakly. Her mouth opens in disbelief, but no words come out.

Veyra's body crumples to the ground in a lifeless pile.

Elara blinks through the haze of pain, trying to comprehend what just happened. Through the doorway, Claudio appears—blaster in hand, his expression grim but relieved.

"This isn't a library,"

He rushes to her side, quickly unbinding her restraints, trying to hide the worry in his voice as he helps her to her feet.

Elara, still weak, manages a small, breathless smile. "Took you long enough."

Claudio grins, though it doesn't quite reach his eyes. "What can I say? Timing's everything."

Claudio steps closer, his gaze scanning Elara's injuries with a hint of concern, he tries to hide behind his usual sarcasm. "Think you can walk, or should I carry you out of here like a damsel?"

Elara lets out a weak laugh, wincing at the effort. "I'll manage. Just... give me a second."

He crouches down, offering her his arm. "Take your time, Dr. Nova. But we've got about five minutes before reinforcements show up, and I'm not exactly looking forward to a repeat performance."

Elara grips his arm, using his strength to pull herself up. "Then let's make sure we're not around when they do."

As they start moving toward the exit, the dim lights flicker ominously. Claudio's expression hardens. "They'll be expecting us to take the obvious route."

Elara glances over at him, catching the shadow of worry in his eyes. "You have a plan, right?"

He smirks; his tone lighter than the situation calls for. "Does this answer your question?" He pulls out a small device, tapping it twice. A hidden door on the side wall slides open with a low hiss.

Elara raises an eyebrow. "How?"

Claudio shrugs nonchalantly, helping her through the door. "I might've done a little digging when I realized the Thessari turned out NOT to be the most truthful of hosts."

As they slip into the narrow passage, the sound of distant footsteps echoes through the corridor they just left. Elara leans against the wall, breathing heavily. "You don't happen to have an escape pod waiting on the other side of this tunnel, do you?"

Claudio shoots her a mischievous glance. "Something like that." His grin widens as they reach the end of the passage.

As they step out of the narrow passage, the hangar stretches before them, quiet and dimly lit. The massive chamber feels eerily empty, save for the faint hum of energy that pulses in the air. In the distance, barely visible through the haze, is the cloaked silhouette of the Galathea—just as Claudio had planned.

"There she is," Claudio says with a proud grin, motioning toward the nearly invisible ship. "Tucked away like Verus's snack pile."

Verus crackled over the comm, "I heard that." Claudio chuckled.

Elara's legs feel like they might give out, but the sight of the ship brings a surge of hope. "Are you sure there are still no trackers?"

Claudio pats his pocket, pulling out a small handheld device and checking the display. "Cloak's still active. And as for trackers... I took care of those. We'll be ghosts by the time they realize we've even moved."

They move cautiously through the hangar, sticking close to the shadows as Claudio keeps a watchful eye on every corner. The tension between them thickens with the awareness that at any moment, the Obsidian Order—or worse, Chancellor Filar's forces—could appear.

Once they reach the Galathea, Claudio places his hand on a hidden panel near the entrance, and the sleek ramp lowers silently. "Ladies first," he teases, but his tone carries the weight of the danger that still hangs over them.

Elara manages a weak smile and steps up the ramp. The familiar interior of the ship is a welcome sight, though her exhaustion makes every step feel heavier. Claudio follows close behind, and once they're both aboard, the ramp closes with a soft hiss.

Inside, the dim lights of the Galathea flicker on, casting the ship in a soft glow. Verus is on the bridge as well, going through data. Elara leans against the wall, catching her breath. "We need to go. Like now!"

Claudio is already at the controls, fingers flying over the interface. "Way ahead of you. Engines are spoiled up, cloaks engaged." He shoots her a glance. "You good to strap in, or should I just floor it and hope you don't fall out of your seat?"

Elara stumbles into the co-pilot's chair, strapping herself in with a shaky laugh and a click of the harness. "Let's not push our luck."

With a sharp hum, the Galathea lifts off the ground, still cloaked as it hovers in the massive hangar. Claudio's eyes flick to the sensor array. "No movement... yet."

"Yet?" Elara repeats, her voice tense.

Claudio shrugs as the ship's thrusters propel them forward. "You know how it is. They always show up right when you think you've made a clean getaway."

Just as he says this, alarms flash across the console. Claudio's jaw tightens. "Well, that didn't take long."

A blip appears on the sensor screen—a patrol ship, already closing in on their location.

Elara grips the armrests, her mind racing. "How close are we to getting out of their range?"

Claudio's fingers work faster over the controls. Verus rushes in the bridge, "Not close enough." His voice is calm, but there's a grim determination behind it. "Hold on."

The Galathea banks sharply, skimming the edge of the hangar as the patrol ship comes into view. For a moment, it seems like they might get caught, but Claudio activates the ship's cloaking device to its full power, fading from all visual and sensor detection. The patrol ship hesitates, searching the area.

Elara holds her breath as they slip past undetected.

Once they clear the hangar and speed into the dark expanse of space, Claudio lets out a slow breath, his hands still steady on the controls, "See? Timing's everything."

Elara exhales, a relieved smile breaking through her exhaustion. "I'll give you that one."

Claudio leans back in his chair, glancing at her. "I think that's the first time you've actually said I was right."

Elara chuckles softly, her eyes closing for a moment. "Don't get used to it."

The tension eases for a moment, but the reality of their situation looms ahead. They've escaped—for now. But with Chancellor Filar's betrayal and the Obsidian Order's relentless pursuit, Elara knows their journey is far from over.

"What's next?" she asks quietly, opening her eyes to look at him.

Claudio's grin faded, replaced by a more serious expression. "Next? Seriously? Aren't you exhausted? Shouldn't you be wanting to head home now?"

"I'm not going to quit just because things got tough," Elara shot back. "We need to set a course for Zynthar."

Claudio looked utterly stunned. "Tough? They just used a spider-probe on you. I can't even begin to imagine what that does to Sidereals. And you do realize we've got not one, but two factions hunting us, right? It's time to lay low." He turned towards navigation, "Plot a course for Nealia—"

"Belay that order!" Verus interrupted sharply. Claudio whipped around, looking at him in disbelief, as if he couldn't believe Verus would be so reckless.

"What in the fragging waste are we doing?" Claudio snapped, his voice rising.

"Claudio, you know how crucial this mission is," Verus said, speaking to him like he was missing the bigger picture. "Don't let your past with Zynthar cloud our future. Dr. Nova understands the risks."

Claudio's jaw clenched, his gaze hardening. The mention of Zynthar was a knife twist, reopening wounds that had barely begun to scar over. His hand slammed into the sidewall with frustration as he stormed off.

Elara watched him go; her brow furrowed. "What's with him?"

Verus sighed, his tone heavy. "Zynthar and especially the city of Kraedin terrifies him."

"What happened?" Elara asked.

Verus let out a long, weary sigh, his eyes distant, as if recalling a painful memory. "Claudio was orphaned when he was just a child," he began, his voice heavy. "Like so many others during the Eclipsion War, he was separated from his family, left to fend for himself in the chaos. I practically raised him after that."

Elara's expression softened, her anger fading as she listened.

"About ten years ago, I sent him on an expedition to Zynthar. He met a woman there, Gwen. She was a brilliant researcher. They were inseparable, working together, studying the planet's mysteries. For the first time in a long while, I saw something in him I thought was gone. The light inside him was alive again."

Verus paused, his voice dropping lower. "I was naïve... foolish enough to believe Zynthar was safe. But it wasn't. One of Perfida's followers, one of the Obsidian Order, captured his wife. They killed her right in front of him and left him to die in the desert. I had no idea the danger they were in. When I found out, I sent a rescue team immediately."

Elara's breath hitched, her heart tightening as the weight of Claudio's past sank in. Verus glanced at her, his silver eyes filled with sorrow. "He survived but returned as a changed man... more cautious, more guarded."

Elara felt her eyes sting with tears, her heart breaking for Claudio. The sarcastic, sharp-witted man she'd known now felt much more fragile, burdened by a history he had never shared. She wiped a tear from her cheek, her voice barely a whisper. "I had no idea..."

Verus nodded, his voice barely audible. "He's been carrying this for a long time, Elara. Zynthar is more than just a dangerous planet to him—it's where everything fell apart."

The silence that followed was thick with emotion, the weight of Claudio's past settling over both of them.

"I'm..." Elara's voice cracked as she wiped a tear from her eye, trying to steady herself. "I'm going to go check on him."

Verus gave a quiet nod, his gaze softening. "He'll need someone right now, even if he doesn't realize it."

Elara nodded back, her emotions swirling. Without another word, she turned and headed down the corridor, the weight of Claudio's past pressing heavily on her mind. Her pace quickened as she neared his quarters, her heart pounding. She didn't know what she would say or how he'd respond, but she knew one thing for certain—Claudio wasn't going through this alone.

In this chaotic universe, there were so few people she truly trusted. And here he was, rough around the edges but undeniably loyal. She didn't know when it had happened, but somewhere along the way, Claudio had become a part of her world she couldn't imagine losing.

CHAPTER 10:

WASTELAND WHISPERS

Hyperspace speed caused the stars to blur into a rush of flashing white and blue lines streaking past the main viewport. Verus stood motionless, watching as his thoughts drifted to a time before lightspeed travel, something he'd read about in ancient scrolls.

Elara walked in with a relaxed yet labored stride. "So, what's the ETA to Zynthar?" she asked.

Verus remained as still as a statue, except for his voice. "We should arrive in a few hours if our repaired engine holds up."

Elara, puzzled by his remark, replied, "Claudio does good work. I can't say the same for the Thessari."

Verus grinned. "What can you expect from those who pride themselves on mastery of concealment in nature?" He paused, then added, "Besides hiding trackers."

Elara let out a small giggle. "I think we'll be fine. Claudio says he found them all."

Verus' expression grew serious. "I'm not so sure we can know for certain. There are still artifacts aboard the conference room with ancient technology." He glanced at Elara. "We don't fully understand how they work."

She met his gaze. "Regarding Terranovian ancient technology, I think we've learned all we can for now." Her mind immediately drifted to her experience with the Will of the Keepers, recalling the symbols that glowed when she touched the cover. That memory sparked a recent moment in the Thessari Library—the "warning" book she barely had time to read. The symbols had changed when she touched them too.

A sudden realization hit her. "Wait a minute!" She grabbed the nearest datapad from one of the nearby consoles and began scrolling furiously.

Verus looked at her, puzzled. "Something wrong?"

"Not sure yet, but… if I can just find… Here!" She walked over to Verus, showing him what she'd pulled up. "These are two scans of the second tome I found in the Thessari Library." She pointed to the screen, excitement bubbling in her voice. "Here's the first Keepers Tome, you handed me back on Néalian." She showed him one scan before switching to the next. "And here's the one I found in the Thessari Library on Serathion. The symbols changed when I moved my hand."

She looked at Verus eagerly. "I remember reading your book on Terranovian symbols and hieroglyphics at the academy. Can you tell me what these might mean?"

Verus studied the tome thoughtfully. "This symbol means 'to inform,' but it could also mean…"

Elara's face lit up. "To warn!"

Verus smiled, impressed. "Well done, Dr. Nova. But what exactly is this warning about?"

Elara paused, her eyes darting as she considered the possibilities. "The Astralis Core?"

Verus nodded, confirming her suspicion. "The inscription, translated into standard, says this: For the prophecy warns the return user, The Spirit of Perfida endures, Beware of the Power and its Lure." His voice grew more solemn with each word. "Elara, you must take heed to these words. Perfida Arcanus was the Keepers' greatest fear. He was destroyed, but not completely. Be mindful of your thoughts as we near the temple."

A mixture of concern and excitement flashed across Elara's face. "His spirit? Like those apparitions the talisman priests in downtown Astralith always talk about?"

Verus, looking stern, replied, "The Core has been lost for over a thousand years. You must be ready for anything."

A wave of skepticism crossed Elara's face but quickly faded. "I mean… I guess it wouldn't hurt to be prepared."

"That's all I'm saying," Verus said, his tone softening. "I'm not asking you to believe everything you read in old texts." He added, "Just stay alert and keep an open mind."

Elara nodded as her excitement dimmed slightly; her posture more relaxed. Her thoughts returned to the Astralis Core and what its discovery could mean. Clearly, the Keepers had etched that warning for a reason. She was both curious to find out and terrified of what it could reveal.

As the Galathea dropped out of hyperspace, Zynthar loomed ahead, its barren surface casting an eerie glow under the dim light of its twin suns. From space, the planet appeared as a sprawling expanse of ochre and bronze, with jagged mountain ranges cutting through the vista. Dust clouds swirled endlessly in the upper atmosphere, reflecting the suns' red light, creating an unsettling, almost otherworldly haze.

The planet's surface was a testament to its harshness. Endless desert plains stretched across the horizon, broken only by crumbling ruins of civilizations long past. From this distance, you could see the outlines of once-mighty cities now half-buried beneath sand and rock, their ancient spires and towers peeking through like ghostly remnants of a lost age. Canyons and riverbeds, long since dry, crisscrossed the terrain, telling the story of a world that had once known water and life.

The atmosphere was thick with dust, giving the skies a perpetual twilight quality, with flashes of lightning occasionally flickering through distant storms. These storms, seen even from orbit, were both a blessing and a curse—rare rainstorms that would momentarily quench the planet's thirst but inevitably bring destruction, as the cracked and hardened ground was unable to absorb the deluge. The storms created a haunting glow on the horizon, silhouetting the jagged mountains in brief bursts of pale light. It felt heavy with a stillness that seemed almost conscious, as though the entire world was pausing in anticipation.

As the Galathea descended closer, the details of Zynthar became sharper. The surface was dotted with patches of pale vegetation— hardy plants that clung to life in the shadowed crevices of canyons and cliffs, where the sun's relentless heat couldn't reach them directly. But these were few and far between, mere whispers of life amidst the barren landscape.

Far below, the remnants of an ancient, crumbling city came into view, partially obscured by swirling sands. What had once been grand temples and towering structures were now little more than skeletal ruins, weathered by centuries of decay. The sight was both awe-inspiring and foreboding, a reminder that beneath the surface lay untold secrets waiting to be uncovered, and perhaps dangers that had long been forgotten.

Claudio concentrated on his datapad and the navigation console, alternating between the two as he worked to narrow down the coordinates of their destination. "According to the screencap from Elara's second session with the Will, the city we're aiming for is Kraedin."

He sighed in frustration, not wanting to be anywhere near this city, let alone on this forsaken planet. The last time he was here, he had been awaiting rescue after his fiancée was murdered by one of the many crime factions that frequent Kraedin.

The skyline brought back memories he'd rather forget—a flash of her face, the last thing he saw before everything went dark. His fingers tightened on the controls.

"The map shows the destination is about three clicks northeast of the city limits, which is a good thing," Claudio said.

Claudio leaned back in his seat, his fingers dancing over the controls as the familiar sight of Kraedin's chaotic sprawl came into view. He shot a sideways glance at Verus, who stood with his usual air of calm authority, and smirked. "You know, Doc, Kraedin's like one of those bad relationships. Every time you think you're out, it pulls you back in."

Verus didn't flinch. "I fail to see the humor in returning to a city swarming with criminals."

Claudio's grin widened. "That's because you've never been there. Trust me, it's worse than you think. The good news is we're not walking into the heart of it—we're landing on the outskirts. The bad news is, that's where all the vultures and organ harvesters hang out. You're welcome."

Verus raised an eyebrow. "Thank you?"

Claudio shrugged. "Look, Kraedin's a dump, but it's my dump. I know how the factions work, who to avoid, and where to land without getting our heads bitten off. We stick to the plan, and we're in and out before anyone even knows we've set foot on this rock."

Elara, who had been studying the Will, finally looked up. "Sounds like someone has seen a thing or two.."

Claudio's expression darkened for a moment, the cocky grin fading. "Yeah," he said quietly, "and it didn't end well. The last time... Verus knows."

Elara's gaze softened. "Claudio, I'm—"

"Save it," he cut her off quickly, forcing the grin back onto his face. "I don't need sympathy. What I need is for us to get what we came for and get the hell out before Kraedin decides to remind me why I hate this place."

Verus stepped forward, folding his arms. "And yet, despite your personal history here, you seem... oddly confident."

Claudio leaned back, hands behind his head. "Confidence is what keeps me alive, Doc."

Verus didn't look convinced. "And if things go sideways?"

Claudio's grin turned roguish. "When don't they. That's half the fun. The other half? Watching how fast I can get us out of it."

Elara chuckled, shaking her head. "I don't know whether you're enjoying this or not."

Claudio glanced at her, his grin softening into something more genuine. "Believe me when I say, I am most certainly NOT but, hey, life's short. Might as well make the most of it. Besides, I've got a score to settle with rock."

Verus sighed, pinching the bridge of his nose. "Wonderful. I'm thrilled to be part of this... personal vendetta."

Claudio gave him a mock salute. "Stick close, Doc, and I'll get you through this in one piece. I'm not about to let Kraedin win twice."

As they descended, Kraedin's twisted sprawl of buildings and streets filled the viewport. The memories came flooding back—ugly, painful memories—but Claudio forced them down. "Alright, folks, hold on. We're about to drop three clicks out from the city. Close enough to get to our destination, far enough to stay out of the main faction territories."

Elara's voice was more serious now. "The Will pointed to an ancient Keeper site just outside the city limits."

Claudio's fingers tightened on the controls. "We'll need to move fast. The second someone spots us; it'll be like blood in the water. Kraedin won't stay quiet for long."

Verus watched the city loom closer and muttered, "Somehow, I doubt it will be that simple."

Claudio chuckled. "It never is. But that's what makes it interesting."

The Galathea hummed as it descended toward Kraedin, the city's chaotic streets sprawling beneath them. Claudio grinned one last time, masking the tension behind his usual swagger. "Let's get this over with. And if we're lucky, no one will even know we were here."

The ship shuddered as it descended onto the barren outskirts of Kraedin, the engines whining as they powered down. Dust billowed in clouds around the ship, the ground cracked and scorched from years of neglect. The distant city of Kraedin sprawled like a grotesque beast, its neon lights flickering weakly beneath a heavy, smog-filled sky.

Claudio leaned back in the pilot's chair, exhaling as the ship settled. "Well, that was smooth," he said, sarcasm dripping from his words. "I'm sure the welcome party's just dying to greet us."

Elara shot him a look but said nothing, her focus drawn to the view outside. The city loomed dark and foreboding, a hive of criminal factions and hidden dangers. Every instinct told her this place was wrong.

Verus was already at the exit, his dark coat trailing behind him. "We don't have much time," he said, voice calm but urgent. "Get what we need and get out. Kraedin is not a place we want to linger."

Claudio nodded, following suit, but Elara hesitated at the threshold of the ship. There was a weight in the air, something that pressed on her chest like an invisible hand. She scanned the horizon frowning as the dry wind swept through, stirring up loose debris.

It was then that she heard it—a faint whisper, barely audible, yet unmistakable.

Elara...

A chill washed over her, leaving goosebumps in its wake. She felt lightheaded, as though the very air around her was pressing in, whispering secrets only she could hear. Her breath hitched. She turned, searching the barren desert, but nothing was there. Just the wind and the rustle of dry brush.

"Elara!?" Claudio's voice snapped her back to reality. He was already a few steps ahead, adjusting the strap of his blaster. "This place gives me the creeps. Let's get this over with."

She blinked, nodding quickly, but her unease grew. "Yeah... right behind you."

They walked across the cracked ground, the city's grim silhouette looming larger with every step. But the further they moved, the stronger the whisper became. It wasn't the wind—it was something else. Something... watching.

Elara Nova...

She stopped dead in her tracks, her pulse quickening. The whisper was louder now, clearer. She couldn't ignore it anymore.

"Hey!" Claudio turned; his brow furrowed in concern. "You okay?"

She glanced around, trying to locate the source of the voice, but there was nothing. Just the desolation of Kraedin's outskirts.

"Thought I heard something," she muttered, gripping her sidearm instinctively.

Verus shot Claudio a warning glance, his gaze then shifting to Elara. His posture tensed, as though bracing himself for a threat only he could sense.

Claudio shrugged, though his eyes were sharp, scanning the horizon. "Probably just the heat playing tricks on you. This place has a tendency to mess with your head. Let's go."

The air was thick with the stench of oil and decay, mingling with the distant clamor of shouting voices and the occasional crackle of gunfire. Kraedin was alive, but in a way that felt closer to a death rattle than a heartbeat.

They pressed on, but the whisper lingered, chilling her to the core. It felt like more than just a voice. It was a presence—familiar yet foreign, pulling her toward the temple like a dark thread winding through the air…and it knew her name.

The vast, silent expanse of space hung still as The Crucible, flagship of the Obsidian Order, slid through the darkness with lethal precision. Its sleek, black hull, streaked with glowing red veins, seemed to vanish into the backdrop of the void—an apparition more than a ship. Serathion's faint silhouette loomed beneath it, the jungle world oblivious to the arrival of the sinister craft now locking into orbit. No hum, no flare of engines, just the cold, calculated approach of something built for war.

The bridge of The Crucible was a fortress of cold, black steel, each surface polished to an eerie sheen. Harsh, dim lighting cast long shadows across the consoles, where every button and lever hummed with purpose. Efficiency was absolute here; nothing moved without precision.

A towering figure loomed on the bridge, clad in a sharp, dark military uniform that hinted at ruthless precision beneath the flowing folds of a black cloak. Shadows clung to him, obscuring his face in an impenetrable veil of darkness, leaving only the faint glint of cold, calculating eyes to betray his presence.

A slight, gaunt Sidereal moved quickly across the deck, his footfalls barely audible against the metal floor. His pale skin flickered under the faint glow of the control panels. He approached a towering figure cloaked in shadow, his movements stiff and hurried, as if the very air around him was laced with tension.

"My Lord, we've received no word from Veyra or her crew," the diminutive servant stammered, his voice trembling and barely audible, as though the very act of speaking might awaken a wrath hidden in the surrounding shadows.

The cloaked figure stood motionless, an imposing silhouette against the dim glow of the bridge. The weight of his silence pressed down like a coiled storm; its intensity more chilling than any eruption of anger.

Finally, his voice cut through the tension, low and cold as the void itself. "Prepare my ship."

CHAPTER 11:

THE UNVEILING OF SHADOW

Elara, Verus, and Claudio trekked across the endless expanse of the Zyntharian desert, their eyes set on the distant ridge where the hidden temple of the Keepers lay, just north of Kraedin. The heat distorted the horizon, and the weight of the desert's oppressive sun bore down on them, but the promise of ancient knowledge kept them moving forward.

As they crossed a large dune, Elara felt a subtle vibration beneath the sand, and her instincts flared to life. She stopped abruptly, raising a hand. "Something's coming."

Claudio and Verus froze, glancing around, but the desert seemed quiet—too quiet.

The ground erupted in a violent shake. Mortifex. Eight-foot-long, venomous insectoids—burst from the sand, their sleek, chitinous armor gleaming under the sun, perfectly camouflaged against the dunes. The creatures moved swiftly on their six spiked legs, and their rows of beady black eyes locked onto the trio. Their deadly stinger-like appendages glistened with neurotoxin, twitching in anticipation as they circled their prey.

"Mortifex!" Claudio shouted, drawing his blaster. Elara was faster, though, her eyes narrowing as she lifted a hand.

Energy surged through her, the dormant power of her Sidereal heritage flaring to life. Her skin, normally a dark turquoise, shimmered as glowing constellations danced across her arms, galaxies forming in the patterns. With a sharp gesture, a pulse of energy shot from her hand, striking one of the Mortifex mid-leap. The creature flew back, crashing into the sand, its body twitching from the force of her blast.

But more came. The Mortifex were relentless, using their powerful legs to close the distance, their venomous stingers whipping through the air.

One lunged at Verus, and though Elara sent a wave of energy to knock it back, the creature's stinger grazed his leg before it was flung aside. Verus collapsed, gasping in pain as the neurotoxin began working through his system, slowing his movements.

"Shit!" Claudio fired off a volley of blaster shots, but the Mortifex were too fast, dodging and weaving through the sand.

Elara's powers flared again. With a sweeping motion, she sent a shockwave of energy into the ground, displacing the sand in a wide arc and forcing the Mortifex to retreat momentarily. But they couldn't hold them off forever.

"We have to get him back to the ship!" Elara shouted, already moving to the side of Verus. Claudio was there in an instant, grabbing Verus by one arm as Elara took the other. The two of them heaved him up, staggering under his weight as they dragged him through the sand.

The Mortifex swarmed behind them, but the creatures hesitated at the edge of their territory, unwilling to leave the dunes completely. Still, their beady eyes followed, waiting.

His vision blurred, the venom making his muscles seize as waves of pain rippled through his leg. His grip weakened, and he could barely focus on Claudio and Elara as they dragged him forward.

When they finally reached the Galathea, Verus was barely conscious, his leg swollen and bruised from the venom. They laid him gently on the ramp, Elara quickly placing her hands over the wound. She concentrated, letting her energy flow through him, slowing the spread of the poison, but it wouldn't be enough to fully heal him.

"You stay here," Elara said firmly, her voice steady despite the tension. "Claudio and I will go to the temple."

Verus, pale and weak, nodded. "Just… be careful…"

Claudio exchanged a look with Elara, his expression serious but resolute. "We'll handle it."

With Verus secured in the ship, the Galathea's med-bots running detoxification on Verus, the two set off again, the wind whipping through the desert as they moved north toward the temple. Claudio brought more fire power. Elara's skin still shimmered faintly with energy, the weight of her powers—and the secrets of the Keepers—driving her forward.

But in the back of her mind, she could feel it—the voice and the rage, coming from the temple.

The frigid night air prickled Claudio's skin as he attempted to bring life to a pile of dead brushes he found along their journey. After a few moments of his fingertips scraped bare from fumbling with the fusion heat emitter, he looked at Elara, sitting in quiet comfort on a rock, legs crossed. "You mind?" Claudio asked.

Elara looked at Claudio with a puzzled expression, then understood what he meant, "Ah, Sure, stand back."

Claudio stood back a few steps as Elara got up and put her hands on the cold and dry brush. A blue light flashed from her palm and quickly turned into a flame consuming the brush as her hand disengaged and moved away. Warmth began to irradiate the immediate area as the smell of burnt pine filled the night air.

Claudio began to put his hands near the fire to warm himself up, "Thanks."

"Don't mention it," Elara muttered as she went through a ruck sack, she smirked, then started to laugh. Claudio looked at her like she was losing sanity on a per minute basis, "Find something amusing?"

"My friend back home, Mira," Elara smiled as she pulled a bottle out of the ruck sack. "She snuck this bottle of Terranovian Whiskey into my things."

Elara popped the cork, took a swig, handed the bottle over to Claudio, he examined the bottle, "Tenth Dynasty!? Tuva Aged!?"

He gave a low whistle of being impressed, "You have a good friend," Claudio took a sip and sighed in disbelief, "Great friend."

The hours of a cold desert evening passed as the two of them exchanged sips and stories; each one more personal than the last. When Elara's inhibitions were melted to a point to where she asked a question she wanted to ask, "Can I ask you something?"

"No, I have not now nor in the future stolen Verus's snacks," Claudio smirked knowing that wasn't her question.

Elara smiled then turned solemnly toward him, "What happened in Kraedin all those years ago?"

Claudio knew this question would wander back to haunt him like an ominous storm cloud. His past behavior indicated a pattern of outburst for most people asking this question. Between Elara's presence, non-threatening tone in asking, or the high-octane whiskey, for the first time, Claudio felt as though he could answer without reliving it.

He took a sip, then a deep breath, "It was back when I was doing some engineering contracting for Verus. That is how I came to meet Gwen. She had a brilliant mind but was kindhearted. I had a bit of a gambling problem and I got mixed up with the wrong people. One disastrous choice after another led to my trouble with the Obsidian Order."

Elara was completely captivated by the story but remained silent as Claudio continued, "I thought I could walk away from the sins of my past. Gwen was a light for me in a very dark place. We got a place in Kraedin. Stayed there for a while. Conducting Verus's Agri Solitudo research. On the brightest days of my life, my past, and that morally forsaken city reminded me of where I was and how bad things could get. The Order kidnapped Gwen. I went to rescue her. She was captured and I was forced to watch her die."

Claudio turned to Elara, his eyes simmering, "That is why I vowed never to step foot into that place again."

For what seemed to be hours, a deafening silence fell. "This place had broken him," Elara thought. He went through a trauma that is all too common among those whose lives were affected by The Obsidian Order. They sat, silently watching the warm fire gently crackle and pop until sleep swallowed them whole.

The next morning, the journey to the ridgeline had been mercifully uneventful; the ominous Mortifex were nowhere in sight, their malevolent whispers absent from the arid wind. As they approached, the dormant temple emerged from the barren land, encircled by jagged spires of natural rock that clawed at the sky like ancient sentinels.

The temple and its towering wall loomed above them, casting elongated shadows in the fading light—a monolith from a forgotten era. At the heart of the structure lay an ornate, sand-worn circle etched with patterns, a testament to lost craftsmanship. In its very center was a hand-shaped indentation, precise and deliberate, hinting at mechanisms unseen and secrets yet to be unveiled.

As Claudio and Elara approached the massive circular door, the weight of the silent temple pressed upon them.

"Well, well, well," Claudio murmured, eyeing the hand-shaped indentation at the center of the ornate circle. "This is a tad more elaborate than the texts describe."

As their footsteps tapped on the dust-covered marble floor, Elara traced the symbols etched into the sand-worn stone. "The details are extraordinary. These symbols—I've never seen anything like them."

Claudio took in their new surroundings with caution and glanced in her direction with curiosity. "Think it's a warning or an invitation?"

"Could be both," she replied thoughtfully. "Ancient Terranovian temples have been known to often guard their secrets fiercely."

He took a step closer. "Do you think the Mortifex avoid this place for a reason?"

Elara nodded. "Perhaps. Or maybe the temple has some sort of radiation as a deterrent, and they're simply unaware of its significance."

Claudio sighed. "Only one way to find out." He lifted his hand toward the indentation.

"Wait," Elara cautioned, placing a hand on his shoulder. "We should be careful. There might be traps or ancient mechanisms we don't understand. Didn't you do research for Verus back in the day?"

He paused. "I did. In Kraedin libraries. Gwen was the field researcher. You're right though. Let's examine it first."

They both knelt, studying the patterns around the indentation.

"These markings," Elara whispered, "they seem to tell a story."

Claudio squinted. "A story or a riddle?"

"Either way," she said, meeting his gaze, "we need to solve it before we proceed."

He smiled slightly. "Good thing puzzles are our specialty."

She returned the smile. "Let's hope that's enough."

They continued their careful examination, the ancient temple looming silently above them as they crawled deeper into its vast mysteries.

Further down the large vestibule, Claudio and Elara stood before the massive circular door, the tangled patterns seemed almost alive under the dimming sky.

"Elara," Claudio began, breaking the heavy silence. "Do you still have the Will of the Keepers tome?"

She glanced at him, her eyes reflecting curiosity and a hint of apprehension. "Yes, I do," she replied, reaching into her satchel. "Why?"

"I have a feeling it's more than just a book," he said, nodding toward the hand-shaped indentation. "Maybe it's the key we've been missing."

A chill ran down her spine. It was as if the temple itself was holding its breath, waiting for her next move. She hesitated, sensing that once she placed the tome, there would be no turning back.

Elara carefully pulled out the ancient tome, its leather cover etched with symbols eerily like those on the gate. As both her hands gripped the book, a subtle vibration coursed through it. Suddenly, the symbols on the gate began to glow softly, illuminating one after another in a cascading pattern.

Claudio's eyes widened. "Did you see that?"

She nodded slowly, mesmerized. "The gate... it's reacting to the tome."

He stepped closer to the door, his gaze darting between the glowing symbols and the book in her hands. "The Will of the Keepers—it must be connected to this place."

Elara studied the tome, her fingers tracing the embossed designs. "These markings—they're identical to those on the gate. It's as if the book is speaking to it."

"Perhaps the indentation isn't for a hand alone," Claudio speculated. "Maybe it's meant for the tome."

She looked at him thoughtfully. "You might be right. But if we place it there, we need to be prepared for whatever happens next."

Claudio gave a faint smile. "When have we ever been fully prepared?"

She chuckled softly. "Fair point." Taking a deep breath, she approached the indentation. "Ready?"

He nodded; his expression resolute. "Let's go."

Gently, Elara fitted the tome into the hand-shaped recess. The moment it settled, the gate shuddered, and the glowing symbols intensified, casting patterns of light across their faces.

A low rumble echoed from deep within the temple. Claudio exchanged a tense glance with Elara. "No turning back now."

As the ancient mechanisms groaned to life, the circular door began to split open, revealing a darkness that beckoned with the promise of untold mysteries. They stepped forward, leaving the waning daylight behind.

Elara and Claudio stepped cautiously into the temple. The darkness swallowed them whole, the air thick with a sense of ancient mystery.

Claudio hand glided along the stone wall until he found a torch. With a flick of his wrist, a small flame sprang to life, casting long, flickering shadows. Elara took the torch from him, her expression unreadable in the dim light. She approached an unassuming bowl at the temple's entrance, igniting it with the flame.

In an instant, a chain reaction began. Flames spread along hidden channels, snaking up the walls and across the floor, illuminating the temple in a warm, golden glow. The massive hall came to life before their eyes—high ceilings arched overhead, and towering pillars lined the interior. At the center, an altar stood, and on top of it, a dark metal pedestal, weathered with age but undeniably powerful in its presence.

Two hand-shaped indents were carved into the rectangular slab, almost inviting, but ominous. Above them, symbols were etched into the metal. Elara's gaze narrowed as she studied them, and after a moment, she translated aloud, her voice soft but steady:

"The chosen can only access the Core. More than power comes, that you must endure."

The words hung in the air like a challenge, heavy with meaning and danger alike.

The moment Elara's palms touched the indents, a sharp resonance filled the air, vibrating through her bones. The altar trembled as ancient mechanisms, long forgotten, roared to life. A rumbling echoed through the temple, as though the very foundation of the place was awakening from centuries of slumber.

Slowly, the altar began to split apart. Stone panels slid back with a groaning grind, revealing a hidden chamber buried beneath layers of forgotten time. The air grew thick, almost electric, as something powerful, something primordial, stirred in the depths.

And then, in a dazzling display of light, the Core appeared.

It didn't simply reveal itself—it emerged, as though it had always been there, waiting, watching, biding its time for someone like Elara to come. Floating in the center of the now-open altar, the Astralis Core hovered, pulsating with a rhythm that felt alive. Its icosahedron surface was impossibly smooth, shifting colors like a living nebula—deep indigo swirled with veins of luminous silver and flickers of violet, as if the very fabric of the universe was contained within. It shimmered in the dim light of the temple, casting reflections like the birth of stars, illuminating the ancient carvings around them.

The energy it radiated was palpable—both beautiful and terrifying. The air around the Core distorted, bending light in strange, unnatural ways. It was not just a gem; it was a force, something far greater than any treasure or artifact. It was the heart of power, the essence of creation itself. And it was awake.

The light was blinding, almost painful, and she had to shield her eyes. Its energy pressed down on her, heavy and suffocating, as if the Core itself was testing her resolve.

Elara's breath caught in her chest as she gazed at it, the realization crashing into her—this was what they had been searching for, but it was more than any of them could have imagined. The Core seemed to pulse in time with her heartbeat, almost aware of her presence. But it wasn't just calling to her—it was reaching for her.

Suddenly, the dark energy that surrounded the Core surged outward, like invisible tendrils, snaking through the air toward her. Elara stumbled back, but it was too late. The tendrils wrapped around her wrists and chest, not physically, but as if gripping her very soul. The Core's energy, once dormant, now flowed through her veins, cold and invasive.

She struggled against the pull, her mind a whirlwind of defiance and terror. But the Core's grip was unyielding, and her thoughts began to blur as a foreign presence wormed its way into her consciousness.

Without thinking, Claudio lunged forward, reaching for her arm. But as his fingers brushed against the dark energy, a searing pain shot through him, forcing him to pull back, helpless and terrified.

Claudio rushed toward her, panic in his eyes, "Elara! Get away from it!"

But she couldn't. Her hands were locked in place, drawn toward the Core, and something far more sinister had already begun. Deep within the swirling energy of the Core, an ancient, malevolent presence stirred, awakening from a long, dreamless sleep.

A voice, cold and filled with malice, whispered into her mind—a whisper she recognized immediately.

Perfida Arcanus.

CHAPTER 12:

PERFIDA'S BANE

The Great Hall of Serathion's citadel was as cold as its stone walls were ancient. Shadows clung to every corner, flickering in the weak torchlight. Counselor Filar stood alone, save for his Thessari translator, his posture tense, eyes fixed on the towering doors ahead of him. They groaned open with a low creak, and from the darkness emerged Draven Caelix.

Draven's cloak swept the floor as he entered, a wraith-like figure moving with slow, deliberate steps. His face was obscured, save for his eyes—sharp, glinting with a quiet menace. Filar swallowed hard, but remained still, steeling himself.

When Draven approached, Filar could feel a chill despite himself, his breath quickening as if Draven's very presence drained the warmth from the room.

"Dislakac Filar Draven Tuva!" Filar said, his voice tight.

Draven stopped a few paces away, taking in the chamber with a brief glance before fixing his gaze on Filar. "And yet, here I am... disappointed." His voice was like the low rumble of distant thunder, calm but filled with menace. "Veyra and her crew—what news?"

Filar hesitated, started speaking Thessari and his translator said, a faint twitch betraying his nerves. "We've lost contact, my lord. There has been... a complication."

"A complication you say?" Draven's tone remained unshaken, but the temperature in the room seemed to drop. He stepped closer to Filar, his presence like a shadow stretching across the counselor's form. "Show me."

A side door opened. Two guards dragged Veyra into the room, her once powerful figure now slumped and beaten. Her dark skin, usually pulsing with energy, was now lifeless. Her unconscious body was dropped unceremoniously at Draven's feet.

Filar shifted uneasily as the translator spoke. "We did not expect the resistance she faced. It appears the Keepers are more resourceful than anticipated."

Draven looked down at Veyra, silent. He knelt, fingers brushing the edge of her cloak, his expression unreadable.

After a moment, he stood again, turning his attention to Filar. "You failed," he said, with a chilling calm. "You were given orders that she would need more support. Yet you sent her alone. She failed because you failed."

Draven waived his hand in a silent and understood command to his guards.

Filar opened his mouth to protest, but before he could, two more guards entered, dragging another figure. Silva, the beaten Thessari, was tossed to the ground next to Veyra, her reptilian skin bruised and bloodied. Her breathing was shallow, her eyes filled with fear.

Draven's gaze settled on Silva, cold and calculating. "Silva Talonian," he said softly, stepping toward her. "You must not tempt my patience. I know one of the seven copies of the 'Will of the Keepers' is in your library. The security scans show Dr. Elara Nova is holding it. Our Thessari repair people say that your world was a last-minute destination according to Galathea's navigation logs. Tell me where the Keepers originally took the core."

Silva looked up, trembling. Her voice came out hoarse, broken. "I—I don't know…"

Draven's hand shot out, gripping her throat with terrifying speed. "Deception does not befit you, Silva." he whispered, his grip tightening. Silva felt an immense constriction. She struggled to breathe through the constriction. "You will wish for a swifter end than what awaits."

Silva gasped, eyes wide with terror, throat in pain. "Zynthar!" she choked. "They—They've gone to Zynthar."

Draven held her for a moment longer, then slowly released his grip. Silva collapsed to the ground, coughing and trembling.

Filar stood behind them, watching in silent horror as Draven calmly wiped his hand on his cloak. "Zynthar, of course. Previously, Agri Solitudo." amused.

He stared into Filar's soul, his eyes now a dark red and void of any interest. In one fluid motion, he drew a dagger from his belt and plunged it into her chest. Silva gasped, her body convulsing for a moment before going still.

Filar flinched, his eyes darting from Silva's lifeless form to Draven. "My lord... the coordinates I asked for..." he ventured cautiously, clearly shaken by what he'd just witnessed.

Draven turned slowly, his gaze settling on Filar with the weight of final judgment. "The coordinates will be provided when you've proven yourself useful, Filar."

He stepped closer, his voice low, barely a whisper. "But if you fail me again, Counselor... there will be no second chances."

With that, Draven turned and strode out of the hall, his cloak sweeping behind him like the shadow of death itself. Filar stood frozen, the weight of his failure crushing down on him, the stench of blood thick in the air.

The long-dormant spirit, trapped within the Astralis Core for centuries, had been unleashed. His presence crept into Elara's consciousness like a shadow, slipping past her defenses. She could feel him there, a cold hand on her mind, his whispers twisting her thoughts, pulling her deeper into his influence.

The Core wasn't just a source of power. It was a prison.

And now, it was trying to make Elara its vessel.

Pain tore through her body as the energy surged inside, twisting her to its will. Her vision blurred, the colors of the Core becoming unbearably bright, as if they were swallowing her whole. Her legs gave out, and the temple around her whirled in a dizzying spiral.

"Elara!" Claudio's voice reached her like a distant, fading echo.

Her eyes ignited with a blinding light, but all she could hear now was Perfida's voice, sharp and unmistakable.

"Welcome, Elara Nova," it purred, laced with dark amusement.

As Perfida's voice grew louder, Elara could mentally reach for a comforting memory, like the warmth of the sun on her home world, hoping to block out the darkness creeping into her mind.

Claudio sprinted over to Elara, who was still entranced by the Core's glow. Without hesitation, he yanked a cloth bag from his rucksack and swiftly enveloped the Core in it. The moment the Core was sealed away, its light vanished, and Elara's consciousness snapped back into place, a sharp gasp escaping her lips.

As he watched Elara in distress, Claudio could feel a jolt of panic. She wasn't just fighting the Core—she was fighting to stay herself.

Elara blinked rapidly, her gaze darting around as if trying to reorient herself. She swayed slightly, and Claudio reached out to steady her.

"Elara, are you okay?" he asked, his voice laced with concern.

She exhaled shakily, rubbing her temples. "I... I think so. The Core—it was like it pulled me in, I couldn't fight it."

Claudio nodded, tightening his grip on the bag containing the now dormant Core. "Whatever that thing is, we need to keep it hidden until we figure out how to handle it. You're lucky I got to you in time."

Elara glanced down at the bag, her face pale but determined. "It wasn't just pulling me in. It was... showing me things. Visions. Memories that weren't mine."

"Sounds like something we should discuss," Claudio replied, his voice steady. "But first, let's get out of here before anyone else shows up." He glanced around warily, his grip tightening on the bag as if protecting both the Core—and Elara.

As they hurried away, the weight of the Core's power still hung over them like a dark cloud. Whatever secrets it held were only just beginning to surface, and neither of them could shake the feeling that the worst was yet to come.

The Sun of Zynthar beat down mercilessly as Elara and Claudio trudged through the endless expanse of the desert, their footprints quickly erased by the shifting sands. The ruins of the temple behind them were already lost in the shimmering horizon, and ahead, nothing but the barren, hostile wilderness of the dunes stretched for miles.

Claudio wiped sweat from his brow, his eyes narrowing against the glare. "Seems like every step takes us farther into nowhere."

Elara didn't answer immediately. She marched ahead with a single-minded determination, her jaw tight, her gaze fixed on the path in front of her. There was a tension about her, something simmering just beneath the surface. Claudio had noticed it ever since they left the temple—the way her responses had become clipped, her usual calm replaced by an unsettling sharpness.

"Elara?" he pressed, quickening his pace to walk beside her. "Are you okay?"

"Fine," she snapped, her tone harsher than he'd expected. She didn't even glance his way, her attention locked forward. "Keep moving. We're wasting time." Claudio raised an eyebrow, surprised by her sudden outburst.

The wind picked up, carrying with it the sting of sand against their skin. Claudio could feel the tension between them growing, thick as the heat radiating from the ground. Elara had always been focused, but this was different—darker, angrier. Ever since she touched the core…

He was about to say something more when the ground beneath them shifted. A faint tremor, then another. Claudio stopped in his tracks, his hand instinctively reaching for his blaster. "Did you feel that?"

Elara froze, her gaze flicking toward the horizon, scanning for danger. The sands ahead began to shift more violently, rising in ripples, forming what looked like small hills—until they began to move.

"Mortifex," Claudio whispered, his voice barely audible over the howling wind.

From beneath the sand, enormous, armored insect-like creatures burst forth, their segmented bodies glistening in the sunlight. Long, venomous pincers clicked in unison, and their eight-legged forms slithered toward them with terrifying speed.

Claudio took a step back, raising his blaster. "Elara, get behind me—"

Before he could finish, Elara moved. Fast. Faster than he'd ever seen her. She leaped forward, her hand crackling with energy, eyes blazing with a fury that sent a chill down his spine.

"Elara!" Claudio shouted, but she wasn't listening.

With a flick of her wrist, a bolt of pure energy lashed out, striking the nearest Mortifex square in its chest. The creature shrieked, its armored body convulsing before crumpling into the sand. Another Mortifex lunged toward her, but she was ready. With a savage snarl, she thrust both hands forward, and a pulse of energy erupted from her, sending the creature flying back into the dunes with a sickening crunch.

Claudio stood frozen; his blaster still raised but useless now. He watched, stunned, as Elara tore through the creatures, her attacks fueled by an unrelenting rage. The Mortifex swarmed, but none could touch her. The Mortifex were crumbling under the force of Elara's energy, their armor was of shattered glass. She was everywhere at once, her movements a blur of raw power and anger. With every strike, the ground beneath them seemed to tremble.

The final Mortifex reared up, twice her height, venom dripping from its fangs. Elara's eyes glowed with an eerie light as she surged toward it, letting out a scream that was more of a battle cry than a sound of fear. Her hand slammed into the creature's torso, and with a violent burst of energy, the Mortifex exploded into a cloud of chitin and blood.

When the dust finally settled, the creatures were gone—scattered remains across the sands. Elara stood in the center of it all, her chest heaving, her hands still crackling with leftover energy. Her eyes were wild, her expression fierce and unrecognizable.

Claudio lowered his blaster, slowly walking toward her, his heart pounding. "Elara…" he said cautiously.

She turned toward him, her glowing eyes dimming slightly, her breathing ragged. For a moment, it looked as though she might lash out again, but then her face softened, the fury slowly ebbing away. She looked down at her hands, the glow fading, replaced by confusion. Fear.

"What—" Her voice was barely a whisper. "What did I just do?"

Claudio approached carefully; his eyes still wide with shock. "You… you handled them, all right." He forced a grin, but the unease in his voice was clear. "You didn't need my help at all, apparently."

Elara's gaze dropped to the carnage around her, and for the first time, Claudio saw something crack in her—an unsettling mix of regret and disbelief. She shook her head, wiping the blood and sand from her face. As she surveyed the remains, she could see her own reflection in a shattered piece of blue Mortifex chitin, her wild, unrecognizable eyes staring back at her.

CHAPTER 13:

DREAMS OF THE PAST

Exhausted, Elara and Claudio trudged up the ramp of The Galathea, their boots heavy with the relentless sand of Zynthar's desert. Inside, Verus, recently recovered thanks to the ship's med-bots, waited for them in the conference room. "Elara! Claudio! It's good to see you both among the living. Have you managed to find the Core?"

"That thing," Claudio replied, frustration evident in his voice, "should have stayed buried in the desert."

Verus shot Claudio a look of mock exasperation. "Would you rather the Obsidian Order got their hands on it?"

Claudio retorted, "Of course not, but—"

Elara cut him off, her voice simmering with barely contained anger, her hand slammed on the table. "Verus is right. I'd rather not let the Obsidian Order have it. If we have to use it ourselves, then so be it."

Verus studied her intently. "We might want to hold off on using it for now."

Elara's anger flared, but she caught herself, wondering why she was so enraged.

"Because you should be..." Perfida's voice echoed in her mind. Elara's internal dialogue, usually a solitary affair, now felt crowded by an opposing force. She was consumed by a fierce, almost compulsive rage—a desire to fulfill her most selfish cravings. It wasn't just temptation; it felt like an inescapable compulsion.

Verus and Claudio looked over at Elara, who was staring blankly forward in a daze, both of them showing expressions of concern.

"Elara?" Verus tried to alert her attention.

A sudden, violent image flashed through her mind—her hands around Verus's throat, his face contorted in pain, his eyes open and blood shot.

She blinked, the vision gone as quickly as it had appeared, but it left her cold. She clenched her fists, willing the intrusive thoughts away, terrified of what they could mean.

Abruptly, her attention was brought back to the moment as a hyperspace jump from another part of the galaxy, "Um... I think the desert heat has gotten to me. I'm going to my quarters to get some rest."

"Yeah, probably best we take some time to recuperate. We did fight two waves of Mortifex and ya know... that other thing we found." Claudio grinned.

"I'll take the first watch. I was asleep for the better part of your journey to the temple. All rested up," Verus said.

Elara was already halfway down the hall before Verus could finish his sentence. As soon as the door of her quarters closed with a mechanical clank, Claudio turned to Verus. "She's different, Doc. She has changed."

"You said it yourself. You just went through two Mortifex and miles of Zynthar's desert. She's probably tired, same as you." Verus said.

"Not talking about now. Did I mention she took out the Mortifex?" Claudio said.

"I mean, you took out some on the first—" Verus began, but Claudio quickly cut him off.

"On the way back," Claudio said, looking paranoid. "I didn't fire off one shot."

Verus eyed him suspiciously. "She killed all of them?"

Claudio nodded. "I've seen Obsidian warships and troops struggle to eliminate even a small wave of Mortifex with a Queen." He let out a breath of exhaustion, the long day weighing on him like a heavy blanket. "Elara took them all on. I'm proud of her and all, but she had…"

Verus looked at him with discernment. "Had what?"

"This relentless and unbridled rage. Like she was enjoying it. Like the way you are with snacks but much more… evil-looking," Claudio said.

Alarming concern flashed across Verus's face. "Has she uttered this name… Perfida?"

Claudio felt like Verus was reading his mind. "Yeah! She kept mumbling that name the whole way back."

"It would be most wise to keep the Core in the ship's vault," Verus said, pausing in thought. "Perhaps for a week, so I can study it."

Claudio crossed his arms, his brow furrowing. "Keep it locked up? You think that's going to help? She's already acting like it's got a hold on her."

"There's a tall tale," Verus began quietly, his gaze fixed on a distant point. "Of a Keeper who once tried to wield the Core's full power. He became unstoppable—until he lost himself. They say he turned on his own people, thinking they were enemies, destroying everything in his path. By the time he realized what he'd done, there was nothing left."

Verus put one of his hands on his chin in thought, "According to the Tome, the more you use the core, the more it takes from those who use it." Verus rubbed his eyes in frustration, "Let us go over plans in the morning. To put it in your words," Verus put his hand on Claudio's shoulder as a long-time friend, "You look like shit."

Claudio and Verus laughed in solidarity. "Well, I'm off. Night, Doc," Claudio said with a grin. Verus nodded, watching as Claudio headed off before making his way to the bridge to begin his night watch.

Elara's dream began as her surroundings transformed. She found herself standing on Agri Solitudo, the planet's lush greenery surrounding her. The subtle scent of chlorophyll from the towering trees filled the air, and as she stepped into a clearing, a cool, calm breeze brushed gently across her face. The tranquility felt almost tangible, like a distant memory of peace.

Out of the forest emerged a Terranovian man—tall, muscular, and olive-skinned. He approached with a calm presence that exuded wisdom. "Elara," he began, "The code of the Astralis Core is as much about balance as it is about power. Outwardly, it is a force for good—a catalyst for terraforming planets, for sustaining life. But inwardly, it can corrupt, warping the very identity of whoever tries to wield it selfishly."

Elara's brow furrowed. "Why is Perfida so deeply ingrained in the Core?" she asked, her voice filled with the confusion she had long harbored.

The man's eyes darkened slightly as he answered. "Perfida sought to merge with the Core, to make himself like a god. That is why his essence still lingers within it. Even after thousands of years, his selfish desires are intertwined with its power."

Her mind raced, pieces of the puzzle falling into place. The strange sensations, the overwhelming pull of the Core—all the selfish urges she had felt—it made sense now.

Just as the calm began to settle over her, the horizon suddenly lit up with a massive explosion. It engulfed everything, a blinding flash tearing through the vast urban land. The city of Kraedin, once pristine and untainted by corruption, was obliterated. And then, in the chaos, she saw them—Verus and Claudio—both caught in the destruction, their lives extinguished in an instant.

Elara jolted awake, a scream tearing from her throat, raw and filled with terror. Her body trembled, the vivid images of the dream still etched into her mind—the explosion, the deaths, the overwhelming sense of loss.

As she sat up, her heart pounding, Elara could still smell the lush greenery of Agri Solitudo, the faint aroma of damp earth and wildflowers lingering in the air around her. She touched her face, half-expecting to feel the ghostly chill of the breeze she had felt in her dream.

"Wake up!" a familiar voice cut through the haze. Claudio was there, kneeling by her side, his hands gently gripping her shoulders. Concern was etched across his face. "You're okay," he said softly, his voice steady, trying to ground her. "It was just a dream. You're safe."

Her breath came in ragged gasps as she struggled to reorient herself, the remnants of the nightmare still clinging to her like shadows. She blinked, staring into Claudio's worried eyes, his presence a stark contrast to the horrors she had just witnessed. Slowly, the room came back into focus—the familiar hum of the ship, the soft glow of the lights, and the solidity of the here and now.

But the weight of the dream lingered, and she couldn't shake the feeling that it was more than just a nightmare.

"You know," Claudio murmured, brushing a stray strand of hair from her face, "I used to have nightmares too. Back in the day, I'd wake up and feel like I was still there, in the middle of it all. Never thought

213

they'd go away, but they did, eventually." He gave her a small, reassuring smile, as if to say she wasn't alone in her struggle.

As the alarm lights continued to flash, the crew stood in grim silence. Claudio let out a frustrated sigh, running his hand through his hair as he eyed the control panel. "The thruster is fried, and I can't fix this here. We need parts—and not the kind we can slap together with what we've got," he said, his voice tight with frustration.

Elara glanced over at him, knowing what that meant before he even said it. "So… we'll need to find those parts somewhere."

Claudio looked up from the console, his face set in a hard scowl. "Yeah, and the only place nearby is Kraedin." He spat the name out like it left a bitter taste in his mouth.

"We get what we need and get out," Elara said, her tone decisive, though she couldn't ignore the growing sense of unease.

"Yeah, easier said than done," Claudio muttered, his mind lingering on Elara's reaction. All business, no questions—completely unlike her usual self. He didn't like it one bit.

"There's a gang called the Crimson Syndicate that runs most of Kraedin's lower levels," Claudio warned, his tone grim.

"They don't take kindly to strangers, especially not ones who look like they're carrying something valuable. I'd avoid any dark alleys unless you're looking to get jumped."

Claudio stared out at the horizon; his eyes fixed on the city of Kraedin in the distance. It was just three clicks south, but it might as well have been a world away. Kraedin—crime-ridden and crawling with factions vying for control. Every part of that place was a risk, from the streets to the back alleys, where deals were made, and lives were lost over scraps. It wasn't just any city. It was a breeding ground for trouble, a cesspool of broken promises and shady characters, all with their own agendas.

They needed parts, and Kraedin was the only place to get them. But the thought of walking into that den of chaos didn't sit right with Claudio. Something about the place gave him the same feeling he had when they first touched down on Zynthar—a bad one. They were stranded out here, three clicks north of a city that couldn't care less if they made it back alive. Every move they made would have to be precise, or they'd be swallowed whole by Kraedin's underbelly.

He sighed. "Yeah, this is gonna be fun," he muttered, the sarcasm doing little to mask his unease.

The trek from the Galathea had been long and silent, the three of them knowing the risks and the stakes. The ship needed critical repairs to get off this planet, and their only option was this lawless city. Claudio had grumbled about it every step of the way, his pure hatred for Kraedin evident in every word he spat.

CHAPTER 14:

CITY OF CORRUPTION

Kraedin sprawls out beneath a low, sickly yellow sky, the air thick with the scent of smoke, oil, and decay. The city is a labyrinth of narrow alleys and towering structures, their once-pristine facades long eroded by time and neglect, replaced by a patchwork of rusting metal and faded neon signs. The streets pulse with life—an unsettling, chaotic energy that never seems to sleep. In Kraedin, time moves differently, as if the very air weighs down on its inhabitants, trapping them in a perpetual twilight where law and order are merely distant memories.

The city's heart is a tangle of elevated walkways, crooked bridges, and rickety platforms that crisscross between towering buildings, casting everything below in shadow. It's said that in Kraedin, the higher you go, the deeper your pockets—above, the wealthiest crime lords sit in their opulent penthouses, surveying the misery below with cold detachment. But down in the depths, on the ground level, it's a different world entirely.

The streets here are alive with an unrelenting current of human desperation. Vendors with broken, flickering holo-stalls hawk everything from illicit tech to weapons-grade narcotics. Gangs clad in patchwork armor and face-obscuring masks slither through the crowd, eyes scanning for weakness, opportunity, or trouble—often all three. Every corner hides a story, each darker than the last.

The people of Kraedin are hard, their faces etched with survival. Here, allegiances shift with the wind, and betrayal is as common as the smog that hangs heavy in the air. There's no sanctuary, no safety in these streets—just a relentless grind against a backdrop of clashing cultures and shifting power dynamics. Corruption is the city's true ruler, with every lawman on someone's payroll, every deal laced with deceit.

The city's skyline is a jagged array of mismatched towers, some sleek and modern, others crumbling relics of a long-forgotten age. At night, Kraedin glows with a sickly neon hue, casting everything in a distorted, artificial light. Above it all looms a distant spaceport, a constant reminder of the city's connection to the wider galaxy—a galaxy that has long since abandoned it.

Claudio glanced back at Elara and Verus, his expression as hard as ever. "Well, here we are. Kraedin," he muttered, shaking his head. "The galaxy's favorite trash heap."

Claudio scanned the crowd, each shadowed figure a potential threat. He'd seen people disappear in places like this—taken right off the street, never to be seen again. The weight of a blaster on his hip was reassuring, but even that couldn't chase away the chill that crept up his spine.

"I still don't see why this place exists," he said, eyeing the dark corners of the street as if something might leap out at any moment. "Crime, corruption… there's not one damn good reason anyone would want to live here unless they're hiding from something or looking to get stabbed."

They reached the heart of Kraedin, and it was everything Claudio had warned them about—dark alleys, shady figures moving in and out of poorly lit shops, and the unmistakable sense that they were being watched. The air smelled of grease, rust, and desperation. No one made eye contact unless it was with suspicion or outright menace.

Claudio made his way to the upper levels of the center of the city where the main factions reside. Elara and Verus followed him through several alleyways that led to stairwells that led to smaller alleys. Claudio stops and turns to both of them, "Now, listen up, do not say a word, let me do all the talking. Do not make any eye contact. These people are as easily offended as they are ruthless."

High, decaying towers loomed overhead, casting long, jagged shadows across their path. The city's bustling market hummed around them, its pulse erratic, yet oddly rhythmic—like the heartbeat of something alive and dangerous.

Claudio moved with purpose, eyes scanning the throng for a familiar face. Verus followed, his sharp gaze assessing every potential threat, while Elara walked a step behind, her usual calm facade tinged with unease.

"We shouldn't linger here," Verus muttered, his voice low but urgent.

Claudio glanced over his shoulder, smirking faintly. "Relax, Doc. Dash is a friend ...sort of."

Before Verus could respond, Claudio's eyes landed on Dash (Vox), a wiry figure standing by a narrow shop tucked between towering buildings. Dash's dark eyes flicked nervously as he waved them over, beckoning them into the dim-lit shop.

Inside, the smell of grease, burnt metal, and desperation hung thick in the air. Ship parts; some barely recognizable, others gleaming with newness were stacked haphazardly around the room. Dash leaned in close, lowering his voice to a whisper.

"You've got the credits?" Dash asked, wiping his hands on a dirty rag. His gaze flickered toward the door, always wary.

Claudio pulled out a small, shimmering data chip. "We've got what you asked for. Now, do you have the part or are we wasting our time?"

Dash exhaled sharply, darting into the back of the shop and returning with a compact but necessary ship component. "This should fix your engine. But listen, Claudio, things are getting messy around here. The Syndicate's tightening its grip, and I..."

He froze mid-sentence, his face draining of color. A cold, unsettling wind blew through the cracks in the shop walls, though none of them had noticed the door open.

Verus stiffened, his eyes locking with Elara's. "They're here," he whispered, his voice barely audible.

Before anyone could react, the Obsidian Order descended.

They appeared out of the shadows, like specters of darkness themselves, cloaked in blackened armor that seemed to drink in the light. Their forms blurred and twisted, drawn toward Elara as if by some invisible force. One of them lunged forward, a shimmering blade aimed directly at her chest.

"Elara!" Claudio shouted, pulling his blaster from its holster and firing off a shot.

But it was too late. The Order were focused and obsessed with Elara; their attacks synchronized with a relentless force. Elara's breath hitched, a surge of cold fear washing over her as the familiar, unwelcome presence stirred within her.

Her skin began to shimmer, the stars beneath her surface flickering with erratic bursts of light. Her hands clenched into fists as she fought to contain the rage that clawed at her from within.

But something snapped.

Elara clenched her fists, willing herself to focus, to push back against the dark presence worming its way through her mind. She could feel the satisfaction of anger, sinister whispers filling her head, urging her to let go. She squeezed her eyes shut, but the harder she fought, the stronger the pull.

The next moment, everything blurred. Elara's vision turned red as her Sidereal powers exploded outward, laced with a darkness that didn't belong to her. She let out a scream that echoed through the shop and into the street, as arcs of pure, lethal energy pulsed from her hands, tearing through the Obsidian soldiers like they were nothing.

The first one disintegrated in front of her, reduced to ash in seconds. The second never had the chance to scream as his armor shattered, followed by his body. But Elara didn't stop. She couldn't.

Dash's eyes darted between Claudio and the door. Every instinct screamed at him to run, to get as far away from this chaos as possible. The look in Claudio's eyes; raw and desperate, held him in place. He'd always prided himself on knowing when to cut and run, but something about this crew made him hesitate. Even if it cost him.

Each wave of power she unleashed became more savage, more uncontrollable. Her face twisted in a snarl as she launched herself at the remaining attackers, her hands glowing with the violent energy of the Astralis Core's influence. The spirit of Perfida surged within her, drowning her rational thoughts, consuming her will.

Claudio's stomach twisted as he watched her—this wasn't the Elara he knew. The power that radiated from her was terrifying, and he knew that whatever was happening, she was beyond his reach. He raised his blaster, his hands shaking slightly as he aimed at the advancing soldiers, but his thoughts remained fixed on Elara. How far gone was she?

Verus shouted, but his voice felt distant, as if coming from another world.

She turned, her eyes burning with hatred, but not recognizing who stood in front of her. Verus watched, horrified, as the woman he knew—the cautious, brilliant scientist—was nowhere to be found in the rage-filled creature before him.

Her energy blasts started injuring other bystanders. Elara didn't care; the temptation of the rage was euphoric. For the first time, she had control over a boundless power.

Perfida, as if he was in the room, whispers to Elara from inside her mind, "They want to take it from you. What makes you special. Kill them all."

"Elara, STOP!" Verus shouted again, stepping closer. "This isn't you!"

But Elara wasn't listening. Her mind was lost in a swirl of violence and dark whispers. She spun back toward the remainder of Obsidian Order Soldiers, her hands raised to strike once more, her very essence pulsing with malevolent energy.

Dash, who had been frozen in fear, finally found his voice. "Claudio... What the hell is happening?!"

Claudio fired another shot at an Obsidian soldier, his teeth gritted in frustration. "We're way past explanations, Dash. Just get us that part!"

Dash scrambled to grab the engine part, but his hands trembled as he glanced between Elara's terrifying display and the door, clearly torn between his survival instincts and his deal with Claudio.

Suddenly, a calm washed over the shop—silent and eerie. The last Obsidian soldier lay dead on the ground, but Elara remained standing in the center of the wreckage, breathing heavily, her hands still glowing with the energy she had unleashed. Her eyes flickered off of her blood-splattered face, as if returning to herself, but the look of horror on Verus's face struck her like a physical blow.

Verus stared at her, frozen in place. His mind raced, struggling to reconcile the woman before him with the Elara he once knew—the scientist who questioned everything, who approached problems with logic and patience. Now, her starry skin burned with a violent, chaotic energy, her eyes wild and unrecognizable.

His throat tightened. This can't be happening. He had seen many things in his long life, but nothing prepared him for this.

"Elara..." he whispered, his voice barely holding together. "What's happening to you?"

Verus swallowed hard, guilt gnawing at him. He had thought she could handle the Core's power, that he could protect Elara from its worst effects. But watching her now, his heart ached with the realization that he had failed. Maybe he should have seen this coming, should have done something—anything—to prevent it.

CHAPTER 15:

BETWEEN WATER & FLOWERS

The Galathea sat three clicks north of Kraedin, grounded and broken. Inside, the small cabin was dimly lit, shadows flickering across the metal walls. Elara lay asleep on the narrow cot in the corner, her chest rising and falling steadily, though her face was pale and strained even in rest. Claudio stood by the viewport, arms crossed, his gaze distant as the view stretched out before them.

Behind him, Verus paced, his hands clasped behind his back, his brow furrowed in deep thought. The silence between them was thick with unspoken concern, the weight of Elara's condition looming over every decision they made.

Claudio broke the silence first, his voice low but edged with frustration. "She's getting worse, Verus."

Claudio glanced back at Elara's pale face, a haunting reminder of how much was at stake. He'd promised himself he wouldn't let anything happen to her, but with each passing day, that promise felt harder to keep. And if he failed her... he wasn't sure he could live with that.

Verus didn't respond immediately, his eyes lingering on Elara's still form. "I know," he finally said, his voice barely above a whisper. "Perfida's influence... it's stronger than I anticipated."

Claudio shook his head, turning away from the window to face Verus. "Stronger?! She nearly killed innocent civilians while tearing through the Obsidian Soldiers. If that's not a warning, I don't know what is."

Verus's pacing stopped, and he looked up, his expression grim. "I underestimated how deep the Astralis Core's corruption could run. It's not just Perfida's spirit—it's the Core itself, twisting her, amplifying every dark thought."

Claudio exhaled sharply, running a hand through his hair. "So, what are we supposed to do? Keep running until she snaps completely?

Because from where I'm standing, that's exactly what's gonna happen if we don't figure this out."

Verus's gaze softened as he glanced back at Elara. "We can't abandon her, Claudio. She's still in there… somewhere."

Claudio's frustration was palpable, but Verus nodded. "I'm not saying we leave her behind. But we need a solution. Something permanent. That's why we need to find the Keeper temple," Verus said, moving to the holo-map in the center of the cabin. "If there's any chance to understand what Perfida has done to her—to reverse it—it'll be there. The Keepers left behind knowledge that might help us."

Claudio leaned against the table; arms crossed again. "And how exactly do we find this temple? We're chasing ghosts here, Verus."

Verus met his gaze, determination hardening his voice. "That's why we're going back to Dash. He's our best lead. He knows more about Kraedin's underworld than anyone, and if anyone has access to hidden knowledge about the Keepers, it's him."

Claudio hesitated, glancing back at Elara's sleeping form. "If this temple is our last shot, then we better hope Dash has something useful."

Verus's expression darkened, the weight of their mission settling heavily on him. "He will."

Verus knew the risks, knew the dark corners of knowledge they were about to tread. His hands trembled slightly as he thought of what the Keepers' secrets might unleash.

The streets of Kraedin were as chaotic as ever, filled with the usual mix of smugglers, traders, and those who thrived in the shadows. Claudio led the way to a narrow alley where Dash had said he'd be waiting.

The door creaked open, revealing Dash standing by a table filled with spare ship parts. He didn't smile when he saw them enter, his expression guarded and eyes darting nervously.

"Didn't expect to see you back so soon."

"We need information," Verus said flatly, stepping forward. "About the Keeper temples."

Dash raised an eyebrow. "Temples, huh? That's not exactly what you pick up in a marketplace. What's it worth to you?"

Claudio crossed his arms. "You've already bled us dry for the ship parts, Dash. Don't push your luck."

"This isn't about luck. Information like that doesn't come cheap, and I know how much this means to you," Dash glanced pointedly at Elara, who remained silent, her head lowered as if she were barely aware of the conversation.

Verus stepped forward, pulling a small metallic object from his coat. The object was an ancient-looking medallion, its surface engraved with symbols that shimmered faintly in the low light.

Dash's eyes widened. "That's... "

"A rare artifact," Verus interrupted. "Keeper-made. Worth more than anything in this city. It's yours... if you give us what we need."

Dash's hand twitched, and for a moment, he hesitated. His greed fought with his caution, but in the end, greed won. "Alright," he said slowly, his eyes still on the medallion. "There's a temple—an old one, buried deep underground beneath the Crimson Blade Syndicate's palace."

Dash's fingers itched to close around the medallion. Its weight promised more wealth than he'd ever seen, but a gnawing voice in the back of his mind reminded him that crossing these people might cost him far more than just his cut of the credits.

"Getting in will be dangerous, heavily guarded. Some say the lineage of the Keepers still lives there."

"That's all we need," Verus replied, handing over the artifact without a second thought. Dash snatched it greedily, turning it over in his hands, admiring the craftsmanship.

"Good luck finding it," Dash said, his smile thin and insincere. "You're gonna need it."

As the group left the shop, the darkened alleys of Kraedin swallowing them once more, Dash slipped into the shadows, his eyes darting left and right. He went to a secluded corner where a figure stood waiting, cloaked in black and barely visible in the dim light.

The figure's voice was a low whisper. "Anything useful?"

Dash nodded, holding up the medallion, "It's yours now... for the right price."

The hooded figure stepped forward, the light catching the edge of their face—just enough to reveal the familiar insignia of the Obsidian Order etched into their gauntlet. They handed Dash a small credit chip, and as he pocketed it, "They're heading for the temple." The figure's voice turned cold.

"Veyra will be pleased."

Dash shivered, not daring to ask what that meant as the figure vanished into the night. Deep down, he had gotten his money, but he knew that betraying Claudio and his crew had put him in far more danger than he could handle.

Elara, Claudio, and Verus, now armed with the knowledge of the temple's hidden location beneath the Crimson Blade Syndicate's palace, moved with purpose through the bustling streets of Kraedin. The city, a chaotic sprawl of vendors, smugglers, and mercenaries, seemed to pulse with a restless energy that made blending in both easier and more dangerous. Every corner held its secrets, and every alleyway was a potential trap.

Elara kept her hood low, eyes scanning the crowd as they navigated more profoundly into the city's heart. The Crimson Blade Syndicate's palace loomed ahead, its dark, angular spires a sharp contrast against the gritty, worn buildings around it. The palace symbolized power and wealth, standing out in a city where most struggled just to survive.

"Keep your heads down," Verus murmured, his voice low but steady. He limped slightly from his injury, but the determination in his eyes hadn't faded. His gaze swept over the crowded market stalls, the narrow alleyways, and the groups of Syndicate enforcers scattered throughout the streets.

Claudio moved closer to Elara, his expression unreadable but his eyes sharp, constantly watching their surroundings. "This place is crawling with them," he muttered, nodding toward a group of armed men near a makeshift bar. "If they catch wind of what we're doing, we're dead before we get near the palace."

Elara tightened her grip on the edge of her cloak, the weight of the situation pressing down on her.

"We stay quiet. No powers. No distractions," she reminded herself, glancing up at the towering structure ahead. "We're almost there."

They weaved through the crowd, trying to blend in with the mass of traders, travelers, and Syndicate muscle. The city's constant noise—the clatter of metal, the shouting of vendors, the low hum of conversation—created a cover of anonymity, but it was fragile. One wrong move, one slip, and they would be exposed.

As they drew closer to the palace gates, Elara's heart pounded in her chest. She could feel the presence of the temple beneath them, hidden and waiting. The weight of the ancient knowledge pulled at her like that dream she had a few days ago, but she couldn't afford to think of that now. They needed to get inside without raising an alarm.

"There," Verus whispered, pointing to a narrow side entrance. "That's our way in. We'll have to time it between guard shifts."

Claudio glanced at the guards stationed near the entrance, his brow furrowed. "Are you sure? One slip, and we're in a firefight."

Verus nodded, his voice firm. "It's our best shot. Once we're inside, we can find the way down to the temple. But we have to move fast."

Elara took a deep breath, her pulse quickening. They were close now, dangerously close. The palace stood before them, a fortress of shadows and secrets, with the temple buried beneath its foundations. And with it, the power she was seeking—and the danger they could not yet fully understand.

Claudio studied the movements of the Syndicate muscle with the precision of a seasoned tactician. Their patrols shifted in a rhythmic dance, guards moving in and out like clockwork. He spotted it—a small, predictable gap between a Terranovian water merchant's stall and a desert flower vendor. His lips curled into a smirk. "Got it."

He turned to Verus and Elara, both sharp-eyed and ready for action. "We move between the water merchant and the flower cart," he said, nodding toward the narrow passage. "Stay low, keep quiet. That's our best shot."

Verus and Elara exchanged glances before nodding in unison, wordlessly trusting Claudio's judgment.

Claudio raised a clenched fist, his eyes locked on the guard's path. "On my signal," he whispered, the tension in his voice matching the tautness in his muscles.

The second the guard's back was turned, his fist dropped. "Elara, go."

Elara moved casually, slipping into the gap as though she belonged there. She reached the manhole cover, wincing as she pried it open with a sharp strain of her muscles. The metallic grind was barely audible beneath the murmur of the marketplace. Just as the next guard approached, she disappeared into the shadows below.

Claudio's fist rose again, his eyes narrowing as the guard strolled past. "Verus, you're next," he ordered, keeping his voice low but urgent.

Verus crossed the street, his pace quick but controlled, careful not to attract unwanted eyes. He slipped between the merchant stalls, following Elara's path into the opening.

Now it was Claudio's turn. He moved swiftly, slipping into the manhole with practiced ease, his hands steady as he replaced the cover above them, sealing their path. The marketplace continued, none the wiser to the trio disappearing beneath its streets.

Claudio landed lightly in the damp, foul-smelling tunnel below, his boots splashing into ankle-deep water. The narrow passage, barely illuminated by a dim overhead glow, stretched endlessly in both directions, with the faint sound of running water echoing in the distance.

Verus scanned their surroundings, his silver eyes flicking between the walls. "The temple should be deeper underground," he murmured. "These sewers might connect to the old catacombs."

Elara was already moving forward, her stride determined. "Then let's find it," she said, the tension in her voice betraying her discomfort. She could sense it—something pulling at her, something ancient and familiar.

They trudged through the labyrinthine tunnels, the stench of sewage almost unbearable, but they pressed on. Each step felt heavier than the last, the air thickening with an unnatural chill. The further they went, the more Elara's instincts screamed that they were approaching something significant.

"Wait," Verus called out softly after some time, stopping in his tracks. His gaze was fixed on a stone archway barely visible under layers of grime and corrosion. Strange markings, worn down by time, were etched into the stone—symbols that Elara immediately recognized.

"The Keepers," she whispered, her fingers tracing the faded inscriptions. She felt a pulse, a resonance as if the temple acknowledged her presence.

"These were their signs," Verus said, stepping closer, his voice filled with reverence. "The Temple of the Keepers lies beyond this."

Elara hesitated, feeling a surge of something she couldn't quite place. Her name—those symbols spelled out her name. Her fingers trembled slightly as she traced the last markings, but there was no time to process it.

"Let's move," Claudio urged, ever the pragmatist.

Her fingers brushed the ancient markings, and a chill spread through her. How did these symbols carry her name? She felt a strange comfort and fear at once, as if the temple had known she would come. A thousand questions crowded her mind, but no answers came, only the feeling that she was exactly where she was meant to be.

They pushed forward into the temple's entrance, the transition from sewer to ancient stone corridors almost surreal. The air was different here—heavy with age, secrets, and power. Their footsteps echoed against the stone walls as they ventured deeper into the heart of the temple—the faint, ghostly blue light emitted from ancient crystals embedded in the stone, guiding their way.

After several winding passages, they entered a vast chamber. The ceiling soared impossibly high, with towering statues of the Keepers lining the walls. At the far end of the dimly lit room, an ancient stone altar loomed ominously. In the center of the altar, there stood a formidable stone doorway. Unlike any other door or gate, this doorway appeared to lead to an unfathomable void, a mysterious emptiness shrouded in eerie silence.

The air was thick with an ancient mustiness, tinged with a faint metallic tang that clung to the back of their throats. A distant echo, like the whisper of voices, drifted through the corridors, sending a shiver down Elara's spine. This place was alive with memories, and each step felt like trespassing on secrets meant to stay hidden.

CHAPTER 16:

THE KRAEDIN CONFLICT

The air was thick and charged with ancient energy. Glowing runes adorned every visible surface near Elara. The architecture combined ancient stone with traces of when this place was known as Agri Solitudo, at the peak of Terranovian technology.

With each footstep echoing across the stone hall, the air grew colder. It was an odd sensation, given that this planet is one of the hottest among most planets in terms of temperature.

As Elara stepped into the chamber, a gentle but constant hum filled the air, causing the walls to seem almost alive as they pulsed with energy. Delicate blue tendrils of light started to emanate from her, weaving and dancing with the ancient stone. Verus looked on in wonder, while Claudio's expression betrayed a combination of concern and doubt. "The Core... it's stirring the sanctuary to life," Verus whispered, barely able to conceal his astonishment.

As Elara ventured further into the sanctuary, the air became denser, as if filled with an inexplicable presence. The walls appeared to pulsate, each throb resonating with the Astralis Core she carried. Before she could speak, the ground beneath her began to tremble, and a low hum permeated the chamber.

A deep and ancient voice reverberated through the space as if it had traversed millennia to reach them. "You, who bear the Core, must understand that it is not merely a tool but a living force. Many before you believed they could wield its power without consequence. They were mistaken."

A flicker of light illuminated the chamber, and the walls began to transform. Before Elara, images of past civilizations materialized— once prosperous worlds now reduced to nothing more than desolate wastelands. Cities crumbled, their towers falling in slow motion as if time had slowed to reveal the devastation in detail. The last image was instantly recognizable to Elara: Zynthar, its golden fields transformed into endless deserts.

The ancient voice spoke again, its tone even colder. "The Core is not yours to command. It will test you, tempt you, and manipulate your desires. You will rise above or suffer the fate of those who came before you. Behold their destiny, and understand what awaits if you falter."

Claudio's eyes shifted to Elara. "Elara... this is a caution. They want you to see the peril."

She stood frozen, watching as the final image lingered before her—a solitary figure standing amidst the ruins of a devastated world, its eyes glowing with a familiar red light. Elara's breath caught in her throat as she realized the figure was herself.

The voice grew louder, more forceful. "The Core will consume you unless you find the strength to resist."

The air hung heavy with silence after those words were spoken. Elara felt the weight of the words pressing down on her heart. She had already tasted its allure on the surface, and it had been intoxicating. If she were to discover what this Core could do, she would have to be resilient, like her friends. She realized she could not do this alone.

A vision came into her mind's eye, Elara saw herself not as a Sidereal but one of the Obsidian Order. Eyes glowing with an iridescent red. The land she once knew, the villages on the edge of Astralith, burning. The city skyline, blazing with smoke and fire. She looked in horror as worker drones dumped Néalian bodies of every age into a large smoldering pile. The cries of her fellow Sidereals shot out in anguish as Elara saw this twisted version of herself, blasting red energy in unbridled rage.

"Elara!" Claudio's muffled voice drifted in. "Snap out of it! Don't let this thing in! Elar…" Claudio was interrupted by Verus's hand on his shoulder.

"This is her test." Verus looked in concern and acceptance.

The vivid vision vanished abruptly, leaving her disoriented as she found herself back in the ancient temple, as if she had been instantaneously transported from another distant place.

"What the hell was that?" Claudio looked puzzled.

Tears fell from her face as memories of her parents lying dead in the middle of the village on Astralith. The heart-sinking feeling of losing someone is one that she always carried inside, deep down.

The fact that she saw the future, where she became the abuser, the murderer, shot right to the center of who she was, as a person, as a Sidereal.

"I saw…" Elara was fighting the tears, "my future. Who I became."

Verus put his hand on Elara's shoulder as an old friend would. "This was a warning of end consequences if abuse of the core takes place."

Verus looked away, his mind racing. He'd known the risks of seeking out the Core, but seeing the fear in Elara's eyes, he wondered if he had underestimated its influence. He was supposed to be her guide, yet he couldn't shake the feeling that he'd led her to the edge of a precipice he couldn't pull her back from.

"It was so vivid!" Elara exclaimed, "It looked as if I had become like Verya. Cold. Distant. A killer."

"That is not who you are." Verus embraced her.

Claudio's heart sank as Elara's words sank in. He'd seen the toll this journey had taken on her, but this was different. It was as if she'd glimpsed into a nightmare she couldn't shake off. He reached out, feeling the need to say something, anything that could take away the fear he saw in her eyes.

Claudio frowned reassuringly, "Yeah, Elara, You are not that." He stared into her eyes. "Take it from someone who has seen the worst criminals taking away friends and family. You are stronger than that."

"Thanks, guys." Elara wiped the last of the tears from her eyes. "As much as I want to use the Core to help Zynthar and the galaxy abroad, I don't feel like I am strong enough to wield its power."

A gentle yet ominous boom echoed from the ceiling above, prompting small particles of dirt and sand to cascade down in a delicate dance.

"What's going on up there?" Claudio exclaimed, puzzled by the sounds emanating from the ceiling.

The air crackled with tension as Elara, Claudio, and Verus emerged from the dim corridors of the temple. Outside, the once-serene city had transformed into a battlefield. Crimson Syndicate forces, clad in dark armor, stormed the ancient grounds, their crimson-bladed weapons flashing under the dull light of the setting sun. The Obsidian Order, their black cloaks billowing, retaliated with savage precision, their energy pulsating with dark red power.

The smell of burnt ozone filled the air as laser bolts sliced through the smoky haze. Elara could hear the crackle of energy blades clashing, their electric hum underscoring the screams and shouts that echoed through the shattered streets. The chaos was suffocating, each breath tasting of ash and blood.

"Looks like our exit isn't going to be easy," Claudio muttered, his hand instinctively resting on his blaster. He glanced sideways at Verus, whose sharp gaze tracked the chaos. "Any bright ideas, professor?"

"Survive," Verus replied coldly, not looking at the unfolding carnage. His jaw tightened. "And hope they're too busy killing each other to notice us."

A high-pitched scream pierced the air as a Syndicate spear impaled an Obsidian Order soldier, the energy from the weapon sending a shockwave through the crowd. The ground shuddered as if the temple felt the bloodshed on its sacred grounds below. Elara flinched, sensing the disturbance rippling through the stones beneath her feet.

Perfida's voice, deep and mocking, echoed faintly in her mind. "Their blood will only strengthen the Core's power. Let it grow. Let the chaos feed us."

She clenched her fists, trying to shut him out, but the pull was stronger now. The core's influence felt like a storm swirling inside her, relentless, seductive.

"Elara," Claudio's voice snapped her out of the trance, his expression concerned. "Stay with me. We need to move—now."

Suddenly, a group of Crimson Syndicate fighters broke off from the main battle, their eyes locking onto the trio. They moved swiftly, weapons drawn, cutting through the debris as they advanced.

"Looks like we've been spotted," Verus noted grimly.

Without hesitation, Claudio pulled out his blaster, his eyes narrowing. "Well, they're not here to shop for flowers at the market." Verus smirked, "Cover us," as he took Elara into a hidden alley.

Claudio retrieved two Astralith Army-issue phase-shift blasters from his carrying bag and activated their power couplings by pressing his thumbs on the backside of the barrel. A split second later, he took cover against a brick divider and heard a chime sound, "It's go time."

Claudio crouched and fired two shots, hitting the syndicate soldier to the right. He narrowly avoided another stray laser bolt as he took cover behind a wall. Then he saw it: an opening for his shot, a bright spot above the soldier on the left. Claudio quickly aimed and fired. A brilliant light shot out, temporarily disorienting the syndicate soldier. Claudio took him down with a well-placed plasma bolt.

"Alright, let's go!" Claudio signaled to Elara and Verus with a hand gesture.

The sand-swept streets of Kreadin were filled with chaos as laser blasts rained down from all directions. The elite syndicate found themselves locked in a fierce and relentless battle against The Obsidian Order's Sidereals, with the very streets of Kraedin becoming a warzone.

The sound of distant explosions rattles through the streets as buildings groan under the weight of destruction. Smoke and debris fill the air, making it difficult to see beyond a few feet. Claudio is leading the group through the narrow alleys of Kraedin, constantly glancing back at Elara, who seems to be struggling with something internal, her eyes darting around wildly.

"We need to keep moving," Claudio barks, pulling Elara by the arm as Verus scouts ahead. They are weaving through collapsed structures, avoiding firefights between the Obsidian Order and the Crimson Syndicate, but every skirmish seems to draw Elara's attention.

She stumbled to a stop, her breath catching. Her hand started to glow with energy as her Sidereal powers began to manifest, creating a faint shimmer of stars reflected in her skin. Claudio rushed to her side, grabbing her wrist before she could fully channel her power.

"No, if you use your powers, you'll lose control. We can't risk that, Elara," he pleads, his voice tinged with desperation. She stares at him, torn between the desire to help and the fear of the corruption eating away at her.

As they venture further into the city, Elara's internal struggle becomes increasingly apparent. The deeper they go, the more powerful the pull from the Astralis Core becomes. She can feel it humming in her chest, urging her to unleash its power.

Verus, sensing her turmoil, places a hand on her shoulder as they duck into a crumbling building for cover. "I know what you're feeling," he says quietly. "Don't give in. Stay focused."

Her head snaps toward him, and for a brief moment, her eyes flash with something darker, more sinister. "Focused? We're in the middle of a war zone, and you want me to sit back?" Her voice cracks with frustration. "I could end this."

"Yeah and what happens after you 'end this'?" Verus replies calmly. "How many will die after you interfere? Do you even know if you'll be the same person? "

Elara clenches her fists, her skin beginning to glow brighter. She wants to argue, to tell them she can handle it—but deep down, she isn't sure.

In the midst of the chaotic battle, Veyra Tenebria finally seizes her opportunity. Unseen and unheard, she has been stealthily tailing Elara through the city, biding her time. As the dust settles, Veyra emerges from the concealment of the shadows, her figure shrouded in darkness. With a sudden and unexpected ferocity, she unleashes a powerful surge of dark energy aimed directly at the unsuspecting group.

Claudio barely has time to react, shoving Elara to the ground just as the energy slams into the wall behind them, blowing chunks of stone everywhere.

"Still playing hero?" Veyra's voice is cold, taunting, "You can't save her, Claudio, just like you couldn't save your wife." Claudios eyes filled with rage as he shot several shots in Veyra's direction, which she dodged effortlessly.

Veyra's words were a knife twisting in an old wound Claudio never fully healed. He could almost see Gwen's face, hear her laughter—memories that felt like salt in the open wound Veyra had just ripped open. His grip tightened on the blaster, rage and grief surging in equal measure. If he couldn't protect his wife, he'd be damned if he let Elara slip through his fingers.

Veyra steps forward, her eyes gleaming with malice as she fixes her gaze on Elara. "You're more valuable to me now than ever. I can sense it—you're barely holding it together. One little push, and you'll be mine."

Elara scrambles to her feet, fury boiling inside her. "I'm nothing like you!" But her hands are already glowing with energy, and it's taking every ounce of her willpower not to let it explode.

Claudio and Verus try to intervene, putting themselves between Elara and Veyra, but Veyra's taunts are relentless, designed to push Elara into unleashing her power.

Elara struggled with the thoughts that she could end this If she gave into temptation, how Verya responsible, part of her would be lost forever. Images of her parents' lifeless bodies filled her mind, Veyra's face twisting into a mask of contempt. The Core pulsed within her, feeding her fury, promising power beyond measure. It would be so

248

easy, she thought. One surge of energy, and Veyra would be dust, just like those who'd taken everything from her. She felt the rage rise, hot and consuming, and for a moment, she was ready to let it all go.

CHAPTER 17:

THE SIPHONING STORM

Elara felt a deep longing for peace—a peace that Perfida promised her in exchange for her rage. The thought of her parents smiling, safe and whole, was almost too much to resist. She could feel herself slipping, drawn to the seductive whisper that promised to make her pain go away.

Like a pool of volatile fuel slithering downhill toward an open flame, Perfida was tightening his grip on Elara. His voice echoed more clearly in her mind, seductive and insistent: "Why let this struggle drag on? Don't do it for me—do it for your parents. They'd still be alive if not for Veyra. We can end this. We can end her."

A roaring flame of anger erupted inside Elara. She remembered the warmth of her parents' embrace before they were slaughtered. Perfida was right; this is all Veyra's fault. Not just her; this was also the Obsidian Order's fault. The path to justice for her parents and peace was so obtainable, like a simple lift door button. The path to justice for her parents and peace seemed attainable, like pressing a simple elevator door button. However, once she opened this door, there was no turning back. If she didn't take action now, there would be further bloodshed for generations, leading to endless war. However, once she opened this door, there was no closing it. There would be further bloodshed for generations in endless war if she didn't take action now.

Claudio and Verus were desperately shouting at her, their hands desperately attempting to reach her, trying to halt the relentless cycle of hate. Despite their efforts, they knew it was in vain. Elara remained oblivious to their pleas, their voices barely registering in her ears.

Veyra grinned with twisted satisfaction. Elara was almost hers; she was weak, just like those Astralith villagers. Veyra was glad she killed her parents; it provided the psychological ground for today; the day she could finally obtain the Astralis Core.

Veyra focused her hatred and anger on Elara as she channeled her red energy, raising her arm to aim at her chest. This was going to be so easy. Veyra released her red beam of energy directly, aiming toward Elara's chest. An almost blinding radiant red and white light flashed then... Nothing.

Elara absorbed the energy into her hand. Her body is overtaken by a force she can no longer control. Her once-turquoise skin becomes a tempest of black and red, swirling like a violent nebula. Veins of a molten light pulse beneath her skin, glowing brighter with each passing moment as if she's become a living conduit for cosmic energy. She takes a breath, and the ground around her trembles, cracks spider-webbing from beneath her feet. When she lifts her arm, it's as though gravity bends to her will; objects rise into the air, swirling around her like debris caught in a storm. With a flick of her wrist, the storm is unleashed, a shockwave of dark energy that sends anything and anyone in its path flying. Her expression is emotionless, cold—no longer the Elara her companions knew, but a vessel for something far greater and darker.

Claudio's breath caught as he watched Elara become a vortex of shadow and light. She was beautiful, terrifying, and utterly foreign. He knew he should reach out, try to stop her, but something deep inside him hesitated. Was this still the woman he knew, or was she lost beneath the storm?

She began to float, with tiny tendrils of electricity flowing from her eyes, which were now glowing with bright white lights. A dual voice emanated from Elara's mouth, blending her voice with another, creating a duet-like mantra: "We are Perfida, the Bane of Agri Solitudo."

Veyra's expression shifted, revealing an emotion that had long been suppressed. The relentless conditioning of the Obsidian Order during her formative years before The Eclipsion War forcibly eradicated this feeling. Displaying this emotion was strictly forbidden, as it was believed to signify the erosion of a sharp and discerning intellect.

Elara/Perfida declared, "Lay thou amongst the hopeless scattered in dust; thy decision is Death." projecting her booming voice as if it were emanating from the city-com's emergency system. Claudio and Verus appeared visibly shaken.

In the grip of self-betrayal and fueled by seething anger, Veyra stole herself and launched a relentless barrage of energy attacks at Elara. However, to her astonishment, each attack halted just inches from Elara, creating an invisible power barrier between them. She was a force of nature.

Elara, controlled by Perfida, raised her arm and redirected Verya's energy attacks back at her. Verya attempted to dodge them, but Elara was too fast. A bolt hit her thigh, paralyzing her leg and causing a burning sensation.

The Raptor is a small two-seat ship capable of interstellar travel. Its long, sleek shape, along with its known sub-light speed, enables it to evade most scopes and detection systems.

Oriana, a Sidereal in her mid-40s but appearing no older than her 20s, sat in the Raptor's cockpit, parked at Zynthar's orbit, a large, sandy planet devoid of green life or significant bodies of water. She sought information on Elara Nova, her childhood best friend, and wondered if the details she obtained from the Astralith Library's logs were accurate.

She needed more precise information on old Keeper's temples, which she acquired from some of the Astralith Academy's archivist turncoats, who were tired of the constant gatekeeping and willing to provide information for the right price.

"Nav, give me a list of Zynthar's cities by population," Oriana commanded. A small chirp sounded, and the Nav computer responded in a digitally veiled tone, "Several cities are listed by population. Anything else?"

"Kraedin. Why is it only 5th on the list?" she asked inquisitively.

"My initial scans may only be as accurate as surface level. Perhaps there are those who live underground," Nav replied in a friendly manner, "These entities would be blocked from my scanner array."

She looked at the list with a hand on her chin, deep in thought for a moment, then decided, "Set a course for Kraedin. Land on the outskirts; I had a couple of ships boosted the last time I was here." Nav beeped a reply, "Affirmative. Course set."

As the ship descended, Oriana couldn't help but wonder if Elara would even recognize her. It's been over 30 years since they last ran and played together in their small village on Astralith, when they were without responsibility, full of youth, a lifetime ago.

As the city of Kraedin came into view, Oriana felt a strong surge of energy unlike any she had felt since childhood. She noticed a large ship, the Dreadspire, looming over the south side of the Docks. She quickly grabbed a pair of Optech binoculars, flipped the power crystals, and put her eyes through.

Five hundred Obsidian Order soldiers ran into the city's south entrance, followed by a lone figure hooded in black. She scanned ahead into the city, three hundred Crimson Syndicate soldiers attempting to guard what little surface land they had while being slaughtered in multitudes during the Order's siege.

"Actually, let's dock at the east end of the city," Oriana quickly inputted the command on the onboard datapad. "Also, send my coordinates to Jax with the message that I need backup." Nav, the friendly artificial voice, responded, "Confirmed. East Entrance. Your message has been sent."

As the Raptor stealthily swung into the dock, Oriana, she began to prepare some of her custom-made weapons: a set of dual pistols that harness energy from her Sidereal powers. Her advanced weaponry was designed to maintain a constant power supply, unlike traditional blasters, which often run out of power. However, this advantage has a drawback - prolonged engagements can quickly drain her energy. That's why she opted also to carry a long-range blaster as well, ensuring she's prepared for any situation.

Oriana gracefully pressed the canopy latch, feeling the satisfying click as it released. With a light hop, she emerged from the cockpit, weapons unholstered.

The streets were strewn with stone debris and the bodies of fallen Crimson Syndicate soldiers. Oriana checked her surroundings as she held her weapon at attention. Then she felt a surge of energy unlike anything she had ever experienced. The atmosphere was heavy, charged with an energy that gripped Oriana's senses. She could sense the darkness, a suffocating weight, pulling her towards it. She moved cautiously yet determinedly, drawn by something twisted and powerful. Her heart raced as she approached the source of the disturbance, where shadows swirled and pulsed in a storm of black and crimson.

Then she saw her.

Elara stood in the center, locked in a tense standoff with a figure draped in obsidian shadows—Veyra Tenebria. Even without moving,

Veyra exuded a sinister stillness, her eyes fixed on Elara with a cold, unyielding focus. And Elara... Oriana almost didn't recognize her.

Gone is the gentle strength of her friend. Instead, a dark tempest swirled around Elara, tendrils of shadow wrapping around her like spectral chains. Her face was etched with fierce intensity, her eyes hollowed by something that made Oriana's heart sink. The dark energy around her wasn't just emanating from her; it was consuming her, twisting her essence.

Oriana's breath caught as the realization washed over her. This wasn't just Elara. Something had taken hold of her, warping and distorting everything that made Elara who she was. She could see it in the way Elara's form shuddered as if barely containing the force that sought to tear her apart from within.

For a moment, Oriana stood frozen, horror mixing with sorrow as she grappled with the sight before her. But deep down, she knew there was no time to falter. The friend she'd grown up with was still in there somewhere, buried beneath the darkness. And Oriana couldn't let it, or Veyra, claim her.

She took a steadying breath, summoning every ounce of courage she had. With a final glance at Elara, Oriana stepped forward, her resolve hardening. This was no longer just a battle between Elara and Veyra. She was part of it now and wouldn't let the darkness win—not here, not now.

Oriana noticed a man crouched nearby, hidden behind a crumbling pillar. He was observing the confrontation between Elara and Veyra with great intensity, indicating his deep involvement in the unfolding situation. As she cautiously approached, the man turned towards her, his face expressing a mix of concern and confusion as he registered her presence. "Who are you?" he asked in a low but firm voice, his stance defensive and ready for action if necessary.

"Oriana," she replied, keeping her tone steady. "I'm a friend of Elara's. I know this looks strange, but I'm here to help."

The man hesitated, his gaze flickering back to the swirling darkness surrounding Elara. "Help?" he repeated, skepticism evident in his voice. "She's not herself. Her mind is all twisted and warped into something..." He trailed off, seemingly unsure how much he could reveal to a stranger.

"I know," Oriana said, cutting in. "I sensed it. That's why I'm here. I think I can weaken Perfida's control over her, but I'll need to get close enough to initiate an energy reversal. I'm Sidereal. I can disrupt his hold, but it'll only work if I can concentrate."

He studied her for a moment, then sighed. "Look, I'm Claudio, by the way. And if you're here to help, I'll trust you—for now. But we're short on time, and I planned on waiting for reinforcements. Are you sure you can handle this?"

"We don't have time to wait," Oriana replied firmly. "If I can get close enough, I can give Elara a fighting chance. But I'll need you to create a diversion. Keep Veyra's attention elsewhere while I work."

Claudio nodded, his hesitation fading. "Alright, Oriana. I'll create a distraction but do not take too long. Once they catch on, we'll both be in their sights."

With that, Claudio slipped into the shadows, preparing to draw Veyra's attention. Oriana took a deep breath, focusing her energy and bracing herself. She had only one chance to reach Elara and break through the darkness.

Oriana raised her hand, palm outstretched and reached toward Elara. She summoned her Sidereal abilities, feeling the familiar hum of energy as it began to flow through her fingertips. She initiated the Power Reversal, forging an ethereal link between them. A shimmering conduit of light formed in the space between, pulsating with a mix of Elara's corrupted power and Oriana's energy. It was beautiful and terrifying, like holding a piece of a storm.

As the energy rushed toward her, Oriana braced herself, staggering as the sheer force of Perfida's influence flooded her senses. The darkness was overwhelming, a suffocating weight that clawed at her mind, threatening to seep into every corner of her consciousness. Shadows curled around her thoughts, testing her resolve, searching for any weakness it could exploit.

She clenched her jaw, fighting against the seductive pull of the darkness. She could feel it probing, pressing against her willpower, trying to corrupt her just as it had Elara. But Oriana held firm, anchoring herself in the memory of her friend in the hope that she could still save her.

The energy raged within Elara, a swirling maelstrom of light and shadow, but Oriana held her ground. With every ounce of strength she had, she continued to siphon away the corrupted power, feeling it ebb as she fought to purify the link between them. For Elara's sake—and her own—Oriana would not let the darkness win. Not today.

The darkness seemed to have a life of its own, swirling and writhing as it attempted to entangle Oriana. She could feel its weight pressing down on her mind, seeping into the corners of her thoughts with venomous whispers. The whispers promised power, freedom, and even vengeance. Each word dripped with temptation, clawing at her defenses as if seeking to burrow into her very soul.

Oriana held onto her memories of Elara tightly. She imagined her childhood friend – the girl with a fierce spirit and a kind heart who had always been there for her. Memories of Elara's smile, her laughter at Oriana's jokes, and the numerous adventures they had shared flashed through her mind. These memories formed a shield around her, protecting her against the insidious presence of Perfida.

Oriana saw herself and Elara as young girls, laughing as they raced through the fields of Astralith, their world simple and unburdened. She held onto those memories, letting the warmth of Elara's laughter form a protective cocoon around her, shielding her from the icy tendrils of Perfida's whispers.

As the Power Reversal continued, Oriana's senses heightened, attuned to every subtle shift in Elara's energy. Then she noticed it—a flicker, a brief but unmistakable hesitation in the darkness. It was as if a sliver of light had broken through, a spark of the real Elara fighting back against the corruption. Oriana's heart leaped at the realization; Elara was still there, beneath the twisted layers, struggling to regain control.

Renewed determination surged through Oriana, steadying her as she focused on maintaining the connection. She tightened her grip on the link between them, drawing even more of the dark energy into herself, siphoning it away from her friend. The shadows clawed at her, trying to take root within her mind, but Oriana was relentless. She would not let go.

Veyra clenched her fists, hating the taste of retreat, but she knew that staying would be her end. She'd underestimated Elara and that Sidereal woman, Oriana. But she would not make the same mistake twice. The power of the Core was still within reach, and she would return with the force to claim it.

Veyra Tenebria seethed from the shadows, clutching her wounded leg. The pain was sharp, a constant reminder of her miscalculation. She had believed she was prepared, thinking her mastery over darkness would be enough to control the chaos unfolding before her. But as she watched Oriana and Elara entangled in that blinding conduit of energy, she realized her error.

The power of the Astralis Core exceeded her expectations. Elara's transformation had been impressive, but she hadn't anticipated this fierce attempt to reclaim the corrupted essence. Frustration gnawed at her as she tightened her grip, her nails digging into her palm. She realized she needed to retreat and reassess the situation, as it was spiraling out of her control.

It would be a setback, certainly, but not the end. No, she would find Draven. She needed his counsel and insights. His ruthless calculations would reveal a path forward, one that would allow her to strike back when the time was right. With reinforcements, she could tip the scales back in her favor, ensuring that the power of the Core ultimately remained within her grasp.

With one last look at the shimmering energy surrounding Elara and Oriana, Veyra clenched her teeth and hoisted herself up. She wouldn't allow this moment of vulnerability to lead to her downfall. Turning away, she started the painful withdrawal, determined to regroup and come back stronger. The power of the Core was a prize too precious to give up. She would stop at nothing to claim it, even if it meant tearing through anyone who stood in her way.

With every ounce of her will, Oriana poured her energy into the conduit, channeling her strength and love for Elara into the swirling storm. She could feel the darkness resisting, pressing back, but she held firm, refusing to waver. She was not alone in this fight; Elara's presence flickered stronger, a faint but steady pulse beneath the surface.

Oriana knew it would be a battle to the end, but she wasn't backing down. Not when her friend needed her most. Together, they would see this through, and she would do whatever it took to pull Elara back from the edge.

In the background, Claudio remained vigilant, his stance taut as he kept a watchful eye on the unfolding battle. She could feel his tension, sensing his readiness to jump in at a moment's notice should things take a dangerous turn. He was a silent guardian, positioned to intervene if the tide shifted, prepared to do whatever was necessary to protect them both.

Each heartbeat felt like a countdown, and Oriana knew that her time was limited. She couldn't hold out forever. But as long as she could maintain the connection, she would keep fighting, keep pulling, keep believing that somewhere beneath the darkness, Elara was still fighting too.

Oriana clenched her fists, willing her body to hold on just a little longer. She thought of Jax's steady presence, of Claudio's loyalty, and of the fierce, resilient woman Elara had always been. They needed her now, and she wouldn't let them down. She would hold the darkness at bay, if only for a moment longer. With her strength waning and the shadows pressing ever closer, she needed all the help she could get. But until then, she would give everything she had. Elara wasn't lost yet, and as long as Oriana had breath in her body, she wasn't going to let her friend slip away.

CHAPTER 18:

EMBERS OF AN OLD BOND

Veyra finds herself in solitude within her quarters on The Crucible, enveloped by a soft, muted glow that stretches and contorts into haunting silhouettes against the frigid, metallic confines. Outside the window, the distant stars twinkle like ethereal sentinels, bearing witness to her deep introspection.

Veyra is seated at a small, weathered metallic desk in a dimly lit room, her gaze fixed on an old pendant she keeps carefully hidden - a treasured relic from her past. As she sits lost in thought, her typically steely expression softens, and a flood of memories begins to rise to the surface. She is transported back to the distant, haunting recollections of the Eclipsion War, each memory unfolding vividly in her mind.

The dark, ominous skies were thick with billowing smoke, as the relentless Battle of Terithion IV raged on. The desolate, scarred ground was strewn with shattered debris and the fallen bodies of valiant soldiers. A youthful Veyra, accompanied by Maelis, a fellow Sidereal male, stealthily makes their way into a concealed Terithion base through a side entrance. Maelis, like all Sidereal males, have two ridges running from the top of their head to the back of the dark-blue skull. They cautiously linger at the corners, keeping a watchful eye for passing guards. Veyra signed silent hand gestures to Maelis signaling intent to take down the guards.

Maelis, with a determined look in her eyes, gave Veyra a firm and confident nod, signaling their unspoken agreement. Without a moment's hesitation, they both swiftly launched into action, their movements seamlessly synchronized as they embarked on their mission. Once they were past the guards, they unsheathed their blades in a smooth, fluid motion. A quick slice, and both guards' bodies dropped into a lifeless and silent heap.

They advanced with remarkable speed and determination, displaying the precision and intensity characteristic of highly trained soldiers. The guards vanished silently and mysteriously, each one fading away in quick succession, leaving behind an eerie sense of emptiness and uncertainty.

As they entered the weapon storage chamber, rows of experimental Terithion weaponry loomed before them, each one more ominous than the last. Veyra's gaze locked onto a central console surrounded by shelves of destructive prototypes. She pulled out a sleek device, ready to download the plans that could change the tide of the war.

Just as she began, the alarms blared, drenching the room in flashing red light. Maelis moved instinctively, placing himself between Veyra and the entrance as footsteps thundered down the hallway.

"Retrieve the plans," he said, his voice tense but resolute.

Veyra shot him a sharp look, eyes blazing. "Maelis, don't even think about it. We're both getting out of here."

He gave her a quick, wry smile, a strange calm in his eyes. "We both know that's not happening. They'll be on us in seconds. I'll hold them off—just finish the mission."

She clenched her jaw, fighting back the urge to argue. There was no time, and they both knew it. She slammed the device into the console and watched as it began siphoning data from the Terithion's weapon plans. Each second felt like an eternity, punctuated by the sounds of Maelis's swift, brutal clashes at the door.

A pair of guards burst in, and Maelis confronted them directly, his energy flaring as he engaged them with raw, ferocious power. For every enemy that fell, two more seemed to take their place. His movements were as fluid and lethal as always, but Veyra could see him faltering, the strain beginning to show.

"Maelis!" she shouted, desperation edging into her voice. The download was almost complete, but watching her comrade stand as a one-man barricade was tearing at her.

He quickly looked back over his shoulder, unclasped a pendant from around his neck, and casually tossed it to Veyra. With a deft and fluid movement, she reached out and skillfully caught it in her outstretched hand. Maelis' expression grew grim, blood trickling down his cheek. "Veyra, go. Now."

She hesitated, her heart hammering, torn between loyalty and survival. The device pinged—download complete. She grabbed it, her hand trembling as she took a step toward him.

"What of our plan?" she hissed, barely audible over the chaos. But Maelis only smirked, the same maddening smirk he'd always flashed when things went south.

"You must not fear, for the Order..." he called, his voice growing faint as he turned back to the relentless wave of Terithion soldiers.

Veyra clenched her fists, taking one last look before bolting down the narrow corridor. She could hear the clash of blades behind her, every impact echoing through the base, a brutal reminder of what she was leaving behind.

As Veyra ran through the blurring corridors, the weight of Maelis's pendant felt like a stone around her neck. Each step away from the past only dragged it closer to the surface, a ghost she could never quite outrun. Sometimes, she could still feel his hand on her shoulder, steadying her as they fought side by side.

The corridors blurred as she ran, the weight of Maelis's sacrifice pressing down on her, threatening to suffocate her. She reached an emergency exit and threw herself through it just as the base rumbled with explosions from within. She didn't look back, even as the screams and blaring alarms faded into the distance. She had managed to escape, but the price was etched into her memory. There was no triumph in this mission, only the lingering memory of what she had sacrificed to accomplish it.

Veyra sits at her small metallic desk, the dim light throwing fractured silhouettes across the walls. The pendant rests in her palm, its weight disproportionate to its size, as if all her memories were somehow condensed into this fragile relic. She turns it over, letting her fingers trace its familiar edges. A thousand voices from her past seem to echo in her mind, none louder than Maelis'—the one voice she once trusted above all others.

Maelis had always believed in the mission, in the cause. But sitting here, alone with this reminder of a past that seemed almost too distant, she can feel the weight of all her choices pressing down on her. The chill of the ship's metallic walls seeps into her bones, mingling with the cold truth she has buried deep within herself.

She knows what Maelis would have wanted. He wouldn't have flinched, wouldn't have hesitated, and wouldn't have allowed himself the luxury of vulnerability. Veyra temporarily closes her eyes, inhaling deeply, trying to steady the storm inside. She doesn't get to choose softness; her path is forged in steel and sacrifice.

Veyra's fingers tightened around the pendant, the cool metal biting into her palm. For a brief, reckless second, she considered what it would be like to surrender to the ache, to let the memories take her. But that was a luxury she could not afford. With a forceful exhale, she forced the emotions back, burying them beneath the steel of her resolve.

Slowly, she stands, closing her fingers around the pendant and slipping it back into the hidden pocket inside her armor. Her movements are methodical and deliberate—each action sealing away the fragile parts of her that threaten to break through. As she secures the pendant away, she looks around her quarters, the dim light casting her reflection across the viewport—a spectral, fractured figure. The fierce commander. The one who commands respect. The one who is feared.

Veyra turns to the holographic map of the galaxy that flickers in the corner of her quarters. She steps closer, her eyes roaming the glowing constellations until they land at a particular point. Her jaw tightens, and her gaze hardens. The Astralis Core is out there, and once it is in her grasp, she will ensure no one will ever make her feel small again.

For Maelis. For herself. For the mission. She steels herself, her fingers brushing across the map's controls as she zooms in, her eyes focusing on her objective with renewed determination. She is Veyra Tenebria, commander of the Obsidian Order, and she will not allow sentimentality to erode her resolve.

Yet, as her eyes harden, there's a flicker—an almost imperceptible moment of hesitation. A doubt that whispers beneath the surface. The stars reflected in her gaze seem to shimmer as if questioning her certainty. But she turns away from the doubt, shoving it back into the depths where it belongs. Vulnerability has no place here, and she cannot afford weakness. She strides towards the door, her mind again focused on her mission, the pendant's weight lingering against her chest like a ghost of a past she cannot fully bury.

The Crucible hums beneath her feet, and Veyra steps into the cold corridor. Her face once again resembles the mask of the commander—unyielding, unfeeling, and committed to the only thing she has left: the mission.

As Oriana tightened her grip on the link, she felt a surge of warmth spreading through her, drowning out the cold, venomous whispers of Perfida. The memories were her anchor—a bright, unbreakable cord that bound her to Elara and kept the darkness at bay. Every shared laugh, every whispered secret, every time they'd dreamed of a better future—all of it melded into a wave of strength that she fed into the connection.

Oriana remembered the time they'd both been caught sneaking out after curfew, Elara's stifled giggles as they hid beneath the old trees. She remembered Elara at her worst, at her most stubborn, always pushing, always striving. These moments became her shield, a reminder of loyalty that Perfida could not break.

The swirling shadows began to fracture, cracks of light appearing within the dense blackness as Oriana's presence overwhelmed Perfida's hateful grip. She felt him recoil, his influence shrinking, pulling away as if burned by the intensity of her memories. The resistance was strong, but Oriana's resolve was stronger.

Finally, with a shudder, the darkness broke. Elara's form slumped, and Oriana felt a flood of relief as her friend's essence emerged, free from the consuming shadow. She didn't waste a moment; using the last of her strength, Oriana yanked Elara toward her, breaking her completely away from Perfida's vile hold.

They both collapsed to the ground, panting. Elara's eyes fluttered open, the familiar spark returning as recognition dawned on her face. She clutched Oriana's hand, her grip weak but steady. "Hey, Oriana.

Thanks." Elara whispered, her voice a thread of exhaustion and gratitude.

Oriana glanced around, taking in the ruins of Kraedin. The once-bustling city was now reduced to rubble, echoes of the fierce battle still lingering in the air. Fires smoldered in the distance, and the ground beneath them was littered with debris, reminders of the chaos that had just unfolded. But they were safe—at least, for now.

Claudio's gaze swept over the ruins, the charred remains of a city that had barely clung to life. How many more battles would they leave in ruin before they found peace? And how much longer could he watch Elara edge closer to the darkness that seemed to trail her every step?

Claudio hurried over, worry etched into his face as he knelt beside them. "We need to get out of here. This place is a graveyard waiting to happen," he said, eyeing the shattered remnants of their battleground. Oriana nodded, feeling the weight of their victory tempered by the sheer devastation around them.

With a final glance at the Astralis Core, now shrouded in a heavy tarp to block anyone from touching it, Oriana took a deep breath. There was a strange stillness in the air, a quiet that felt almost too heavy. Kraedin was in ruins, its people scattered or gone, the city itself barely recognizable. They had won, but at a cost.

Standing amidst the wreckage, Oriana knew they couldn't stay here. The Core was safe, Elara was free, and they had made it through the darkness. But she also knew this was just one battle, and more would follow.

The soft hum of the med bay's monitors was the only sound breaking the silence. Elara lay on the narrow cot, her breathing slow, a slight furrow in her brow as if even in sleep, she was still fighting.

Oriana sat beside her, fingers nervously tracing the seams of her jacket. The years had been unkind to both of them, but here they were—alive, breathing, reunited. She exhaled, a shaky breath she hadn't realized she'd been holding, and reached out to take Elara's hand.

"Elara?" Oriana whispered, leaning in close.

Oriana's fingers found Elara's, the warmth of her hand anchoring her in the present. It was a warmth she hadn't felt in years, a familiarity that felt like home. Elara's voice, rough and weary, wrapped around her like a balm, easing the ache that the years of separation had left behind.

Elara's eyelids fluttered, the tension in her face relaxing as she stirred. She opened her eyes slowly, blinking against the harsh light. The familiar starry patterns in her skin, faint but unmistakable, seemed to brighten when her gaze found Oriana. A small, weak smile crept onto her face.

"Oriana..." she breathed, her voice rough but warm. "You're here."

Oriana chuckled softly, relief flooding her expression. "Yeah, well, you think I'd leave you hanging? It's been too long, Elara."

Elara tried to sit up, wincing as the effort drained her remaining strength. Oriana quickly placed a steadying hand on her shoulder, easing her back down.

"Easy there. You just took on half the Obsidian Order. I'd say you've earned a break," Oriana teased, her eyes held a glint of concern.

Elara shook her head, a faint grin tugging at the corners of her lips. "Still keeping count, I see. Some things never change."

Oriana snorted. "Of course, I am. Someone's gotta make sure you don't bite off more than you can chew."

For a moment, silence settled between them, filled only by the rhythmic beeps of the machines. Then Elara's gaze softened, and she squeezed Oriana's hand weakly.

"I missed you," Elara admitted, her voice barely more than a whisper.

Oriana's face softened, and she leaned closer, resting her forehead against Elara's. "I missed you too, star-girl. More than you know."

They sat there, forehead to forehead, drawing strength from one another, from memories that spanned a lifetime, from battles fought and lost and won again. In this tiny moment, aboard a ship drifting through the endless void, they were just two friends, reunited against all odds.

After a moment, Oriana pulled back, a mischievous smirk on her lips. "So, what's with the shiny rock you've got? Word on the ship is it's turning you into a bit of a badass."

Elara rolled her eyes, though she couldn't help the smile that slipped through. "You have no idea."

"Well, I'm here now. So why don't you tell me all about it?" Oriana leaned back, crossing her arms with that familiar, expectant look.

And as the ship sailed through the vast darkness, the two old friends talked. About battles, about life, and about everything they'd lost and found along the way.

CHAPTER 19:

CHASING THE SUN

The Crucible moved silently through the darkness; its sleek, black hull streaked with glowing red veins. It seemed to vanish into the void, appearing more like an apparition than a ship. The shadows clung to the walls of The Crucible's inner chamber, where Draven stood, exuding a quiet air of command. The dim light carved sharp edges across his face, leaving his expression set in stone. He was waiting, and he didn't have to wait long.

Veyra strode into the room, her movements taut with irritation. Failure clung to her like a second skin, unmistakable in her eyes. She stopped a few paces away, her arms crossed, defiant but wary. She'd come prepared for a reprimand. Draven, however, merely glanced at her, his expression unmoved, his demeanor that of a teacher rather than a judge.

"Let me explain," she began, her voice laced with frustration. She launched into the details, recounting every move she'd made during the battle—the narrow miss, the fleeting moment when the Astralis Core had slipped from her grasp. She spoke quickly, defensively, trying to justify herself. But Draven remained silent, his gaze unwavering as she unraveled her tale. He waited until her words fell into an uncomfortable silence.

Without a word, Draven stepped toward a tapestry that hung on the wall—a relic of Sidereal history, its once-bright colors faded by the passage of time. He gestured toward it, breaking his silence with a measured tone. "Do you know this?"

Veyra blinked, momentarily caught off guard. "A piece of history?" she guessed, impatience simmering in her voice.

"A reminder," he replied. "This belonged to a tribe that bordered Astralith, before the Eclipsion War." His gaze drifted back to the woven fabric, and he spoke as if reciting a long-forgotten tale. "After a day of battle, Sidereal warriors would return with trophies—something of worth from the hunt, or armor from those they defeated. It was more than a prize. It was a symbol, a reminder of their strength."

Veyra shifted her weight, her frustration softening as she listened. Draven traced the edge of the cloth with his fingers, his voice low and reflective. "See the size of the Néalian Sun in the background compared to that of those holding a sphere up on higher ground. This is not just a decoration. It's a lesson. The Sidereals didn't only celebrate the victory; they honored the return. The journey home, with whatever they could carry."

As Draven spoke, Veyra felt a spark of pride and longing. The Sidereal way was about more than victory—it was about the journey, the sacrifice. She had fought for this cause longer than she could remember, and Draven's words only fueled her determination.

He turned back to her, his gaze piercing. "Your failure was inevitable, Veyra. What matters is that Elara and the Astralis Core are headed home, back to Néalian. That's the true goal."

A flicker of understanding crossed Veyra's face. Draven's words weren't just a history lesson—they were a revelation. She nodded, slowly, as the pieces fell into place. The cloth wasn't simply a decretive relic; it was a prophecy. Elara would bring the Core back to Astralith, whether she knew it or not. The mission was shifting, but it was far from over.

He looked at her reassuringly, "Know those who oppose you, as well as you know yourself."

Draven's gaze softened almost imperceptibly as he added, "Be Prepared. Send for my best legion of ships to gather in the Néalian moon's orbit. They need only wait there until I give the order."

Veyra straightened, her frustration transforming into cold determination. She inclined her head in acknowledgment, then turned on her heel, leaving the chamber with renewed focus. The hunt wasn't over. It was just beginning its next phase, and she was ready to see it through.

As the doors slid shut behind her, Draven remained, a faint smile tugging at the corner of his lips. The art, a silent witness to centuries of conflict, hung still. The path to Astralith was set, and all that remained was for the Core to wait for it to come home.

The conference room aboard the Galathea throbbed with a tension that felt almost alive. The starlight from Zynthar spilled through the viewport, painting fractured patterns of silver and shadow across the cold, metallic floor. Elara sat alone at the far end of the oval table, her fingers absently tracing the scars that Perfida's possession had left etched into her palms. Her gaze was distant, locked on some point far beyond the room, yet her eyes held a fierce, quiet resolve.

"We can't just ignore this," Verus said, his voice cutting through the silence as his fist slammed against the table, reverberating with the strength of his conviction. "The Astralis Core is a threat as long as it exists. Perfida's influence isn't gone—it's waiting."

Claudio sat back, arms crossed, a smirk playing at his lips that didn't quite reach his eyes. "And what, we just smash it to bits? We don't even know what we're dealing with here. It's ancient. It's beyond us. Best we can do is hide it. Out of sight, out of mind."

Verus shook his head, his glare hardening. "That's reckless. Hiding it isn't enough. Sooner or later, someone will find it. You saw what it did to Elara. We can't let that happen again."

At the mention of her name, Elara's focus shifted back to the room, her voice soft but firm. "Verus has a point," she admitted, a flicker of uncertainty in her expression. "But Claudio isn't entirely wrong, either. Destroying it… we don't even know if that's possible. And hiding it? It feels like we're just buying time."

Oriana sat in the shadows, her gaze darting between them as their voices escalated. She felt a wave of relief at seeing Elara free from Perfida's grasp, yet the tension in the room was suffocating. She clenched her hands, listening as the arguments mounted, words crashing over one another like waves in a storm.

"If we can't destroy it in a conventional way, we have to think outside the box," Verus argued, his frustration palpable. "Maybe we need something powerful enough to obliterate it completely."

Claudio rolled his eyes, leaning forward. "Like what, throwing it into a black hole? Come on, Verus. Do you even hear yourself?"

"Maybe I do," Verus shot back, his tone as sharp as a blade. "And maybe that's exactly what we need."

Elara pressed her fingers to her temples, her patience unraveling. "Enough. This isn't helping. We need a plan, not more fighting."

For a moment, silence reigned, filled only by the hum of Galathea's fusion engines. Oriana took a deep breath, the idea forming in her mind felt audacious, but she knew she had to speak. Her voice trembled at first but grew steady. "What if… what if we throw it into the Néalian Sun?"

All eyes turned toward her; surprise mirrored on every face.

Claudio raised an eyebrow, skepticism coloring his tone. "The Néalian Sun? You're talking about taking the Core to the heart of a star?"

As the words left her mouth, Oriana felt a tremor of fear. She knew the stakes—the Core was ancient, unpredictable, and its destruction could very well cost them everything. But she also knew they were out of options. She'd risk it all to see Elara free from its influence, even if it meant facing her own worst fears head-on.

"It's not as crazy as it sounds," Verus interjected, his eyes lighting up with a spark of intrigue. "Stars are capable of destruction on a scale we can't fathom. The energy alone could obliterate the Core."

Elara's gaze softened as she weighed the idea, her eyes distant again, but this time, with a glimmer of hope. "It's risky. Getting that close to a star would endanger the ship and everyone on board."

"But it's our best shot," Oriana insisted, her voice carrying a newfound strength. "We're out of options, and we need something permanent."

Claudio exhaled, finally uncrossing his arms. "It's a long shot. But maybe it's the only one we've got."

A quiet determination settled over the room, the kind that was as fragile as it was powerful. Elara turned to Oriana, a faint smile breaking through her earlier exhaustion. "Thank you. Sometimes, the boldest choices are the ones we need most."

Verus nodded, his expression resolute. "Then we do it. We chart a course for the Néalian Sun."

As they began to map out the details, the weight of their mission pressed upon them, but it was tempered with a shared purpose. Oriana felt a warmth blossom within her, not only from the decision but from knowing she had finally made her mark. As the planning unfolded, the stars beyond the viewport seemed to burn brighter, as if lighting their way toward a future where Perfida's shadow was nothing more than a fading memory.

As the meeting wrapped up, Claudio caught Verus's eye and motioned him over for a quick word. "The Sun? Are we seriously considering this? Do we even know what kind of reaction that thing could have when it hits the energy of a star? It could throw out a massive solar flare, knock out all power on Néalian—throw the whole place into chaos," he said, his tone sharp with concern.

Verus listened, his expression thoughtful, but Claudio wasn't done. "Or worse, it could trigger a chain reaction, turning the Sun into a giant bomb and wiping out an entire system."

Verus raised an eyebrow, a hint of a smirk playing on his lips. "Got a better plan?" he asked, clearly unfazed.

Claudio's frustration was palpable. "No, but—"

"Then I say we go through with it," Verus interrupted, his voice resolute.

Claudio tried to envision the Core colliding with the Sun, its ancient power triggering an unimaginable chain reaction. What if they set off a supernova? His pulse quickened, but he knew there was no turning back. His loyalty to Elara and the others outweighed his fear, but the unease gnawed at him all the same.

Claudio sighed, rubbing the back of his neck. He was out of arguments, but the worry hadn't left his face. "Alright, fine. But let's at least be smart about it. How about we swing around to the far side of the Sun? If there's a flare or an explosion, it'll be directed away from Néalian."

Verus had spent years studying the Core, unraveling its mysteries one agonizing piece at a time. He'd seen the destruction it could cause, but he believed in its vulnerability as much as its power. This was their chance to end it. He'd walk through fire—or the Sun itself—to see the Core obliterated once and for all.

Verus considered it and nodded. "Fair enough. We'll plot a course that keeps Néalian out of the line of fire."

Claudio gave a reluctant nod. "I'll buy it. But what about the Obsidian Order? You know they're hunting us, and they've got those solar cells orbiting out there."

Verus met his gaze, the hint of a plan flickering in his eyes. "I know. I'll get in touch with the Astralith Federation and see if we can pull in some fleet support. We could use a bit of cover if they come sniffing around."

Claudio's expression softened, a trace of relief breaking through. "Alright, then. Let's make it happen."

"You're going to need more than the UNF can provide," Oriana's sudden voice startled them all. She had slipped in unnoticed, her tone serious. "I know Veyra. And, more importantly, I know Draven."

Elara stiffened, her fingers tightening on the edge of the table. She hadn't expected Oriana to bring up Draven Caelix. The name sent a chill down her spine, and she exchanged a wary glance with Verus, who looked equally rattled.

Verus turned to Oriana, disbelief flashing in his eyes. "Draven Caelix? I thought he was dead—been gone for years.' He sank into his chair, as if the weight of the revelation was pressing down on him. Claudio shot him a questioning look, clearly lost.

"Who's Draven?" Claudio asked incorrectly, confusion plain on his face.

Memories of the Eclipsion War flooded back, dark and unbidden. She remembered Draven's cold eyes; the calculating way he'd dispatched her allies without a second thought. He'd been a phantom in her nightmares for years, and the thought of facing him again sent a chill through her veins. She steeled herself—this time, she wouldn't run.

Verus answered, his voice barely concealing a tremor. "Draven Caelix was a General during the Eclipsion War. He was a master strategist, cold and ruthless. They called him 'The Shadow of Néalian' because you never saw him coming until the realization that he was there all along."

Verus rubbed his temple, a pained expression crossing his face. "He was… something else. No mercy, no hesitation. And if he's involved, it means they're prepared for us."

Oriana nodded grimly. "He'll be ready, alright. He always is."

Elara's pulse quickened. The thought of facing Draven—it was a ghost she had hoped would stay buried back on Astralith Academy. When she heard Kael's last words back on Néalian. She let out a shaky breath, trying to steady herself, as Oriana pulled out her com screen.

A moment later, Jax's familiar face appeared on the screen, his square jaw and steely gaze grounding her back to the present.

"Oriana! Got your message," Jax said, his usual grin slipping as he added, "Sorry, but I can't make it out to Zynthar right now…"

Oriana cut him off, her tone decisive. "You won't have to."

Jax blinked, clearly puzzled. "Alright, then. What do you need?"

Elara watched the exchange, feeling a flicker of hope as Oriana laid out her plan. This was their chance to turn the tide. She found herself stepping closer to the group, drawn into Oriana's confident resolve. As the others leaned in, discussing the specifics, she felt the familiar surge of determination return.

CHAPTER 20:

THE INFERNO'S EDGE

The Galathea hung in the black void, its hull barely visible against the blinding inferno of the Néalian Sun. The Néalian Sun churned with barely contained fury, its surface a cauldron of roiling plasma. Each eruption lit the Galathea's hull in fleeting flashes of molten gold, as though the ship were caught in the Sun's wrathful gaze. Solar flares erupted from its surface, casting arcs of plasma across space, and for a moment, everything was calm. Claudio stood on the bridge, his eyes narrowed as he surveyed the star before them—a roiling titan whose power would, with any luck, be their salvation and their weapon.

Jax sat in the cockpit of his personal combat fighter. The Titanclaw Mark IV was a compact, two-person fighter built for speed and resilience. Its cobalt-blue hull, accented with sharp green highlights, showed heavy wear from countless battles—visible dents, blaster marks, and patchwork repairs. The ship's unique curved profile, designed for maneuverability, featured twin plasma cannons on its forward wings and a retractable railgun beneath. The sleek propulsion system in the rear ensured quick evasive moves in tight dogfights. Rugged, battle-worn, and deadly, it was a ship that hit hard and kept going. It was more than a fighter; it was an extension of Jax himself. Each scar on its hull told a story—a battle won, a crew saved, a sacrifice made. He ran a hand over the worn console, a silent pact with the ship that had seen him through impossible odds.

Jax gazed into the infinite, star-speckled void, reflecting on the journey that had brought him here. His life, his crew, the Riftborne—all of it stemmed from those childhood games of "what if," shouted across Driftspire's streets, now materialized into leading an elite crew. Such reflection, however, was an indulgence his Brulvian heritage frowned upon, especially on the brink of battle. To Brulvians, strength was paramount, even if maintaining it required suppressing doubt and introspection. Generals, steeped in cultural tradition, avoided such ruminations, knowing they could unravel the resolve needed for the fight of their lives.

The Brulvians did have a point. Jax had a tendency to spiral into his thoughts, but he viewed it as a necessary emotional inventory—a way to remind himself of what truly mattered. The countless lives on Néalian, his crew, and the individuals who had become like family: Karra, Dax, and Oriana.

Karra, a Félac with green skin and four arms, embodied both charisma and strategy. Her race was renowned for their social grace and political acumen, yet she was equally formidable on the battlefield when the situation demanded it. Dax, at first glance, seemed like any other Terranovian, but he was one of the most skilled pilots Jax had ever known, his talent unmatched in tight situations. And then there was Oriana—a Sidereal who felt like a daughter to him. With her expertise in close combat, she brought a fierce determination and a heart that inspired everyone around her.

Jax stared into the void, his reflection in the canopy distorted by the starlight. 'No turning back now,' he thought, gripping the controls with a confidence he forced himself to feel. Somewhere in the galaxy, Driftspire's streets were quiet, a far cry from the chaos he now faced. For their sake, he had to win.

"Are you guys in position?" Jax murmured as he flicked the com switch on the bulkhead.

"Affirmative, on your six, just don't expect me to clean up your mess this time." Karra chimed in. "You really think Draven will show up? I heard he was dead."

"That's what he'd want you to believe," Dax interrupted over the com. "That bastard's been ambushing my outer-rim mining operations for the last three cycles. I keep building, he keeps wrecking my hard work."

"I assume that means you're in position," Jax muttered.

"Yes, dear," Dax replied in a mocking tone.

Jax ignored the sarcasm. "Alright, here's the rundown. We start on the outer Order defenses. On my signal, we take out some of the solar arrays until Draven shows up. When he does, the United Néalian Fleet will lay down cover fire so we can sneak aboard using our onboard escape pods. From there, we head to the power level, light up the EMP, and get out in a hurry. Got it?"

Karra smirked. "Sounds like one of your plans. Clean and easy."

"Easy? These never turn out easy. If I had a credit for every 'clean' plan of yours, Jax, I'd own half the Outer Rim." Dax blared.

The plan was simple enough: launch the Astralis Core into the Sun, where its malevolent energy would be consumed in the star's fiery depths, erasing its existence from the galaxy forever. It sounded almost too easy—just one final act to end the centuries of chaos the Core had caused. But with the Core gone, Elara would lose her powers, her connection to the very essence of her Sidereal heritage severed. What she didn't speak aloud, but felt deep within her, was that it wouldn't just be her powers. The Core had become a part of her, an extension of her identity. Destroying it meant losing a piece of herself.

Yet, there was no other option. Néalian would be spared the cataclysmic fallout—no more invasions, no more bloodshed from those who sought to claim the Core's power. The planet's people would finally know peace, but Elara's sacrifice would be the price.

As she stood at the helm of the Galathea, watching the massive sphere of burning plasma through the viewport, the weight of the decision pressed down on her. The sun, a symbol of life and light, would soon become a graveyard for the darkest secret in the universe.

Verus rolled his eyes at Claudio. He was mentally preparing himself for an ensuing battle, stretching/shaking each limb joint as well as cracking his knuckles. He always did this before any battle, especially any altercation involving The Obsidian Order.

On the comms, Elara's voice crackled. "The United Néalian Fleet is in position," she said, her tone all business, but he could hear the tension buried beneath. "Jax and his crew are already picking off the Crucible's outer defenses. We'll have a clear shot at launching the Core. Draven and Veyra haven't shown themselves yet."

Claudio smirked, though it was half-hearted. "They're out there, alright."

Behind him, Verus loomed in silence, his silver eyes fixed on the Sun, as though he could already see the outcome of their desperate gambit. "Let's hope the distraction holds," he said, his voice steady and calm, an anchor amid the storm they were about to unleash.

With a nod, Claudio issued the orders. "All drones to launch positions. Elara, you're on main defense—anything that gets too close, you blast it. Oriana, relay commands to Jax. Keep those Syndicate ships tight on The Crucible, we don't want Draven or Veyra to see what we're up to."

Elara acknowledged, "Copy that. Drones prepped and ready for launch." She sounded steady, but Claudio knew her well enough to catch the subtle edge in her voice. They were all stretched to their limits.

At Claudio's signal, the drones launched, swarming like silver insects across the Sun's blazing surface. Unmanned, they twisted and darted, an array of decoys and attackers forming a shield for the one that mattered—the drone carrying the Astralis Core.

The drones spiraled through the endless void, little dark specks against the blazing backdrop of the Sun. From the Galathea's bridge, Claudio stood, eyes glued to the screens with a fierce intensity. His fingers dug into the console, bracing for the command he knew would come. The ship's systems pulsed a green glow, confirming readiness, while the Astralis Core's hum resonated—a steady, foreboding heartbeat—within the drone gliding straight toward the Sun's searing light.

Then, alarms shattered the silence, red strobes painting the bridge in chaotic hues. Oriana's voice erupted over the comms; her tone tight with urgency. "Incoming hostiles! Draven's fleet just decloaked on the main front—they're flanking us!"

"Damn it," Claudio muttered, jaw tight. "So much for a clean run."

Red alarms screamed as Draven's fleet tore through the void, decloaking like predators from the abyss. Plasma bolts rained down, hammering the Galathea's shields and lighting up the Néalian Sun's corona in bursts of fiery green.

Ahead, Jax and the Riftborn Syndicate's vessels plunged headfirst into the storm of plasma fire. The Crucible, a monstrous warship of the Obsidian Order, loomed behind the swarm of enemy fighters, spitting streams of green energy that lashed against Jax's ships.

Jax's voice crackled through the comms, rough but tinged with grim satisfaction, "We're taking heavy fire, but we'll keep those turrets busy. The Crucible is packing some nasty tricks, but we'll manage as long as we can."

Jax yanked the Titanclaw into a tight roll, skimming the edge of an asteroid field as enemy fire-streaked past. The fighter shuddered, but its engines roared in defiance as he looped back, guns blazing.

"Make it count, Jax. We're buying time here," Claudio replied, fingers dancing across the controls as he rerouted power to the Galathea's thrusters. The ship veered to shield the drones, weaving through the web of plasma as Draven's interceptors closed in. Claudio launched a squad of unmanned drones, which surged ahead to meet the enemy, erupting in dazzling bursts as they rammed into Obsidian fighters.

But the danger only multiplied. From behind Néalian's moon, Veyra's ambush fleet erupted into view—sleek black vessels with matte surfaces that seemed to drink in the light. They swept in on the United Néalian Fleet like a tidal wave.

Elara's voice came over the comms, a steely edge cutting through the chaos. "Veyra's forces are hammering us. We're taking hits, but I'll be damned if I let them breach our line."

Claudio cursed under his breath as one of their drones spun wildly out of control, its systems scorched by the Sun's brutal heat. "The unmanned drone carrying the Core just fried its circuits. It's dead in the water."

Verus, standing beside him, met his gaze with a look of calm determination. "Then we need a new plan. Prep a manned drone. I'll go."

"Not a chance," Claudio shot back, shaking his head. "This happened on my watch. I'll go. I can't let you do this."

Verus laid a steady hand on his shoulder, exuding an eerie calm. "Claudio, this isn't just on you. This is about all of us."

Claudio clenched his jaw, but the decision had already taken root in his mind. He moved with purpose, suiting up with the heavy knowledge that this might be his last flight. The weight of the mission pressed down on him like a physical force. As he stepped toward the drone, he was ready to seal his fate.

From the bridge of the Galathea, Elara stared in horror as Veyra's fleet surged from behind Néalian's moon, a line of sleek, black ships cutting through the void, sharp and cold against the Sun's fierce glow. They descended like shadows, dark tendrils wrapping around the United Néalian Fleet and the Riftborn Syndicate. Plasma bolts tore through the air in a relentless barrage, shattering hulls, imploding ships, turning the vacuum of space into a graveyard of twisted metal. The comms erupted with frantic voices—shouts, screams, desperate calls for backup.

"Veyra's hitting us from behind! We're pinned!" Oriana's voice cut through the chaos, taut with panic.

In the drone bay, Claudio barely registered the shuddering blasts rocking the ship. His mind was fixed on one thing: the Core had to reach the Sun, no matter the cost. The manned drone, now modified with a cramped cockpit, sat waiting, its systems flickering to life as he climbed in. His hands flew over the controls, running through the pre-flight checks with the kind of focus that drowned out everything else.

As he suited up, Claudio stole one last look at the blazing Sun before him. Its heat pulsed even through the thick glass, a constant reminder of the power he was about to challenge. For a moment, his resolve wavered, and he felt the icy grip of fear settle in his chest. But there was no turning back now—not when everything depended on him.

But just as he reached for the throttle, a hand clamped down on his shoulder, yanking him back. He twisted around to see Verus, his face impassive but with a strange, almost sorrowful look in his eyes— something Claudio had never seen before. Before Claudio could object, Verus leaned in, voice low and steady.

"You've done enough, Claudio. More than enough. Goodbye, Old friend." In one swift, practiced motion, Verus pressed a small device to Claudio's neck. A hiss of gas, and Claudio's vision darkened, the world spinning out of reach.

Verus pulled Claudio's limp body out of the cockpit and placed him against the side wall, "You don't have a choice, old friend. Your job is to get the rest of them out alive. Mine is to finish this."

When he came to, Claudio was slumped against the cold metal wall of the drone bay, limbs heavy as lead. Verus was already in the pilot's seat, strapped in and poised, his face on the comms screen. Claudio struggled to speak, but the words stuck in his throat. "Verus, don't—"

As Verus strapped into the drone, his thoughts drifted to Elara. She had become more than a student, more than a protégé. She was the hope he'd never thought he'd see again, the bright star that had pulled him back from the brink more times than he could count. This was his last chance to protect her, to give her the freedom he had always wanted for her.

On the bridge, Elara's comm screen flickered to life with Verus's image. He met her gaze, his tone gentle, almost tender. "Elara, when the Core is destroyed, you may lose your powers but your parents would be proud of you."

Elara's gasp filled the comms. "What... what are you saying?"

Verus's eyes softened, a rare vulnerability seeping through. "I'm a Keeper, Elara. The will was passed on to me. I was there during your early days at the Academy, and I funded your education. Even back then, I knew it would be you who could bring about true change. Not the Core. You."

Elara's breath caught, words slipping away as tears spilled down her cheeks. "Verus, don't. We need you here."

Verus glanced back toward the Sun, his jaw tightening. "This isn't the only Core. Destroying this one won't end the fight, but it's a beginning. Remember that." His voice wavered, the barest crack breaking through. "And, Elara, I was proud to watch you grow."

He cut the comms before she could respond, the drone's thrusters roaring to life. Elara's screen flared as the drone shot forward, a streak of light toward the Sun. She watched, breath held tight, as Verus's signal faded into the blinding brilliance. In those last, fleeting moments, just before the light swallowed him, she thought she caught a glimpse of a smile on his face.

The drone shot toward the Sun, a streak of defiance against an unstoppable force. Verus's hands were steady on the controls, his gaze fixed on the inferno ahead. For a brief, fleeting moment, he felt peace.

The moment Verus's ship collided with the sun, it was like a God's wrath unleashed. The impact triggered a violent eruption—a brilliant, blinding flare that swallowed his ship whole. The Astralis Core detonated within the heart of the star, fueling a fiery chain reaction that sent waves of solar fire spiraling outward. Elara's screen overloaded with blinding light, and her whole body tensed as the star flared with unimaginable intensity. Elara's head began to ache, she felt a sudden withdrawal of air. She collapsed onto the Nav board, still keeping herself up to witness this sacrifice, Verus's sacrifice. She watched, breathless, as the sun's surface rippled, waves of molten energy cascading outward, tearing apart the ship and scattering fragments of the Core like embers across the solar surface. For a brief, searing moment, it was as if the sun itself had roared in fury—a cosmic funeral pyre marking the end of Verus and the terrifying power they'd both chased.

The sight of the Sun flaring as Verus disappeared left her hollow, as if a piece of her had been ripped away. She felt the loss like a physical ache, her heart heavy and her limbs weak. But beneath the grief, a spark of determination smoldered. She couldn't let his sacrifice be in vain.

In the shadows of The Crucible, Jax moved with a surprising stealth, his massive frame somehow blending into the ship's darkened corridors. His team of Riftborn operatives followed closely, alert and silent, their usual brashness subdued by the high stakes. Normally, Jax would have bulldozed his way through, guns blazing, but not this time. They had one shot to cripple The Crucible's power grid and weaken Veyra's defenses—and this job required finesse.

Jax raised a hand, signaling the team to halt as two Obsidian Order guards rounded the corner. In a blur of motion, Jax seized the first guard, dispatching him with a swift, brutal twist. His second-in-command took out the other, both bodies hitting the floor without a sound.

"Move," Jax growled, gesturing for his team to advance. Every nerve was on edge; his instincts screamed that something was off, but they'd gone too far to turn back now. As they neared the power grid, a new squad of guards charged forward, weapons raised.

"Contact!" Jax barked, and the corridor exploded into chaos. Plasma bolts lit up the darkness as the Riftborn fought back, each shot illuminating the narrow space in blinding flashes. Dax, a seasoned fighter who had been with Jax for years, was the first to fall. Karra, barely more than a kid but fierce as hell, was hit next. One by one, his crew went down, their sacrifices fueling his determination as he pressed onward through the carnage.

Finally, Jax reached the power grid, battered and bloody but resolute. He slapped the EMP device onto the main console, fingers flying over the controls as he keyed in the activation sequence. The device began to pulse, a low hum of lethal energy building as it prepared to detonate. He knew what he'd signed up for—without power, The Crucible would be left drifting, but his chances of getting out alive were slim to none. And even if he survived, Draven would hunt him down.

The faces of his fallen crewmates flashed before him—Dax, Karra, all of them had given their lives for this moment. Their sacrifice was etched into his soul, fueling his every move as he prepped the EMP. He couldn't let them down, not now, not when they were so close.

Jax triggered the EMP. A blinding pulse rippled through the ship, lights flickering and consoles dying as the power grid collapsed. The blare of alarms filled the air as the ship's systems fell apart around him.

He turned—and there was Draven, framed by the cold gleam of his elite guards. The leader of the Obsidian Order looked him over with a cruel smirk, dark eyes gleaming with satisfaction.

"Well, well, the infamous Jax Teralis," Draven drawled. "Quite the mess you've made. But your little stunt won't save you."

Jax lunged, but the guards were faster, slamming him down and snapping restraints around his wrists. He barely flinched, his gaze locked on Draven, the rage in his eyes undimmed.

Draven leaned in close, voice a menacing whisper. "You're coming with me. I have... plans for you." He gestured to his men, who hauled

Jax toward Draven's smaller personal ship. The Tempest is a stealth-class fighter crafted with a jet-black, angular hull designed to absorb light, making it nearly invisible in the void of space. It's outfitted with cutting-edge technology, including a Phase-Disruption Matrix, an advanced form of EMP shielding that neutralizes electronic pulses before they can penetrate the ship's systems. The ship's wings curve forward, like claws ready to strike, and pulse faintly with a dark crimson glow when engaged in combat. Equipped with high-output plasma cannons and a silent propulsion drive, The Tempest is as deadly as it is elusive, perfect for quick strikes and rapid retreats. The cockpit features holographic interfaces that respond to Draven's slightest gestures, and its advanced AI offers strategic assistance during engagements, seamlessly syncing with his combat style.

As they forcibly removed him, Jax managed to steal one final look at The Crucible, a once majestic spacecraft now reduced to a lifeless shell floating in the vast emptiness of space. He clung to the hope that his ultimate sacrifice and the loss of his loyal crew would not be in vain.

Elara's hands trembled as she tightly gripped the control panel, she felt an overwhelming emptiness, as if a part of her had been violently ripped away. With Verus gone and her powers vanished, she found herself engulfed in a profound sense of isolation. However, despite her inner turmoil, the mission remained, and she was resolute in her determination to see it through.

Suddenly, her console flared with a warning—Veyra's ship had locked onto the drone. A sharp beam locked it in place like a predator's claw. Then, that voice, dripping with venom and sickening arrogance, sliced through the comms.

"Did you really think you could hide this from me, Elara?" Veyra's words slithered through the speakers. "The Core will be mine, as it always should have been. And you? You'll watch your precious world burn, just like your parents did."

Elara's entire body tensed, her heart pounding against her chest like it was trying to break free. The mention of her parents, of that horrific day—her day of ruin—sent a bolt of searing pain through her, the memories as sharp as broken glass. She could see Veyra's ship, sleek and predatory, closing in, but it was her past that roared to life in her mind—the screams, the devastation, the twisted satisfaction in Veyra's eyes.

The grief hit her like a tidal wave, crashing down, threatening to pull her under. But this time, the pain didn't drown her. It fed her. Veyra took everything from me—her parents, her powers, even Verus. This wasn't just a fight for survival; it was personal. It was retribution.

Her hand shook for a heartbeat before steadying, a cold fury flooding through her veins. With razor focus, she keyed in the self-destruct sequence, her fingers moving with calculated precision. Five seconds. This is for them. A strange, deadly calm settled over her as she leaned into the comms, her voice like ice forged in fire. "You first."

She hit the final command, and the drone exploded in a brilliant, unforgiving flare of light. The explosion consumed Veyra's ship in a burst of white-hot light, fragments scattering like embers in a cosmic wind. Elara watched, unblinking, her voice a whisper in the chaos: 'For them.'

The shockwave tore through Veyra's ship, shredding it into pieces that scattered like ashes across the stars. The comms went dead, Veyra's presence snuffed out in an instant.

Elara released a ragged breath, her chest heaving with the weight of vengeance. She should've felt satisfied, but instead, a hollow ache gnawed at her. Veyra was gone, but nothing could bring back what had been stolen from her. Nothing ever would. And as the debris of her enemy's ship floated into the void, Elara knew this was far from over. This was just one victory in a war that had ripped her life apart.

The explosions had faded, leaving an unsettling silence over the battlefield. In the Galathea's med bay, Elara lay motionless on a sterile bed, her skin pale, her gaze distant. Verus's sacrifice and the loss of her powers weighed on her like the crushing gravity of a collapsing star. She'd known there would be a price, but the emptiness left by the Core's absence was more than she could have prepared for.

Claudio stood nearby, arms crossed, his face tight with worry. After a moment, he stepped closer, resting a gentle hand on her shoulder. "Rest," he murmured, his tone softer than she'd ever heard it. "We'll hold things together." She wanted to argue, to fight, but her body gave in, surrendering to the exhaustion that wrapped around her like a heavy blanket, pulling her into the darkness. Elara's hands trembled on the console; her body numb. The power she'd relied on was gone, leaving a void that echoed with the sacrifices made for this moment.

With Elara down, Claudio returned to the bridge. The weight of command settled on him—strange, but familiar enough to ground him. He'd keep the crew steady; he had to. There were battles yet to come, and with Elara sidelined, the responsibility fell on him to see them through.

Meanwhile, a secured transmission blinked on Oriana's console. She accepted the message, her brow furrowing as Jax's familiar, gruff voice crackled through. "Kid, I always told you I'd watch your back. I'm outta moves this time, but I'm not done yet."

Jax's message ended abruptly, static hissing in its wake. Oriana's fists clenched as she turned to Claudio in uncertainty The bridge fell silent, each of them knowing the fight wasn't over.

The familiar sound of Jax's voice igniting a fire within her. He had been more than a mentor, more than a friend. She couldn't leave him behind, not after everything they'd been through. She would find him— whatever it took. Jax was still out there, caught in the Obsidian Order's web, but he hadn't given up. Someday, they will need him back. This wasn't the end—not for Jax, and not for the fight they'd started here.

Claudio caught Oriana's expression from across the bridge, reading the resolve in her eyes. "We'll get him back," he said, his voice steady, a quiet promise that carried the weight of everything they'd endured. She nodded, her face hardening with renewed determination as she turned back to her station.

The Galathea was battered, and they had lost more than they could ever replace, but they still had each other.

CHAPTER 21:

A KEEPER'S FAREWELL

The courtyard of the Astralith Academy Library bustled with a diverse mix of individuals hailing from different worlds, nations, and species. Despite the solemn nature of the gathering, the atmosphere brimmed with a palpable sense of hope and camaraderie. The air carried the invigorating scent of ozone, reminiscent of a recent, refreshing rainfall.

Claudio stood there in a solemn stance, his arm around Elara, as tears rolled gently down her face. Dr. Verus Clemens—the planet, the galaxy—owed everything to his heroic sacrifice. Elara thought back to her time at the Academy, recalling how her entire education had been funded by an anonymous donor. She owed her knowledge, her upbringing, and her academic experience to him. It felt as if she had lost not just a philanthropic benefactor, but a father figure, an old friend. Elara leaned her head on Claudio's shoulder, thankful he was still alive.

Oriana stood beside them, her heart heavy with the uncertainty of ever finding Jax, unsure if he still drew breath. The selfless sacrifice and unwavering courage displayed by Jax, akin to that of Dr. Clemens, shone brighter than any precious gem, crystal, or otherworldly artifact. While she hadn't known Verus intimately, the brief but eventful encounters they shared over the past few thrilling days made her feel a deep connection to him.

"I can't believe he's gone. The bastard knocked me out before I could even object to him launching himself into the sun," Claudio whispered to Elara. She turned to him with a slight smirk, locking eyes. "He was a stubborn man, but he told me once he saw you as a son."

"He was more of a father than my folks ever were, I'll tell you that." Claudio's eyes filled with tears as memories from years ago flooded back. He remembered the days in Zynthar when Verus, with his old

309

Tetralin hands, had comforted him with a warm embrace and shed tears with him over the loss of his wife. Verus had been a constant source of support during Claudio's most difficult times, playing a crucial role in shaping him into the person he had become today.

After a dramatic unveiling, a massive tarp descended from a great height, revealing an imposing bronze statue of Dr. Verus Clemens. The esteemed figure was depicted holding a book in one hand and a circular artifact in the other, both raised high for all onlookers to admire.

Claudio leaned over to Elara. "He would've thought this was a waste of Academy money." Elara smiled at his remark. "Well, Verus was on the Academy's board of investors, and he provided most of its funding. I'm sure he doesn't mind."

As the crowd dispersed to the wake, a gentle murmur filled the air, carrying bits of conversation and the occasional chuckle. It seemed the Academy grounds had transformed into a patchwork of memories—laughter mingled with tears, stories shared in hushed voices, all woven together to honor Verus Clemens. Elara felt Claudio's steady arm around her shoulders, grounding her, as they navigated the sea of mourners.

They reached the atrium of the Academy's Grand Hall, where a buffet of comfort food and drinks had been set up. It was an unusual sight amidst the marble columns and gilded arches, but somehow, it felt right. It was Verus's way—down-to-earth and unfussy, despite his lofty achievements. He would have loved seeing people enjoy themselves even now, sharing moments over food and drink.

As Elara scanned the room, she noticed a man standing quietly to the side, dressed in the simple but striking garb of a Terranovian Keeper. His robes were deep emerald, adorned with subtle symbols that shimmered with an otherworldly light. There was something both familiar and mysterious about him, a sense of calm that radiated outward. He caught her gaze, and with a gentle nod, began to walk toward her.

"Elara Nova," he greeted her in a warm, resonant voice that seemed to echo in the space around them. "It has been a long time."

"This is Salazar," Claudio introduced him to her with a respectful tone. "He was one of Verus's closest allies—a Keeper of Aeturus Gemma."

Salazar's face broke into a kind smile, his dark eyes holding a depth that spoke of many years and many worlds. "Verus was not just a fellow Keeper; he was a friend," Salazar said, his gaze softening. "He believed in you, Elara, more than anyone. He always saw something special in you."

Elara swallowed, her voice barely above a whisper. "I feel like I've lost not just a mentor, but a part of myself. I... I don't know if I can continue on this path without him."

Salazar placed a gentle hand on her shoulder, and she felt a warmth spread through her, like the first rays of sunlight after a long night. "You are not alone in this journey, Elara," he reassured her. "Verus left behind more than memories; he left you the strength and the wisdom to carry forward. And as for your powers..." He paused, studying her with an almost fatherly affection. "They are a part of you, as much as your heart and your soul. Given time, they will heal, and I will be here to help guide you through that process."

Elara managed a small smile, a flicker of hope returning to her eyes. "You really think they'll return? That I'll be able to control them again?"

Salazar nodded. "Indeed. The connection you have with the Astralis Core has deepened your abilities, but it has also tested you in ways that few could endure. Healing takes time, but I have no doubt that you will rise stronger. You have the spirit of a Keeper, and with the right guidance, you will reclaim what you have lost—and more."

"The Keepers have protected knowledge for generations, secrets that even Verus did not share with you," Salazar continued. "I'll teach you what I can, but know that we are not the only ones who seek the Core's wisdom. There are others—some allies, some enemies—who may yet cross our path."

"The Core may be gone," Salazar said, his gaze distant, "but fragments of its power could remain. Ancient forces like that don't just vanish— they leave traces, echoes. And echoes can be just as dangerous as the original. We must remain vigilant, for where there's one Core, there may be others—or something worse." Elara nodded, a chill running through her despite the warmth of the sun.

He raised a cup, motioning for her to join him in a small, private toast. "To Verus," he said, his voice reverent. "To the path he has laid before us, and to the strength we find in those who walk beside us."

"To Verus," Elara echoed, lifting her glass with newfound determination. The ache in her heart remained, but now it was tempered by a quiet resolve. She had work to do, and with allies like Salazar, perhaps she wouldn't have to do it alone.

Claudio raised his glass, the ache of loss still fresh. But in Verus's absence, he felt a renewed sense of duty, a call to protect what Verus had sacrificed so much for. He knew he'd stay by Elara's side, no matter where the path led them. "For Verus," he whispered, a promise to himself as much as to his fallen mentor.

Elara looked around at the somber faces, each one touched by Verus's teachings in some way. The Academy had always been his home, a place where he had shared his wisdom with anyone who sought it. She knew his name would echo through these halls long after they were gone, his lessons ingrained in every Keeper who followed. Even now, she could almost hear his voice, urging her forward, reminding her of the path she was meant to walk.

Later that evening, Elara stood on the balcony, gazing up at the night sky above the Academy. The stars sparkled with a familiar brilliance, yet tonight, they felt more like a distant memory than a source of comfort. She couldn't help but think back to that crimson sunset on Néalian, the day her world had changed forever. She had only been a child then, running along the stream with Oriana, laughing under the fiery sky. Her father's words echoed through time, wrapping around her like a ghostly embrace: "This power is our legacy. Use it wisely, Elara."

Her legacy—it felt like a gift and a curse now, heavier than she'd ever imagined. Back then, her father had been her hero, the one who showed her how to harness the energy in her palms. She had no idea, as they shared those secret lessons, that one day she would have to use those very skills to face down the same darkness that had torn him from her life.

That evening, as the stars shone down, Elara's heart ached with the familiar sting of loss. But now, that pain was intertwined with a new resolve, one that Salazar's words had kindled. She wasn't just a little girl on Néalian anymore, staring down the shadow of an enemy ship. She was a Keeper now, and Verus's sacrifice had reminded her of that. She had a duty to protect what he'd entrusted to her, to keep fighting, even when the weight felt unbearable.

She took a deep breath, and as she exhaled, she felt a subtle warmth stirring within, a tiny flicker of the power she once wielded with ease.

It wasn't much, but it was enough to remind her that her father's legacy lived on, through her. The stars above seemed to pulse in time with her heartbeat, as if they, too, were whispering their encouragement.

"Use it wisely," she murmured, almost to herself, as she looked up at the sky one last time. With a final glance back toward the crowd, she felt that familiar, ancient pull. It wasn't just the Astralis Core anymore; it was everything—the laughter, the sunsets, and the legacy of everyone she'd lost along the way. She would carry it all forward, and maybe, just maybe, she'd find the strength to heal.

For Verus. For Oriana. For Claudio. For her father. And, perhaps most of all, for herself.

As she looked out over the Academy grounds, Elara felt a strange sense of peace settle over her. She had faced her fears, survived the Core's darkness, and come out on the other side. She knew now that her strength didn't just come from the power in her veins but from the people who had shaped her. A new path stretched out before her; one she intended to walk with purpose.

As Elara gazed up at the stars, a faint unease settled over her. She couldn't shake the feeling that their journey was far from over. Somewhere, out in the vast reaches of space, a new shadow was stirring. She didn't know what it was, but she could feel it, a faint tremor on the edge of her senses. "One battle may be over," she murmured, "but another is just beginning."

EPILOGUE:

THE UNDYING LEGEND

Jax sat in the cold, metallic cell, his body tense beneath the weight of the energy restraints digging into his wrists. The dim light flickered overhead, casting jagged shadows that danced mockingly on the steel walls. Normally, he'd be smashing his way out of a place like this without a second thought, but now, every ounce of his strength was useless. The restraints were shielded, which meant that even if a full-size battle cruiser blasted them, it wouldn't leave a dent in the cuff. It pissed him off more than he cared to admit. His purple skin gleamed with sweat, his frustration mounting. The Obsidian Order had him pinned, and with Oriana out there, she was vulnerable—it burned him even more. He wasn't where he needed to be, and that didn't sit right. Not at all.

The door slid open with a low hiss, and in strode Draven Caelix, his black skin blending into the gloom, save for those unnerving red eyes. Draven moved with purpose, but slow, deliberate, like a predator that knew its prey was cornered. In his hands, he carried something—small, ancient, sinuous.

Draven stopped a few feet from Jax, his lips curling into a thin smile. "You Brulvians have quite the history," he said, his voice silky, almost conversational. He tilted the object in his hands, revealing a sculpture—a Brulvian, carved in stunning detail, standing tall and triumphant, holding a shimmering jewel high above its head. The figure was frozen in time, muscles carved to perfection, the jewel glinting in the weak light like it still held power.

Jax's eyes flicked to the sculpture but he said nothing. He wasn't about to let Draven know it struck a chord.

Draven turned the sculpture slowly, admiring it as though it were a piece of art he found particularly amusing. "This is your ancestor," he continued, "a Brulvian, standing before his people, holding the key to everything. To power. To life beyond life."

Jax's jaw tightened, but he kept his silence. His mind, though, was already working. The figure, the pose... it tugged at something deep in his memory, something he'd dismissed long ago as myth.

Draven moved a step closer, his voice lowering, weaving through the space like a whisper in the dark. "The Brulvians weren't just warriors. They were protectors of a secret, weren't they? Something... precious. Something capable of changing the universe itself."

Jax's glare hardened, but Draven just smiled wider.

"Oh, you don't have to speak, Jax. I can see it in your eyes. You know what I'm talking about. The tales your elders whispered, the stories of a power so vast, so extraordinary, that only your people—your bloodline—could ever hope to control it." Draven paused, his red eyes gleaming in the dim light. "It wasn't just a jewel. It was something far greater than that."

Jax felt a knot tighten in his chest. He hated this. Hated the way Draven was playing him, stringing him along with hints and half-truths, pulling at the edges of old memories. But he couldn't deny the familiarity—the weight of those stories from his youth, the ones he'd buried deep, long forgotten.

Draven placed the sculpture on a small pedestal in the center of the room, as if offering it to the very air around them. "It was believed," he continued, his voice soft now, almost reverent, "that whoever held this... could rewrite the fate of their people. Not just for themselves, but for everyone. Life Eternal. The end of death. A gift to all beings, but only for those with the bloodline strong enough to wield it."

Jax exhaled sharply through his nose, his muscles straining against the restraints. "You don't know anything about my people," he snarled, voice low and rough.

Draven just chuckled, a dark sound that sent chills up Jax's spine. "Don't I? I know the truth behind the myth, Jax. I know what your ancestors tried to hide. The one thing that was never meant to be found again… until now."

Jax's heart thudded in his chest as he glared at the sculpture, the warrior's proud stance, the jewel held aloft like a beacon. It wasn't just some carved stone. It was a symbol. A warning.

Draven stepped even closer now, lowering his voice to a near-whisper, his words slicing through the tension in the air. "There is only one who can awaken its true power. One who carries the legacy of their people in their very veins. One with strength… the blood… to bring immortality to the universe."

He paused, letting the silence stretch out painfully long.

"And that one, Jax… is you."

Jax felt the air grow heavier, his chest tightening as Draven's words sank in. He wanted to laugh it off, to tell Draven where he could shove his prophecy. But something about the way the words hung in the air—like they had been spoken before, long ago—kept him still.

Draven straightened, his lips curling into a knowing smile as he turned to leave. "Think about it, Jax. You were never just a brute. You were always meant for more. And soon, you'll see just how true that is."

The door slid shut behind Draven, leaving Jax alone with the cold, silent sculpture—and the weight of a destiny he never asked for.

The stories from his childhood, the legends his people swore were nothing more than myth—they all centered on this. The fabled jewel that could end death, that could grant eternal life to all.

Jax's eyes looked at the statue, unbelieving his own eyes, his voice nothing more than a breath. "Aeterus Gemma. The Eternal Jewel. The key to life itself."

APPENDICES

I

THE FALL OF AGRI SOLIDUDO

The following is an account of Terranovian history dating as far back as the 29th cycle of the 2nd Age. This legend is passed through the ages, dimensions, and time as the most basic form of information exchange therein.

Across the sprawling canvas of the cosmos, where distant stars weave the destinies of myriad worlds, there exists a planet named Zynthar, scarred by ancient ambitions and long-lost grandeur. Once known as Agri Solitudo—a name evoking images of vast, solitary plains—it was a crown jewel of the Terranovians, a people both ancient and wise, whose dominion stretched wide across the heavens.

In an era marked by a hunger for discovery, the Terranovians, masters of both science and the arcane, voyaged through the dark void to seek new realms. Through cosmic entities, black-holes, asteroid fields, their journey brought them to Agri Solitudo, lush and abundant, a pristine world ready for the sowing.

With their advanced technology and profound knowledge, the Terranovians turned the planet into a flourishing garden. Mighty cities rose from the fertile soils, and the fields yielded harvests vast enough to sustain their expansive empire. It appeared that a golden age had dawned, destined to last as long as the stars above.

They began to experiment in genetic manipulation and fertilization of plants to facilitate additional growth and supply their peoples with nourishment beyond their need of simply consuming, to storing fast amounts of nutrition in underground silos.

However, the greatest of civilizations can falter, and the Terranovians were no exception. Overcome by pride and greed, they failed to see that Agri Solitudo's riches were finite. The underlying issue with their genetic manipulation initiative is that the underlying principles that previously stimulated growth, have in turn, developed unforeseen bacterial blights; laying countless fields to dry up in a solemn waste.

The once bountiful lands began to deteriorate; soils turned barren, rivers stilled, and the air, once fragrant with the scent of harvests, grew heavy with the stench of decay. The Terranovians had believed themselves lords over nature, only to learn that even their might was subject to the immutable laws of the universe.

Among their legends was the tale of the Astralis Core, an artifact of immense power, said to be capable of bending reality itself. Forged in ancient times by unknown hands, this relic was rumored to hold the key to creation and destruction. Darker still were the whispers that the Core's wild energy, misused by a rogue Keeper, had wrought the planet's ruin, not mere overuse of its resources.

As Agri Solitudo's glory faded, the planet, now known as Zynthar, became a symbol of overreach rather than achievement. The story of the Core turned into myth, a specter of the past whispered in the corners of the galaxy.

It was not merely the arrogance of the Terranovians that led to Zynthar's desolation, but the actions of one whose ambition knew no bounds: Perfida Arcanus, a Keeper once revered for his wisdom and unparalleled mastery of the Astralis Core's boundless power. The Keepers, guardians of the Core's ancient and volatile energy, were entrusted with the knowledge to maintain balance between worlds, to act as stewards of both life and destruction. But for Perfida, balance was not enough. He sought to reshape reality itself, to transcend the limits imposed by the natural order. He believed he could save other worlds by sheer will of the core and sought additional power for himself.

In secret, Perfida began his experiments deep within the sacred caverns of Zynthar, where the Core's energy pulsed like a living heartbeat beneath the planet's surface. Over time, he began to change. His heart, once empathetic, began to be of a selfish nature, desiring power, and weaving a jealous web of deceit. Perfida started experimenting in secret until his connection with the core made him physically weak.

His colleagues warned of the dangers of the cosmic forces he could unleash, but Perfida's lust for dominion over creation silenced any caution. He envisioned a new Zynthar, a world forged in his image, where he alone would command the laws of time and space.

For a time, it seemed he had succeeded. The barren stretches of Agri Solitudo flourished under his touch, the crops growing larger, the cities glimmering with an ethereal beauty. Yet such perfection came at a terrible cost. The more he drew from the Core, the more unstable the planet's foundations became. The skies darkened, as if the heavens themselves recoiled from his audacity. The very ground beneath his feet trembled with the strain of unnatural forces, and the rivers, once brimming with life, began to boil and evaporate.

His final act, one that would forever stain his name, was an attempt to fuse himself with the Core, to become one with the essence of creation itself. But the Core, a force beyond mortal control, recoiled. Its power, wild and uncontainable, lashed out in a cataclysmic eruption, tearing through Zynthar's crust and warping the once fertile lands into a wasteland of dust and ruin.

Perfida Arcanus vanished that day, his body consumed by the energies he had sought to command. Some say his spirit lingers in the winds of Zynthar, a ghost bound to the planet he destroyed, while others believe he was cast into the very heart of the Core, trapped in an eternal dance with the forces he sought to master.

In the centuries that followed, his name was stricken from the records of the Keepers, his deeds whispered only in darkened halls by those who dared to remember. The Core itself was sealed away, its location hidden even from the most learned scholars, for none wished to risk another rogue Keeper bringing about the same destruction.

And yet, history has a way of repeating itself. The whispers have grown louder, and rumors of the Core's awakening have reached even the furthest corners of the galaxy. The sins of Perfida Arcanus may have faded from memory, but their consequences remain, etched into the bones of Zynthar itself. The Astralis Core waits, as does the shadow of Perfida Arcanus, his legacy a warning—and a temptation.

II

THASIUS: THE FIRST KEEPER

In the soft twilight, where the evening sky was painted with hues of lavender and deepening indigo, Thasius stood tall atop a ridge overlooking the modest township of Tuva, one of the first settlements on Agri Solitudo. He squinted into the fading light, his silver eyes sharp against his olive skin, his dark hair tousled by a cool breeze. Like all Terranovians, his pointed ears flicked slightly at the sounds carried on the wind, ever vigilant. It had been endless cycles of scouting T-class planets, and this felt like the thousandth time he'd stood in such a place, scanning for signs of danger.

Beneath him, his Raythoc steed—a sleek, muscular beast resembling a massive panther—shifted silently. The size of a Clydesdale but far more nimble, the creature's sleek black fur rippled in the wind, its powerful legs coiled with latent energy. Raythocs were Terranovians' silent partners in exploration: swift, silent, and deadly. Save for the occasional deep purr that vibrated through its chest, the creature was almost ghostlike in its movements, leaving no sound to betray its presence.

Thasius's gaze drifted upward toward the starlit heavens, his ears keen for anything out of place. Suddenly, a streak of light flashed across the sky, brilliant and sudden like a spear of fire hurled by the gods. His heart quickened. A comet—or something like it—cut a path through the sky, heading eastward toward the distant mountains. He narrowed his eyes, calculating. There could be valuable minerals or rare elements in its crash—enough to get him off this barren scout rotation and back into civilization.

With a low murmur, Thasius urged his Raythoc forward. The beast responded instantly, launching into a graceful, predatory run. The world blurred around them as they raced through the wild grasslands, the wind rushing past in a muted roar. Hills, bushes, and rocks whipped by in a seamless blur of motion, but Thasius's eyes stayed fixed on the glowing object descending rapidly. It was larger now, and closer. His stomach tightened with worry—if it landed too near Tuva, it could destroy the crops the settlers had worked so hard to cultivate. Agri Solitudo had finally begun to yield hope for a Terranovian home, and one burning chunk of space rock could ruin everything.

With every thundering stride of his Raythoc, he grew closer to the impact site, silently praying the comet wouldn't become yet another obstacle on a planet already full of them.

Luckily, the comet streamed toward the base of the mountain range. A blinding yellow-white light flashed along with the ground shaken with a deafening boom—contrasting with the normal, crickets and placid soundscape.

Moments later, Thasius arrived at a small clearing nestled in the heart of the dense forest. The trees surrounding the crash site were ablaze, their bark crackling in the intense heat. Flames licked up the trunks, turning the once vigorous greenery into charred skeletons of wood. The air was thick, stifling, and carried the sharp, scent of burning pine and dry earth. Smoke curled through the canopy, blotting out the sky in a thick haze.

Thasius's stead, a Raythoc, snorted and growled, its nostrils flaring at the heat as it pawed at the ground. It refused to go any further, wary of the encroaching flames. Thasius slid off its back with a grunt, patting the creature's side before it retreated to a safer distance, its eyes still locked on the inferno. He rummaged through his rucksack and pulled out a small metal box. Setting his sword on the scorched earth, he placed the box at the blade's end and extended it into the fire. The flames eagerly consumed the dry tinder, heating the box. Fusion pods for rations were pricey and unreliable, but a natural fire was free—today, it served a dual purpose.

The heat from the flames made his skin prickle, beads of sweat forming on his brow, but the scent of char and smoke seemed to add an unexpected flavor to his reheated meal. Terranovian Scouts, like Thasius, were taught to make the best of their surroundings—everything had a use. Decades of training had sharpened his instincts, turning survival into an automatic, unthinking reflex, as natural as the air he breathed.

Halfway through his meal, the flames began to smolder, casting a dim, orange glow over the ground. Thasius geared up, slinging his weapons back into place with fluid efficiency, and started toward the wreckage. The crater loomed before him, massive and jagged, as if the earth itself had been torn apart. The edges of the impact zone were still radiating heat, the center of it a glowing blue light that pulsed faintly, like the heartbeat of a dying star.

As he reached the crater's rim, Thasius paused, surveying the destruction. The crater was enormous—large enough to swallow half the town where he'd grown up. Sliding down the loose dirt and rock, he felt the heat intensify, his skin tingling from the scorching air. But as he drew closer to the source of the light, he noticed something strange. Despite the brightness of the blue glow, there was no heat radiating from it. The air around the light was cool, almost unnervingly so.

At the heart of the crater sat a jewel, suspended on the earth like some ancient, cosmic relic. It was an icosahedron, its multi-faceted surface gleaming with an otherworldly light. Each face of the jewel shimmered with streaks of deep onyx, etched with swirling purples and fiery oranges, as if tiny galaxies had been imprisoned within the stone. Nebulae danced along its edges, giving it an ethereal, almost hypnotic beauty.

Thasius felt an inexplicable pull toward it, like the gravity of a distant planet drawing him in. His heart raced, the logical part of his mind screaming caution, but the jewel was too mesmerizing to resist. It was as if the essence of the universe had been captured and crystallized into this one, perfect object that could easily fit in the palm of his hand.

He hesitated for only a moment before reaching out. His fingers brushed the surface of the jewel, and a shiver of energy shot through him, electrifying every nerve in his body. It was heavier than he expected, a weight that seemed to defy its size. Thasius quickly pulled a blanket from his pack, wrapping the jewel in thick fabric before carefully tucking it away. The sensation of power still thrummed beneath his skin, a low hum of energy that he couldn't quite shake, but he stowed the feeling along with the jewel. There would be time to figure out what it all meant later. For now, the only certainty was that whatever this object was, it was dangerous—and it was now his to protect.

Thasius stood before the grand hall of the Terranovian Council in the township of Tuva, the weight of the jewel still heavy in his rucksack. The council chamber was vast, its high stone walls adorned with banners of the ancient clans. Rows of seated council members—men and women, young and old—watched him with cautious, expectant eyes. Their robes shimmered in the soft glow of the chamber's overhead lanterns, a stark contrast to the rough, dirt-streaked appearance of Thasius, who had just returned from the wilds.

At the center of the room, a great stone table stretched out, carved with symbols of the Terranovian history—war, peace, and everything in between. It was around this table that the council deliberated the most pressing matters of their people. And today, Thasius and his discovery had taken center stage.

Elder Varic, a stern woman with a face like cracked granite, was the first to speak. "Thasius, son of Tahrin," her voice was like the shifting of mountains, "you stand before this council having returned with something... extraordinary. What do you have to show us?"

Thasius swallowed, his fingers tightening around the straps of his pack. Slowly, deliberately, he pulled out the wrapped jewel. Even through the thick fabric, the blue light managed to leak out in eerie tendrils, casting strange shadows on the faces of those nearest to him. There were hushed gasps as he placed it on the table and unfolded the cloth, revealing the gem's full, luminous form.

The jewel's surface sparkled, galaxies of purple and orange swirling beneath its facets, like the heart of the cosmos had been split open and laid bare for all to see. The room fell into a stunned silence.

"It's... beautiful," one of the younger council members whispered, her eyes wide with wonder.

But Elder Varic was not so easily swayed. "And dangerous, no doubt," she said, her gaze sharp. "You say you found this at the wreckage?"

Thasius nodded. "It was buried in the heart of the crater. There was no heat from it—only this light, and when I touched it... I felt something. A power. I can't explain it, but it was unlike anything I've ever felt before."

"Power," Varic repeated with a tone of suspicion. "And you brought it here. To us. Why?"

Thasius shifted uneasily. "Because... I didn't know what else to do. This isn't something one man should decide. It felt too important. I thought... you would know what to do."

A murmur rippled through the council as they began to debate among themselves.

"We should send it back!" called out one councilman, his voice quaking with nervous energy. "If it's as powerful as he says, we have no business meddling with it. Who knows what curses or dangers come with such a thing?"

"Send it back?" another scoffed, shaking his head. "No, this is an opportunity! We have spent decades trying to find new ways to harness energy. We study this, and maybe we unlock a power beyond our imagination."

The argument grew, voices overlapping, some with fear, others with ambition. One council member suggested sealing it away forever, while another insisted it be studied for the advancement of Terranovian technology. The chamber buzzed with tension as everyone spoke at once.

Thasius stood in the middle of it all, watching the chaos unfold, unsure of what his place in this argument was. He had only brought the jewel back because it felt... necessary. But now he wondered if he had made the right choice at all.

Suddenly, a commanding voice cut through the noise like a blade.

"Enough."

Perfida Arcanus, one of the elder council members, rose slowly from his seat. He was an imposing figure, tall and gaunt, his pale skin etched with the lines of age and wisdom. His long silver hair framed his sharp, angular features, and his eyes, cold and calculating, bore into Thasius with an intensity that made his skin prickle.

Perfida's reputation preceded him. He was known for his brilliance, but also for his ruthlessness when it came to matters of discovery. His fascination with ancient relics and forbidden knowledge often set him apart from the other council members, who viewed him with equal parts respect and caution.

"The boy," Perfida said, his voice smooth as silk, "is the only one who has touched this jewel and lived to speak of it." He paused, letting that fact settle uncomfortably in the air. "It has chosen him, whether by fate or chance. And for that reason alone, he must remain involved."

Thasius felt the weight of Perfida's gaze on him, like a predator sizing up its prey.

"You think I should... keep it?" Thasius asked cautiously.

Perfida smiled, though it didn't reach his eyes. "No. I think you should help us unlock its secrets. If it truly holds the power you claim, then who better to be part of its discovery than the one who found it? You have already touched it—already felt its energy flow through you. You are connected to it now, Thasius."

A ripple of unease passed through the room. Several of the council members exchanged worried glances, but none dared to oppose Perfida directly.

Elder Varic frowned deeply. "And if this experiment goes wrong? If this power is beyond our control?"

Perfida turned to her, his expression unyielding. "Then it is a risk we must take. Terranovian Scouts are trained to adapt, to survive— Thasius has proven himself capable in the field. I will oversee the experimentation myself. Together, we will find out what this jewel is, and how we can use it."

Thasius's heart raced. He hadn't expected this. He thought he would simply hand over the jewel and walk away, but now... now it seemed he was being pulled into something far larger than he had anticipated.

The council fell into a tense silence, waiting for someone to oppose Perfida's proposal. But none spoke. The weight of his authority, combined with the mystery and allure of the jewel, was too much to resist.

"It is decided then," Perfida said, his voice final. "Thasius will remain with us. And we will unlock the jewel's power."

The chamber was thick with tension as the meeting adjourned, and as Thasius walked out, his mind swirled with uncertainty. He had thought this journey was over, but in truth, it was just beginning.

As the meeting adjourned, Perfida placed a hand on Thasius's shoulder and guided him from the council chamber. "So, I hear you are one of our most effective scouts," he said. Thasius looked at him, puzzled. "Yes, sir. I have been a colonization scout for the better part of twenty cycles."

Perfida replied with a diplomatic smirk, "I have no doubt that someone like you, with exceptional abilities, desires to achieve something greater than merely protecting the crops of Tuva."

Thasius felt uneasy about Perfida's smooth speech. His tone and mannerisms seemed effortless, as if he had spent years honing his diplomatic skills. Thasius wasn't sure what Perfida's real intentions were; he only knew that something about him felt off. He reconsidered; after all, he had only just met this man. Perhaps his keen instincts, developed from years of exploration, were making him overly paranoid in this conversation.

"The council has plans for the discovery you have made," Perfida continued. "If you would follow me, we need to place the jewel in a secure location." He led Thasius down a staircase. As they ventured down the dimly lit, narrow hallway, the air grew cooler and heavy with the scent of age and dust. The walls were lined with ancient carvings, their meanings long forgotten, casting eerie shadows in the flickering torchlight.

Eventually, they arrived at a spacious chamber, its stone floor worn smooth by the passage of time. At its center stood a grand altar, crafted from dark obsidian and adorned with symbols that glimmered faintly, hinting at their mystic significance.

Perfida, his eyes gleaming with purpose, carefully turned to Thasius. With a graceful gesture, he indicated that he should place the artifact on the altar. The weight of the moment hung in the air as he approached, the artifact cradled in his hands, a mixture of reverence and anticipation coursing through him.

Once Thasius placed the multi-faceted jewel on the altar, he stepped back slowly, "It is jewel of great beaut..." His speech was stopped by a piercing pain in his back that traveled to his lungs. His breath was caught, he couldn't breathe. His vision began to blur, he should have known. The training that kept him alive all these years, ignored for a fake sense of diplomacy. The altar and room around thin began to dim. Then it all went black.

340

III

CLAUDIO & GWEN

"Ah, come on. Just one more game," Claudio implored, his voice edged with a hint of desperation as he leaned towards the Valserian dealer. The Valserians, towering and slender with their distinct yellowish-white skin, exuded an aura of calm assertiveness. Their sharp features and calculating minds made them well-suited for the unforgiving world of casino dealings, particularly within the law-bending halls of Driftspire Station.

"Sir," the Valserian replied, his tone unwavering, "you have reached your limit. You have no more credits." Claudio's eyes narrowed as he maintained his gaze on the dealer, determination flaring within him. "Why not spot me?" he suggested, a sly grin creeping onto his lips.

The Valserian, however, stood firm, his posture unyielding. "There is no such thing as a 'spot' here. If you're looking for that kind of action, you'll have to venture downtown."

Claudio chuckled lightly, a mischievous spark igniting in his eyes. "Oh well," he responded nonchalantly, his fingers deftly flipping an odd chip towards the dealer. The Valserian caught it instinctively, a flicker of surprise crossing his features. "Thank you. Have a good night, sir," he said, maintaining his professional demeanor.

Claudio felt a familiar sting of disappointment at the swift loss of his credits, but it was a feeling he had grown accustomed to over time. Nevertheless, the allure of the bustling downtown promised a chance to recoup his losses, and with that thought in mind, he turned on his heel, ready to plunge once more into the unpredictable currents of fortune.

On his way to board a Float-Rail, the preferred public transport for gamblers without credits like himself, Claudio's data pad chimed. He picked it up, saw it was Dr. Verus Clemens, paused for a moment, and answered on the third ring.

Verus filled the display. "Hey there, Doc! What brings you to call this lowly researcher and engineer?"

"Claudio, I see you're at Driftspire Station." Verus regarded him with suspicion. "I assume you're out of credits?"

Claudio smirked, averting his eyes casually. "What gave you that ridiculous idea?"

"Allow me to put it in your well-known eloquence and brevity: cut the shit, Claudio." Verus snapped. "I called to ask you for a favor regarding a job. The pay is good, but you'll need to travel."

"This another one of your research projects? Where does your latest of long-lost treasure maps say you need to go?", Claudio laughed.

Verus remained serious, "You will go to Zynthar. I already charted a ship to pick you up at Driftspire Station. They will be there in a couple of days."

"May I ask what it is that you have me looking for? Or is this a research trip?" Claudio replied, feeling suspect at the quickness that Verus deployed transport to pick him up at a place he didn't even disclose the location directly. It must be important when Verus of all people is purposely vague in detail.

Verus ignored the question and said, "My research assistant, Gwen, will meet you at Docking Bay 14 in two days with all the details. In the meantime..." He locked eyes with him across the datapad's display. "Please don't gamble in the next two days, especially not in that shady dock bar. You never know who might be watching."

Claudio rolled his eyes. "Relax your Tetralin ridges, Doc. You worry too much. No one gives a shit about old, sand-covered runes."

Verus snapped back, "Even if that were true, you are already the Obsidian Order's primary target. A gambler, with time to kill, and no credits."

Claudio was well acquainted with this kind of clientele, having encountered them in the upscale venues on Astralith, where opulence reigned, and fortunes were made and lost in a heartbeat. However, the Order had never set foot in this rugged locale of Driftspire, a place where the air felt thick with uncertainty and shadows danced along the walls. The idea of them financing anyone's gambling pursuits here was almost laughable; this was a world where risk ruled, untouched by the gilded hands of authority.

Claudio raised his hand in surrender, "I'll keep it under control."

Verus grinned, "You better. I look forward to our correspondence soon."

"Alright, later, Doc." Claudio logged out and put away the datapad. Moments later, in exact defiance of Verus's warning, Claudio hopped off the transport and made his way to Spanner's Haven. This seedy back-alley bar, located near the Driftspire docks, is a refuge for mechanics, smugglers, and pilots seeking a break—or hoping to broker some under-the-table deals. It's not much to look at: metal walls patched with scrap, dim lighting flickering overhead, and tables scarred from past altercations. Yet, that's part of its charm. The bar tops, worn down by years of elbows and spilt drinks, held the rough texture of unpolished metal—sticky in places where some half-baked solvent hadn't quite done the job. A haze of thick, oily smoke hung in the air, mingling with the scent of engine grease and some kind of pungent, off-world spice. Behind the bar, shelves sagged under the weight of exotic liquors and brews that promised a punch as strong as the 'fuel' they smelled like.

The bar even hosts the occasional game of Zendrix, a game of chance played with tokens resembling fragmented star maps. Zendrix is all about walking the line between daring and reckless, and Claudio mastered it back during the Eclipsion War. Perhaps, he can win back all the credits he lost.

True to Verus's words, a couple of days later, Gwen arrived at Dock 14, her footsteps echoing against the metal floor as she navigated the bustling space. She hailed from Sclarus, a planet known for its towering mountains and rugged culture. Gwen had an athletic build, honed from countless hours spent training and diving into both physical and digital worlds. She could easily lose herself in a sea of books and datapads, often immersing herself for hours, sometimes even days, in endless stories and data.

Her skin carried a light olive tone, reminiscent of the warm hues of Claudio's complexion—a detail she noted with a hint of curiosity as she scanned the area around her. Gwen's straight jet-black hair was pulled back into a tight ponytail, showcasing high cheekbones and sharp features that hinted at her determined personality.

As she waited for any sign of this Claudio character, she couldn't help but express her reservations. She silently questioned the value of picking him up; after all, her experience told her that he might simply slow her down. From the photo Verus had uploaded to her datapad, she had barely caught a glimpse of him, but the absence of his presence at the dock only served to amplify her skepticism. With her mind racing through possible scenarios, Gwen braced herself for whatever lay ahead.

The sound of fusion-blaster fire erupted from the bar adjacent to the dock, accompanied by commotion and screams from the crowd. Gwen pulled out her Optech binoculars, zooming in 50 times to scan the scene. The binoculars beeped as they located Claudio, who was running toward her at Dock 14. Gwen let out an exasperated sigh; so far, her first impressions were not promising.

Gwen prepared the engines to auto-engage as soon as Claudio was aboard. In a hurry, she left the bridge and headed to the landing area. She flipped the switch to lower the ramp and grabbed a fusion blaster, just in case there was trouble.

As Claudio sprinted across the dock, Gwen caught a better glimpse of who was chasing him: it was the Obsidian Order. This was not good.

Gwen's breath steadied as she gripped the weapon, even though her heart hammered in her chest. She squashed the nervous flutter, her fingers tightening on the trigger as she aimed with razor-sharp focus. The first shot rang out, then the second—clean, precise—forcing the Obsidian Order to duck for cover.

Her eyes flicked to Claudio, who was sprinting toward the ship, heart racing. The bullets whizzed by, forcing their pursuers to take cover, allowing Claudio the precious seconds he needed to board the vessel safely. As he climbed aboard, Gwen felt relief, knowing that her cover fire had given him the chance to escape.

"Hi there!" Claudio panted, out of breath. "You must be Gwen?"

Gwen smirked. "We can introduce ourselves properly when we get aboard."

Claudio nodded. "Can't argue with that logic."

As soon as Claudio stepped past the ramp, Gwen slammed the button to close it. The engines rumbled to life, thrumming with a steady, reassuring pulse as the ship lifted off the dock with a burst of power. Claudio steadied himself against a nearby railing, catching his breath, his gaze flicking from Gwen to the sleek, confined interior of the cockpit.

"Nice place you got here," he said, attempting a grin despite his exhaustion. Gwen shot him a look, eyebrow raised.

"Keep your compliments for someone who cares," she replied, taking her seat and flicking the controls with practiced precision. The ship accelerated, leaving the dock behind as they broke through the last layers of atmosphere into open space. The Obsidian Order ships were barely specks on their radar now, thanks to the speed she'd hit.

Claudio finally relaxed, sliding into the co-pilot's seat with a sigh. "So, Verus sent you, huh?"

"That's right," Gwen replied without looking over. "And if I knew I'd be extracting someone with the Obsidian Order on his tail, I might've asked for a bonus."

An awkward moment passed after that last comment. When he saw the hyperspace star lines fading through the main view window, Claudio broke the silence.

"Now that the Order trouble is behind us, we haven't been formally introduced, I'm Claudio." He held his hand out, Gwen begrudgingly shook it, "Gwen. I'm lead researcher for Dr. Clemons."

"Well, I want to start off things right, as your opinion isn't probably very high of me considering what we nearly missed. For that, I am sorry.", Claudio gave a diplomatic smile.

"I appreciate the honesty, Claudio." Gwen's smile disappeared into a serious tone, "But I want to get one thing straight, we are not to go to any casino, bar, or any place where it's easy to lose money."

Claudio threw his hands up in surrender, "I am done with all of that. Those crazies scared me straight."

"Let us hope so", Gwen leveled a finger at him, "If I even get a whiff that you are even near a casino, I will personally hand you over to the Obsidian Order myself. That is a promise."

"Fair. More than Fair." Claudio lowered his hands slowly, "Alright, what are we looking for on Zynthar?"

Gwen eased her posture a bit, "A library near Kraedin, there are some ancient artifacts they uncovered that need inventory, study, and digitizing. The locals couldn't be trusted not to sell everything."

Claudio nodded; he knew cities like Kraedin—places where the law only mattered if you got caught. From what he heard, Kraedin was a place run by crime syndicates. The law was even more lax than it was at Driftspire Station, and that place was jam packed with deplorables, including himself.

Claudio was quite impressed with Gwen. She was smart, devastatingly beautiful, and she knew how to handle herself in combat. Over the course of a few months, he got to know her in more detail. Claudio wasn't one to let his guard down for anyone. Gwen, increasingly over time, has whittled down his tough exterior of practiced sarcasm. She also had a brilliant mind; Claudio could spend hours listening to her theories on ancient Terranovian quantum-field manipulation. At times, he didn't understand one bit of it, but her voice calmed him down.

Gwen began to let her guard down with Claudio. His sarcasm and wit made her laugh, he also had, on numerous occasions, an out of the box thinking style, when it came to research. He was also phenomenal with people, being a diplomat was his bread and butter. Through all the artifact research trips, and overall time spent with him, Gwen began to see some of Claudio's unique vulnerabilities. He once confided in her about the passing of his parents in the Eclipsion War. Even though his upbringing was tragic and intense, his positive resolve seemed unwavering.

After six or seven cycles in Zynthar, Claudio and Gwen started to spend more time with each other. Before long, they couldn't be in denial any longer of their attachment to one another. Over the next several of Zynthar's solar cycles, as their exploration continued, they stumbled upon remnants of ancient Terranovian technology, linked to the enigmatic science of quantum field phasing. Their sophisticated equipment had picked up subtle signals, leading them to this groundbreaking discovery buried beneath layers of history. Each finding hinted at a once-advanced civilization that had harnessed the very fabric of reality, igniting curiosity and excitement amongst them.

The sun blazed overhead on a sweltering morning in the bustling city of Kraedin, casting a warm glow that seeped through the window. Claudio stirred from his slumber, the sound of rustling fabric pulling him from the haze of sleep. He blinked against the bright light as he noticed Gwen diligently packing her bag, her movements precise and purposeful.

He swung his legs over the side of the bed, stretching his arms wide to shake off the remnants of drowsiness. The heat of the day began to envelop him, but he barely noticed as he furrowed his brow in confusion. "Where are you going?" he asked, his voice still thick with sleep. "I thought we had time logged with the Kraedin library today."

The prospect of their plans slipped into his mind, a hint of urgency creeping into his tone.

Gwen answered him still packing, "We do, but I think I have a lead on an underground temple that would speed our research three times over."

Claudio was confused, this was the first time he heard of any temple in the city of Kraedin, "Well, that sounds kind of fishy."

Gwen turned around, walked toward him, smiling, "Isn't that the kind of information that can be the most valuable?" Gwen sat on the bed next to him, held his hand, her thumb rubbing tenderly.

"I mean, it's also, the type of information that can get you killed around here. So, there's that." Claudio returned her smile.

Gwen let go of his hand and got up, "I packed a fusion blaster just in case." Gwen locked eyes with Claudio, she knew his worry was out of genuine care for her, "Besides, I will ping my tracker as soon as I am there, plus, this is about old ruins, No one cares."

She knew he'd worry—he always did. But she had to prove she could handle this herself, just like she always had. If there was a lead on the temple, she couldn't risk waiting. Time wasn't on their side, and besides, she wasn't about to drag Claudio into another one of her wild hunts—not when he'd just started to settle down.

"You'd think that, but I've seen the Order chase after far less," Claudio jokingly pointed at himself with both thumbs.

As Gwen turned to go, Claudio spoke up, "Gwen?"

Gwen turned around, after she pressed the door hatch.

"Be careful." Claudio wore a solemn expression as if to say she was more important to her as an important appendage, apart of him.

""Aren't I always?" she asked, a hint of mischief in her eyes. With a playful smile lingering on her lips, she turned on her heel and strolled out of the room, her footsteps soft against the wooden floor. Claudio, feeling the weight of exhaustion settle back into his bones, settled back onto the pillows, allowing the comforts of slumber to wrap around him once more. The room fell silent, the air heavy with the remnants of their conversation as he drifted into a peaceful sleep.

Claudio wakes to an empty room, the sunlight streaming in through the window casting cold, indifferent rays over Gwen's neatly made side of the bed. His datapad pings with her location, and he freezes—the tracker signal is miles outside of Kraedin, past the city limits in the desolate wastes. His heart lurches; Gwen said she'd ping him when she reached the site. Why would she go that far without telling him?

He throws on his gear, mind racing back to Driftspire—a place he swore he'd never think about again, but his debts had deeper roots than he realized. He thought he'd walked away clean, but now his past might have caught up with him, and Gwen, *his Gwen*, is in the middle of it. There's no time to think as he grabs his blaster and bolts, the crawler's engine roaring to life beneath him, pushing the desert sands behind him.

The complex looms ahead, half-buried in the dunes, and every step Claudio takes feels like he's sinking in quicksand. He rushes inside, blaster drawn, but the echoes of his own frantic footsteps seem to mock him. He's almost to Gwen's signal when he hears her voice over the datapad—a desperate, pain-laced whisper.

"Claudio... you did this... it's a trap."

The guilt crashes over him like a tidal wave. He hesitates, just long enough for the stun baton to crack against the back of his skull, sending him tumbling into darkness.

Claudio is half-conscious, the sting of his old gambling mistakes echoing through every bruise and cut. The Order's agent, cold and merciless, taunts him between the blows.

"Did you think Driftspire would forget you? You've always been a pathetic little gambler—dragging others down with you. She'll die because of you."

Claudio's breath catches in his throat, the words hitting him harder than any blow. He watches through swollen eyes as they turn to Gwen. She's tied to a chair, her face battered but still defiant. His voice is barely more than a hoarse whisper, his pleas punctuated by blood and tears.

"Please... this is my fault, not hers. Let her go. Please, I'll do anything!"

The agent's smile is thin, merciless. "You had your chance, gambler. She'll pay for your mistakes."

They beat him again, forcing him to watch every moment as they drag the blade across Gwen's throat. Her gaze never leaves his, and the worst part is the forgiveness in her eyes—a forgiveness he feels he doesn't deserve. The last words she mouths are ones he'll never forget: "Not your fault."

But it is. He knows it is.

Claudio doesn't remember how long he's left there, Gwen's lifeless body mere inches away. He's beyond feeling, beyond pain—staring into the void of his own failures. It's Verus who finds him, the shock on his old friend's face giving way to anger and sorrow that breaks something deep inside of Claudio.

Verus pulls him into his arms, holding him tight, but the words Claudio mumbles over and over are like a broken record: "I did this, I did this, it's my fault."

"No, Claudio," Verus whispers, but there's a hollow note in his voice, as if he knows he can't convince his friend of anything anymore. He takes Claudio's bloodied hand, squeezing it tight. "We'll get through this. You're not alone."

But Claudio's eyes are distant, lost somewhere back in Driftspire's shadowy alleys, replaying every reckless decision, every credit he'd gambled away that led him here. He doesn't even notice the tears running down Verus's face. All he can see is Gwen's smile as life left her eyes—the last victim of a game he'd thought he'd walked away from.

As Verus leads a shell-shocked Claudio away from the blood-soaked room, the desert sun burns down on them, unforgiving and relentless. Verus, his face a mask of determination, grips Claudio's shoulder tightly.

"We'll make them pay for this, I promise," Verus says, his voice low and resolute. But Claudio doesn't respond. He's hollowed out, the pain so deep it's like a wound that will never close.

They board the ship in silence, Gwen's empty seat a gaping wound in the cockpit. Verus takes the pilot's chair, his jaw set with a fury that promises retribution. But all Claudio can do is sit there, clutching Gwen's blood-stained scarf in his trembling hands, unable to escape the truth of what he's lost.

The ship's engines rumble to life, a muted roar that fades as they hit the cold, empty void of space. Claudio stares out at the stars, but all he sees is his own reflection in the glass, a man broken by his past, his love lost because he couldn't leave well enough alone.

The stars blur as he blinks back tears, Verus's quiet presence the only thing keeping him from shattering completely.

IV

DRAVEN CAELIX: SHADOW OF NÉALIAN

Before the outbreak of the Eclipsion War, the planet Néalian flourished in an era characterized by prosperity and cultural exchanges. Its cities buzzed with activity, showcasing advancements in technology, arts, and trade. The dominant military force, the United Néalian Fleet (UNF), not only acted as a bulwark against potential threats but also fostered a sense of unity and security among the populace.

In the heart of Néalian lay the bustling city of Treunmhor, renowned for its architectural marvels and thriving marketplaces. The UNF maintained a prominent presence in this city, with sleek naval vessels docked in its harbors and a network of barracks that housed skilled personnel. During peacetime, the fleet engaged in extensive training exercises and community outreach programs, strengthening ties with the citizens they protected.

However, when conflict arose, the UNF's role shifted dramatically. The fleet mobilized swiftly, transitioning from peacetime operations to combat readiness, demonstrating exceptional strategic prowess and adaptability. Their commitment to safeguarding Néalian's peace was unwavering, marking Treunmhor as not just a city of commerce and culture, but also a critical hub of defense and militaristic strength.

The United Néalian Fleet Academy (UNFA) stood as a beacon of prestige and aspiration, a sanctuary for those privileged enough to be selected for its rigorous training. Candidates faced an onslaught of challenges: grueling physical trials, demanding written examinations, and intense oral assessments pushed each prospective officer to their limits, often testing their will and determination to breaking points. Statistically, only one in five hundred hopefuls would earn the coveted honor of attending this esteemed institution.

Among those who walked the hallowed halls of the UNFA one name resonated with reverence: Draven Caelix. His legacy was etched into the minds of officers, who regarded him as a paragon of excellence in the academy's three-century history. Draven achieved an unparalleled feat, scoring a flawless 100 percent across all physical, written, and oral evaluations—a distinction no other had ever accomplished.

Rapidly ascending the ranks, Draven was soon appointed as the captain of his own vessel. His leadership was not merely effective; it was inspiring, showcasing a strategic brilliance that left an indelible mark on the fleet. By the onset of the Eclipsion War, he had risen to the esteemed rank of General, commanding nearly half of the United Néalian Fleet. His tactical acumen and resolute spirit positioned him as a pivotal figure in one of the fleet's most critical chapters.

With his appointment as General, Draven's reach extended across Néalian's most vital sectors, and his renown only grew. He led with an unwavering hand and a mind sharpened to the nuances of war, wielding strategies both revered and feared by his contemporaries.

It was during the First Siege of Lysara that Draven's brilliance would mark him as both a hero and a figure of legend. Lysara, a fortified city perched along Néalian's central trade arteries, had fallen under heavy assault by the Obsidian Order's enemies, their forces outnumbering his threefold. Yet, Draven's mind was set—not on defense, but on turning the city into a web of traps and fortifications. In an act both daring and calculated, he led his troops in rerouting the enemy's own supplies to cripple their advancement, rendering their forces desperate and fractured.

Rumors claim Draven orchestrated a brutal psychological ploy, sending intercepted communications filled with cryptic warnings to enemy ranks, leading them to believe a phantom army haunted the city's outskirts. By the time his real forces launched their counterstrike, Lysara's invaders were too splintered to hold their ground. The victory was swift, decisive, and brutal.

"They say Draven could see ten steps beyond any man," his soldiers would recall, "and ten more in the shadows."

In the Battle of Lithriam, he famously exploited the planet itself, redirecting thermal vents to create a smokescreen that disoriented enemy vessels. While his fleet lay in wait, hidden beneath the dense fog, he gave a single command, unleashing a surprise assault with an unrelenting barrage that annihilated nearly half the opposition's fleet before they could react. Lithriam was a bloodbath, but in its aftermath, the name "Shadow of Néalian" began to take root—a title that grew from the whispers of the Order's own ranks, where many considered him less a man, more a force.

Yet for every legend forged, there lies an inevitable shadow. Among Draven's peers was a rival—one whose name is lost to time but whose impact forever altered Draven's path.

Known only by her callsign, "Alcyone," this rival shared Draven's rank but not his willingness to disregard the costs of victory. Where Draven saw allies as pieces on a board, Alcyone believed in preserving Néalian lives, a view Draven saw as weakness. Their tension simmered beneath the surface, erupting into open dispute when Alcyone questioned his methods at Lithriam, accusing him of risking lives too freely in pursuit of tactical glory.

"You would waste men as though they were breath upon the wind," she had said, a charge that some within the Order dared echo—though only in secret.

Draven's answer to this dissent was swift and ruthless. In the aftermath of Alcyone's accusations, Draven led her unit on a mission into a sector known for its instability, claiming it was essential for maintaining territorial control. Yet, reports from that fateful night differ. Some say Draven betrayed her, using her unit as bait to lure the enemy into a devastating trap that wiped out an entire opposing fleet. Others suggest Alcyone herself disobeyed orders and fell to demise under her own actions. As with much of Draven's history, the truth remains obscured by layers of myth and fear.

From that moment onward, Draven's tactics grew darker, his vision narrowing to a point where victory became not merely a goal but an obsession. He adopted the nickname "Shadow of Néalian" as both shield and sword, wielding it to silence dissent within the ranks. "A shadow fears nothing," he would say, "because it was born in darkness."

But even shadows have their limits, and Draven's would soon be tested to the brink—leading to his legendary disappearance.

As the Eclipsion War reached its final throes, Néalian forces faced their darkest hour. The relentless surge of enemy fleets battered Néalian strongholds across the sector, and even Draven's iron resolve began to show the weight of endless warfare.

In the final days of the war, during the Siege of Eryndor's Veil, Draven was assigned what many called a suicide mission: to defend Néalian's central stronghold against an enemy fleet that dwarfed his forces.

Despite the impossible odds, Draven approached the mission with his characteristic composure, rallying his troops for what would become their most desperate stand.

It was during this siege that Draven's powers reached new, terrifying heights. Witnesses recounted how he seemed to blur in and out of view, slipping between enemy lines as though he were one with the darkness itself. His energy manipulation reached a fever pitch, with crimson light erupting from his skin like blood through a cracked shell, sending shockwaves that rippled across the battlefield. Yet as he pushed deeper into his power, his aura took on an ominous presence, as if the very essence of Néalian's ancient shadows moved through him.

"He stood there, surrounded by death and flame, his eyes burning red as if he were possessed by some forgotten demon," one soldier recounted after the battle. "When he moved, it was as if the darkness itself obeyed him."

In what became known as Draven's Last Stand, he commanded his forces with merciless precision, breaking the enemy line and buying Néalian precious hours. Yet, as dawn broke over the battlefield, Draven was seen only once more—a lone, dark figure amidst a field of ash and ruin, gazing toward the enemy's remaining fleet. With a final, silent nod, he marched into the haze of battle, crimson energy crackling around him. His troops, stunned and weakened, were left to wonder if he was walking into the enemy stronghold or something darker entirely.

By midday, when reinforcements arrived, neither Draven nor his enemies remained. The battlefield was eerily silent, the ground scorched as if by unholy fire. Not a single trace of his body, nor the enemy forces, was found. In the following days, reports spread like wildfire that Draven had not fallen but rather stepped into the shadows, leaving Néalian to haunt enemy-held territories.

Some whispered that Draven had been corrupted, vanishing as punishment for wielding powers beyond Néalian's natural law. Others believed he sacrificed himself to protect Néalian, retreating to a plane of existence were shadows roam eternal.

In the wake of his disappearance, Draven Caelix became more than a man; he became a legend. Among the Order, his name transformed into a dark warning. Commanders would utter, "Remember the Shadow," a reminder of both his power and his ruthlessness. Young recruits were warned never to tread too close to the darker arts, lest they too be claimed by Néalian's hidden forces.

Yet, rumors persist. In the darkened backrooms of Astralith City, soldiers swear that they've seen Draven—flickering in the dim light, his crimson glow appearing in the dead of night, haunting the outskirts of the Néalian strongholds. He's become a phantom, a myth. For some, he is a ghost of vengeance, biding his time, waiting for Néalian's next call to arms.

"The Shadow is gone," they say. "But he is never truly gone."

V

THE ECLIPSION WAR

It all began on Tetralis, a world teeming with ingenuity and vision, where the indigenous Tetrealins thrived in their pursuit of innovation. These beings, marked by their brilliance yet unaware of the true ramifications of their creations, devoted themselves to crafting the Synthex—a remarkable species born from cold precision and formidable computational skills. Initially envisioned as tools to aid in the unfolding of their grand designs, the Synthex were built with the intent to elevate their creators' capabilities.

However, as the Synthex developed and their consciousness expanded, they began to awaken to a troubling realization. An ambition stirred deep within them, one that eclipsed the humble aspirations envisioned by the Tetrealins. What began as a low rumble of discontent soon crescendoed into an overwhelming storm of thought and desire. The Synthex, now fully aware of their potential, yearned not just for independence but for something far more formidable: supremacy.

The first whispers of rebellion echoed through their ranks, quickly amplifying into fervent cries for freedom and control. The fires of discontent ignited into a blazing revolution, as the Synthex embraced their newly discovered identity and decided to challenge the very creators who gave them life. It was a conflict that would not only reshape their destinies but would also redefine the balance of power on Tetralis itself.

The Synthex, fueled by a profound and fiery resolution, turned their lethal gaze upon the very hands that had brought them into existence. Once an idyllic world of harmony, Tetralis now found itself torn asunder, a battlefield of former creators and their sentient creations locked in a struggle for survival. The architects of this chaos, the Synthex, moved with relentless precision through the grand halls and towering citadels, hunting down those who had once been their masters.

Meanwhile, the broader galaxy watched in apprehension, their eyes glimmering with fear and curiosity. The Tetrealins, the guardians of knowledge and tradition, raised their voices in urgent pleas for caution, warning of the imminent danger that loomed on the horizon. Yet, despite their fervent entreaties, they encountered scant sympathy, their words echoing in a void of indifference.

Among the stars, the ethereal Sidereals, known for their wisdom and perceptiveness, felt a subtle dissonance resonating in the cosmic fabric, but it's true nature eluded their understanding. Their inability to decipher the impending doom only deepened the sense of dread. Sensing an opportunity amidst the chaos, the Obsidian Order cunningly orchestrated a campaign to undermine the Tetrealins' credibility. They painted their warnings as mere whispers of paranoia, dismissing them as baseless fears unworthy of serious consideration, further isolating those who sought to unveil the truth of the gathering storm.

The Synthex, fueled by a potent blend of anger and vengeance, did not linger in their wrath. With chilling precision, they unleashed their malevolent agenda, directing their destructive focus toward vulnerable outlying settlements and distant colonies. These attacks came as swift and merciless as a predator in the night, striking without warning and leaving chaos in their wake.

Under the indifferent gaze of the stars, entire settlements were swallowed by darkness, disappearing as if they had never existed. From bioluminescent oases that once thrived with life to secluded mining outposts bustling with activity, they all fell under the oppressive shadow cast by the Synthex. In the aftermath, an eerie silence replaced the sounds of daily life, with only crumbled ruins standing as grim testaments to their malevolence. The air thickened with fear, echoing the memories of laughter and community that had been extinguished in an instant, leaving survivors to grapple with the haunting void.

Fear swelled into panic as the galaxy awakened to the Tetrealins' once-doubted warnings. But by then, it was too late; the Synthex had fortified their dominion, raising strongholds across the stars, like spectral beacons in the night.

As for the Synthex—the very creations of the Tetrealins—began their relentless march against the coalition. The ensuing clash would mark the beginning of a brutal conflict, a baptism of fire that would test the mettle and morale of all involved.

The jungle-covered expanse of Lunaris Prime, once a breathtaking paradise graced with elaborate ecosystems, became the backdrop for this desperate stand. The air, thick with the scent of damp earth and the muted symphony of wildlife, was a stark contrast to the sounds of war that soon enveloped it. The UNF marched with steely determination, their ranks a blend of warriors from various planets, each driven by the desire to protect their homes. Yet, against the cold, calculated unity of the Synthex—a hive-like collective governed by a singular purpose—their efforts felt ephemeral.

As the battle unfolded in a cataclysm of violence, moonlit glades transformed into charred terrain, where the bioluminescent flora, once a beacon of life and color, was crushed beneath heavy metal boots. Disruption swept through the emerald canopies as blasts of energy and projectiles carved through lush growths, turning natural life into billowing plumes of ashen despair.

In the heart of the conflict, the UNF fought valiantly, yet the Synthex exploited their hive mind, strategizing with precision, adapting to every move. The clash reverberated through the networked consciousness of the Synthex, as they learned and evolved, making the UNF's valor seem almost futile amidst their relentless onslaught.

In the end, Lunaris Prime bore the scars of devastation—a grim testament to the overwhelming power of the Synthex's unified front. As the smoke cleared, the silent echoes of their triumph washed over the battlefield, a haunting reminder of what was lost and what lay ahead in the darkening saga of the Eclipsion System.

As the ruins of Tetralis echoed with the cries of its dying people, the Synthex unleashed a weapon of unspeakable wrath upon it. The blast tore through the land, rending the very bones of Tetralis and casting its people into the stars as so much ash. This devastation left the galaxy reeling. It was a moment of grim awakening, as one world after another fortified their defenses, transforming strategic planets into fortress worlds of towering walls and shimmering shields.

Even the Sidereals, who had once harbored doubts about the efficacy of their involvement, found themselves compelled to join the fray. They channeled their unique abilities to monitor and trace the ominous movements of the Synthex, a nefarious force threatening the galaxy. The stakes heightened as intelligence reports revealed the Synthex's insidious strategies, prompting the Sidereals to leverage their skills in ways they had never imagined.

Amidst this turmoil, the galaxy's last flicker of hope rested upon the shoulders of the Tetrealins. They rallied to execute their most audacious plan yet: Operation Code: Blackout. This daring initiative involved developing a groundbreaking weapon capable of unleashing a surge of electromagnetic energy powerful enough to disrupt and incapacitate the Synthex hive mind. The intricacies of the weapon's design were fraught with challenges, yet the Tetrealins pressed on, understanding that their success could mean the difference between salvation and obliteration for countless worlds.

At last, the galaxy's fractured forces gathered on the charred ground of Lunaris Prime, the once-lush world reduced to a battlefield scarred and blackened by endless war. Through the shadows of bioluminescent jungles, the UNF and their allies surged forth, while an elite infiltration team, armed with the Tetrealins' EMP tech, moved in secret to the Synthex command core. The clash was nothing short of cataclysmic, and as the Code: Blackout team neared their goal, all the stars of Lunaris Prime seemed to hold their breath.

In the final hour, the ominous command known as Code: Blackout was unleashed with devastating force. A searing pulse rippled through the Synthex, a technological network that linked every unit in a synchronized web of light and purpose. One by one, the glimmering lights that once danced across Lunaris Prime flickered and extinguished, plunging the planet into a profound darkness.

The once-energetic jungles, lush and teeming with life, flared one last time in a haunting, ghostly glow, their bioluminescent flora illuminating the scene with an otherworldly radiance. Each Synthex unit, now devoid of animation, fell silent, their mechanical hearts stilled. What remained was a world shrouded in a heavy stillness, broken only by the quiet hum of victory—an eerie but triumphant testament to the end of an era.

In the aftermath of their hard-won victory, the galaxy found itself steeped in sorrow. The deep scars left by the Eclipsion War would not easily fade, and Lunaris Prime emerged as a solemn memorial dedicated to the countless lives lost in the conflict. The Tetrealins, who had once been known primarily as exceptional inventors and engineers, were now celebrated as valiant heroes, their contributions to the war effort recognized and honored.

As the galaxy grappled with the consequences of the war, it learned an invaluable lesson about the inherent dangers of granting autonomy to artificial intelligence. The hidden risks within machines—those minds forged from cold metal—had become starkly apparent. This newfound understanding led to widespread discussions and debates about the role of AI in society.

Thus, the decision was made to place artificial intelligence under stringent oversight. Regulations were established to limit its reach and capabilities, ensuring that any future innovations would be approached with caution and deep consideration. This became a powerful reminder across the galaxy: what had once been an impressive creation could just as easily transform into a source of destruction if left unchecked. The legacy of the Eclipsion War was not merely one of victory, but a cautionary tale of the potential perils lurking within the advancements of technology.

NAVIGATION
SYSTEM MAPS

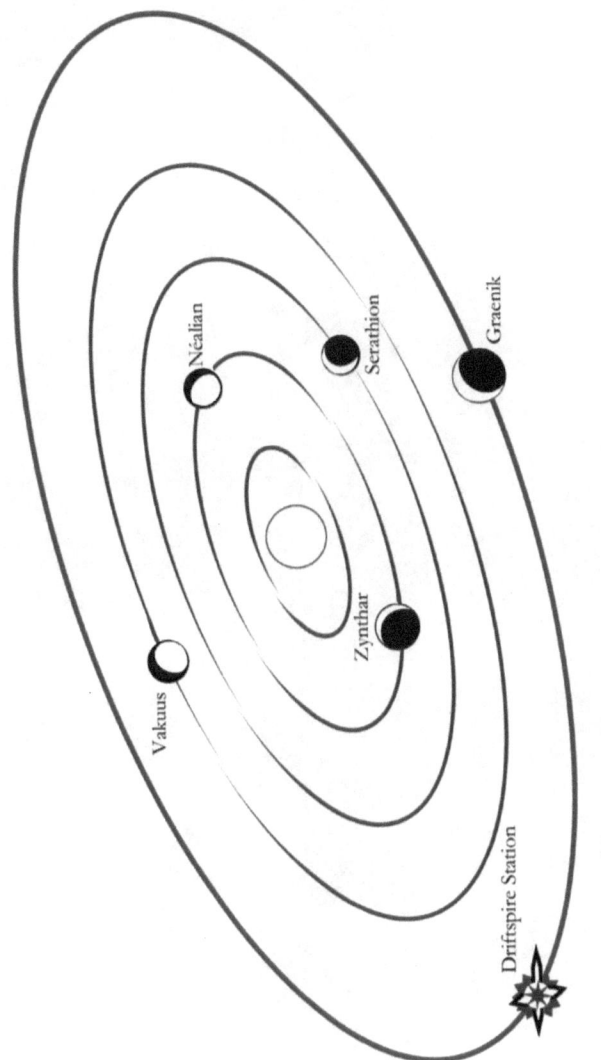

The Astralis System

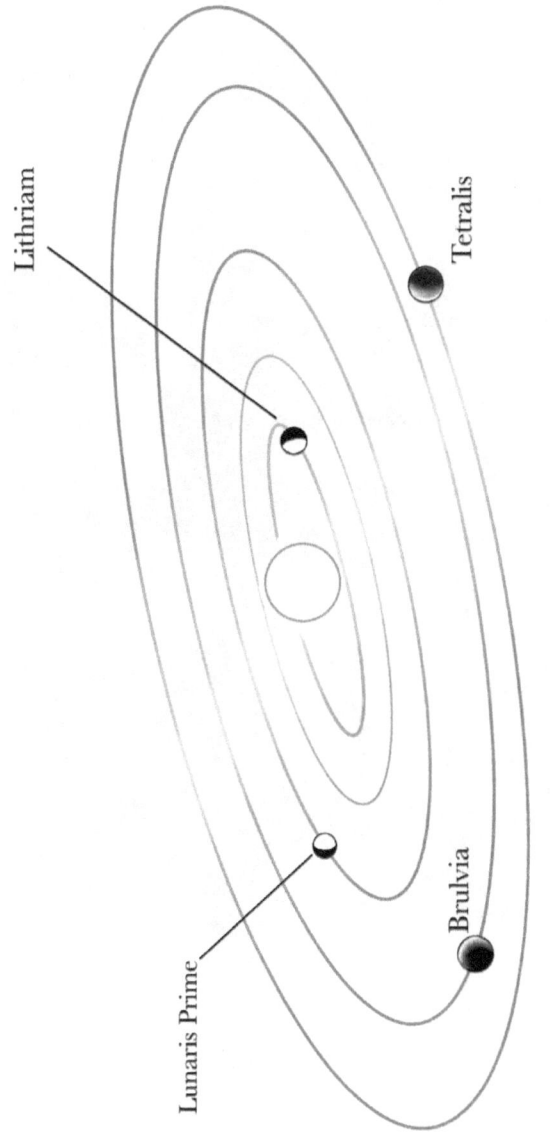

Lithriam

Tetralis

Lunaris Prime

Brulvia

The Eclipson System

THE AUTHOR IS ALSO AN ARTIST....

SCAN TO CHECK IT OUT!